ARISE

MONARCH RISING: BOOK THREE

SYLVANA CANDELA

MONARCH RISING
BOOK THREE

ARISE

FROM THE DARKEST NIGHT
COMES COURAGEOUS LOVE

SYLVANA CANDELA

PEACEFUL WORLD
PUBLISHING

This book is dedicated to YOU, beloved human creature.

May your heart be filled with joy and love,
Shining your light to the heavens above.
When your heart knows sorrow, grief, and pain,
May you reach out to LOVE, once again.

TABLE OF CONTENTS

PART 1: COURAGEOUS LOVE 11

Chapter 1 – Angie..13

Chapter 2 – Alliance..31

Chapter 3 – Philia..47

Chapter 4 – Secrets...61

Chapter 5 – Sisters...75

Chapter 6 – Summit..89

PART 2: FREEDOM RINGING 107

Chapter 7 – Insurrectionist...109

Chapter 8 – Veritas...121

Chapter 9 – Uprising..135

Chapter 10 – Mercy..151

Chapter 11 – Mine...165

Chapter 12 – Beloved..179

PART 3: ONE WORLD 195

Chapter 13 – Trickster..197

Chapter 14 – Farma-ceuticals..211

Chapter 15 – Redemption...225

Chapter 16 – Double-Cross...237

Chapter 17 – Fire...255

Chapter 18 – Birth..269

A MESSAGE FROM ANGEL 281

Acknowledgements...283

About the Author...285

PART 1
COURAGEOUS
LOVE

Chapter 1 – Angie

ANGIE ENTERS THE HEAD OF THE BEAST and descends to the darkest depths of hell. Her love for Kookie gives her strength to face the demon, whose world she has now entered. Her soul is filled with the words of the Creator saying, *I will fear no evil, for thou art with me.*[1] And Angie finds her courage when she hears the thunderous screams of the dark lord raging at her.

"YOU TRICKED ME! YOU TRICKED ME! It is I who was to have tricked YOU!"

The Monarch Angel is now part of Angie's body, giving her the full protection of the Heavenly Father. Angie glows with radiant colors of orange, yellow and white, and her wings are a shimmering, pure gold. Though her body is combined with that of the Monarch, Angie's spirit and will are still her own.

She speaks to the beast. "I AM HERE, fallen one, as you requested."

"I did NOT request, your–your–*companion* to join us!" the beast snarls at her.

With a charming smile, Angie replies, "Oops! Didn't see that one coming myself! What a pleasant surprise!"

Hee Hee! Nice one, human creature! Angie hears Angel speaking to her heart loud and clear.

The beast growls with fury, *"Wicked woman! Evil woman! You have accomplished NOTHING! I will take him, and I will CRUSH HIM! LORD KENNETH WILL BE MINE!"*

Angie looks at the beast and speaks gently to him, "Then I will have no choice but to go back and be with him. The Angel of the Lord who

---

is with me says she can bring me back to him anytime. And you will have lost me forever, fallen one."

"*NOOOOOOOOOOOOOO!*" screams the beast. "*TRICKED ME! YOU TRICKED ME!*"

"It's all right," says Angie, with much sympathy. "I will keep my end of the bargain and keep you company. Like you said, you are misunderstood and very lonely here in your own darkness and misery."

The beast has stopped screaming, but he is still glaring at Angie with fury.

"So, tell me, fallen one, tell me what it is that people do not understand about you?" asks Angie.

Screaming again the beast cries out, "*WHY . . . DO . . . YOU . . . NOT . . . FEEEAR . . . ME!*"

Angie spreads her golden wings and holds her hands out to the beast, "Because I can hear your pain," she says, "And I hear how sad and lonely you truly are. I felt that way once, too."

The beast continues to glare at Angie, but this time he says nothing.

Angie continues, "I know that you were once a magnificent angel, before you fell, and that our Father in Heaven loved you very much."

OOO! Where are you going with this, human creature? Angel inquires to Angie's heart.

Hang in there with me, Angel, and we will figure this one out together! Angie replies, speaking heart-to-heart with Angel.

You got him, sister creature! I'm with you.

Looking at the beast with sadness, Angie continues, "I lost my parents, too, not very long ago. They vomited to death from Ebola right in front of me."

The beast smiles. "Yes! That was a nice touch, wasn't it? I *do* enjoy those messy diseases of my creation!"

As an afterthought the beast says, "Perhaps it will be, how shall we say, *interesting,* to have your companionship, even with that other one there sitting inside of you. Who knows? Maybe I can make some kind of bargain with the Monarch."

Don't count on it, fallen creature!

* * *

Kookie is sitting in a big chair in the living room at the Lord's estate in Johannesburg. Since his cherished Angie disappeared a couple of days ago, he has planted himself in that chair and has not moved. All his friends at the estate have gathered around: Yakov, Neely, Liling, Dumaka, Mimi, Ryan, Doc, Phil, Bem, Tafari, Nassor, the three young ones, and the Chrysalenes from the Village of the Holy Ones. They have been with him day and night, taking turns, not leaving his side.

Number 3 and #4 are also snuggled in tight on either side of Kookie's neck. They miss Angie, too.

The news of Angie's disappearance has reached all the friends of Operation Monarch, including, Judy, Kenny, Lisa, the Alliance of the 36 Lords, and every Chrysalene from all three Continental Territories of One World.

When the Major and Vi heard the news, they immediately made arrangements to go to Johannesburg. Other Lords and Ladies of the Alliance of the 36 are also expected to come and spend some time there. It is rumored that the Alliance has grown from the 36 original Lords and Ladies, although no one knows for sure how many sympathizers there are in total. In fact, the friends of Operation Monarch have now merged with the Alliance of the Lords and Ladies, combining themselves into one force.

It has all happened under the radar of the Council and with great secrecy and caution, for everyone's safety and protection.

The group gathered around Kookie is anticipating the Major and Vi's arrival.

Eve Elli, Suzie of the Seashells, and Emeka have been especially helpful in keeping everyone's spirits from sinking too low, especially Kookie's. In fact, Eve Elli has an idea for which she has enlisted the help of the other young ones.

As the group is about to have their morning meal together, they are aware of a little scuffle going on just outside the living room. All eyes look up and see the three children bringing in Kookie's tuba, moving slowly and with much care not to drop it.

"Aww!" and other mumblings of endearment come from everyone in the living room with a tone of bitter-sweetness and affection. When Kookie sees the children's intense efforts to bring him his tuba, he is moved to feelings of love and grief all jumbled up inside of him. He has thought about his tuba for the past couple of days but has been unable to go near it. Now, he knows that he cannot let Eve Elli, Suzie and Emeka down.

Besides, he thinks to himself, *I'm sure it is what Angie would want.*

The children hand Kookie his tuba as he smiles at them and says, "Thank you very much."

Kookie sits there holding his tuba, thinking about Angie, and staring at the floor. Everyone else fixes a plate of food for themselves from the meal buffet and settles down among the small tables scattered around the room.

Suddenly the soft deep tones of Kookie's tuba fill the living room and the heart of each person.

"Very pretty!" says Eve Elli, as she and Emeka clap their hands.

Little Suzie starts to clap too and says, "Pitty!" bringing a smile to everyone, who all applaud Kookie's efforts.

As they are all finishing their meal, Eve Gerda and Adam Paki arrive from the Village of the Holy Ones. They see the children enjoying the sound of Kookie's music and Eve Gerda goes over to them saying: "My, what beautiful angelic sounds Lord Kookie is making! Just as sweet as the three of you dear little cherubs!"

"Hee, hee, hee," the three cherubs giggle as Eve Gerda sits down on the floor to join them.

Adam Paki shares the news that the Major and Vi have just arrived and are walking to the Big House; and Kookie stops playing his tuba. Upon hearing that his best friend in all of One World is almost here, he is barely able to contain his emotions when the Major and Vi walk in. They both head straight for Kookie, and without saying a word, the three of them put their arms around each other in a tender embrace, and weep.

The room goes silent as all the friends gathered feel the love for Angie and the sorrow of her disappearance. The bond of love between everyone in the room is deepening along with a growing feeling of courage and hope.

The Major finally speaks softly as he looks Kookie in the eye; "I'm so sorry, bro'."

Kookie just nods and looks down as he sinks wearily back into his chair.

Vi looks at the Major. They had discussed something on the way over, and he nods at her giving Vi the go ahead to share.

She sits down on the floor in front of Kookie and says to him, "We heard all the details of Angie's whereabouts from the Chrysalene Adam Tate at Judy's farm, and the Major and I just wanted to share with you what he said."

Kookie looks at her with a hopeful expression on his face.

"First, and I'm sure you have already been told this by the other Chrysalenes, Adam Tate says that he can feel the protection that Angie has from the Monarch Angel. Second, and you may already be aware of this too, Adam Tate can feel what Angie is feeling now, and he wants you to know that Angie is not afraid."

At this, Vi has the complete attention of everyone in the room.

"In fact," Vi continues, "he says that Angie is so *unafraid,* that she is frustrating the beast! She is even speaking to him like a parent speaks, with patience and calm, to an unruly child."

At this the whole crowd begins to chuckle.

Kookie lets out mixed sounds of laughter and sorrow. "Thank you, Vi. I needed to hear that. Yes, Angie has scolded me, too, when I have been a bad boy," Kookie says with a smile and the chuckle around the room grows a bit louder.

The Major adds, "Well, it seems like she is putting that bad dude in his place!"

More gentle laughter and sighs of relief fill the room in response.

Eve Gerda says to Kookie, "Every Chrysalene in One World is praying for Angie, and we are all right there with her in spirit."

"Thank you," says Kookie. "Thank you, dear friends." Turning to the Major, Kookie says, "And we have certainly heard some miraculous things that are happening at Howard Pharmaceuticals these days."

The Major and Vi look at each other smiling, and they proceed to fill everyone in on the story of the purified water and Master Howard's healing of his heart and soul. As the others listen, the hope grows stronger among the friends gathered in the living room.

Adam Paki says to the group, "When we ourselves become Courageous Love, there is nothing we cannot do. It is the Light of Heaven shining through us, and there is no light or force more powerful in all of eternity."

Everyone nods in agreement.

And Vi hears a voice in her heart speaking from another dimension saying, *Amen, human creatures! Amen!*

* * *

Three terminals activate across One World and PA, ES and SPA accept the incoming message. As their screens light up, there is a glowing red light and a deep resonating boom.

A voice comes on and begins to speak:

Voice: *With you I am most displeased! With you I am angry!*
PA, ES and SPA stutter with confusion and terror: "Wh–wh–why? My lord, what have we done? Do you not have the woman? Did we not lure her into your trap, as promised? What have we done, lord? What have we done?"
Voice: *FOOLS! I do NOT have the woman. I have the woman PLUS ANOTHER!*
PA, ES and SPA: "What? My lord! We do not understand! What do you mean? What other?"
Voice: *It seems that you FOOLS sent me a package deal!*
PA, ES and SPA: "A *WHAT?*"
Voice: *Yes, you dolts! She has arrived with an Angel of the Lord embodied in her ethereal corpus!*
PA, ES and SPA: "OH DEAR! HEAVEN FORBID!"
Voice: ***EXACTLY! YOU IDIOTS!***

There is a silence from PA, ES and SPA as the full consequences of what is happening begins to register with them.

Voice: *FOR THIS YOU WILL ALL BE PUNISHED! I shall seal you down below the ice and land. You and your Overlord Contacts and technical people who are all with you now; I shall cut off all communication between the lot of you and the outside world! No one will even know what has happened to ANY of you! THIS IS MY WRATH! MY JUDGEMENT! MY PUNISHMENT!*

The transmission is disconnected, and PA, ES and SPA are left crying out in hopelessness and despair.

* * *

In the northernmost regions of Euroslavica, two men inside a weather station are tracking an incoming storm of massive proportions.

Speaking in Russian:

"Fyodor!"

"Da."[2]

"*FYODOR!*"

"DA, Ivan! What is it?"

"Will you take a look at that Fyodor!" says Ivan, pointing to the screen in front of him. "What in thunderation is *THAT?!*"

The sky blackens with a swift and massive front coming directly at them. Fyodor and Ivan have never seen such a storm front before.

The two men look at each other with just enough time to shriek, "*AAAHHHGGG!*" before they are blanketed with an avalanche of ice and snow.

Ivan had a split second to send out a distress signal . . . if it ever went through.

The terror-stricken cries of PA, ES and SPA are now covered with ice, and lost in the middle of nowhere.

* * *

Lord Jackson and Rita are on their way to Johannesburg, as well as several other Lords and Ladies. More news is coming in from the Alliance, with reports that more recruits from the UC are coming, too.

---

[2] *Russian for Yes.*

With the influx of arrivals on their way, Lady Liling realizes that she, Kookie and Yakov need to start making arrangements for a Gathering of The Alliance.

Liling approaches Kookie and asks him if he is up to joining her and Yakov in "the study, for a little work on the estate;" their code for talking about covert business undercover of the Holographic Imager. Kookie indicates that he is most definitely ready.

Liling, Kookie and Yakov know they will need a team beyond just the three of them "working on the affairs of the estate," so they quietly manage to invite the others to join them.

The group slowly trickles into the study, mindful that they do not appear to be in a hurry, or anxious in any way, to the Council's surveillance system. All they are supposed to be doing is helping out Liling with her chores for the Council. However, no one is aware, yet, that the heads of their adversarial rule, PA, ES and SPA have just disappeared without a trace.

Looking around the room, Liling wants to make sure that everyone is present before she begins. Those in attendance consist of Kookie, Yakov, Neely, the Major, Vi, Mimi, Ryan, Doc, Phil, Bem, Tafari, Nassor, and Dumaka, who of course, is by her side.

Liling has managed to obtain additional Universal Translators, as pendant necklaces, which up until now only the Lords, and a few select Masters, have had access to. She hands them out to all the non-UC people present, with much smiling and nodding of appreciation around the room.

With everyone's Universal Translators turned on, Liling begins. "It is so nice to be able to communicate fully with all of you now!"

The others are amazed at how wonderful it feels to communicate with each other, although they truly do understand one another, already. The love of friendship has given them all the gift of communication from the heart.

"As you probably all have heard by now," Liling continues, "There are many more from our Alliance who are on their way here. We must use this opportunity to press forward with our plans, as no doubt the pro-Council UC are also doing at this time."

All nod in agreement and mutter a variety of responses around the room, "Yes. This is true. We must press forward!"

Liling says, "From all that we have been learning, it seems that our greatest strength against the dark forces of our adversaries is, well . . ." she pauses for a moment and looks around the room at everyone, and then at Dumaka.

Smiling, Liling continues, "It seems that our greatest strength is Courageous Love. And it also seems that we are not alone in feeling this way. I believe that the Light of Love is what has been drawing us to each other and guiding us in our plans. I feel that this Alliance, or Community, which we are creating is central to those plans. In fact, were it not for the oppression of the Council, I do believe that the people already have the beginnings of Community going all over One World. We see it in the Coffeehouses and on the farms, as well as the kindness that we offer to each other. Most recently, we all experienced it in the Harvest Festivals; both here and throughout all three Continental Territories.

"My friends, I do believe that uniting is what we are being called to do, and to help others do the same. We are called to encourage and help the people in our small local communities to become one large family. What we did here the other day by creating a Trader's Market is only the beginning."

There is silence around the room as everyone digests the truth that they have just heard coming from Liling.

Yakov speaks next. "There was a book once that our ancestors used to read all the time. I'm sure we have all heard these wonderful stories handed down as legends. In the beginning, this book describes a beautiful garden. And when I first heard the Chrysalenes calling themselves Adam and Eve, it somehow struck a chord in me, as if it somehow has something to do with this beautiful, perfect garden. Perhaps, Liling, this 'Garden of Ancient Times' is the Community we are meant to help establish."

"Yes, Yakov, I believe that it is," Liling replies. "I see it as a world where we all live in small communities and support one another with food, shelter, and much love. Our garden communities are then connected to each other through Trader's Markets and Community Centers. We can barter and trade our goods that way, as well as share news of the people at the Coffeehouses. The large estates and main houses can be centers of support, where we gather and learn from each other the ways of the earth and nature; combining it all with modern technology. With goodness and mercy on our side, a world of love and freedom is on the way. All things are possible!"

Yakov looks at Neely and says, "And I know that My Lady and I can do a whole lot of great cooking for a whole lot of people in such a world!"

Neely and the entire group fill the room with warm laughter, and she leans over and gives her man a big hug and a kiss.

Everyone begins to mutter amongst themselves with great enthusiasm for what has just been put forward. They are thinking about how it will be a most excellent topic for the Gathering of The Alliance, to discuss, how to move into swift action in the creation of such garden communities, in a world that has become a true paradise . . . a Garden of Ancient Days.

"Well!" says Kookie. "All this has made me hungry for a plate of chocolate chip cookies! Have you got any on hand, my Sister?" he asks Liling.

"That, and plenty of other pastries," she says, chuckling.

"And plenty of coffee, too!" says Yakov.

"Well, that settles it then," says the Major. "Pastries, coffee and chocolate chip cookies. Sounds like a great Adam and Eve kind of garden to me. I'm in!"

They retire to the dining area for their fanciful snack with much to think about and talk over. The big hurdle they anticipate ahead of them is the Council and the others of the UC who are supportive of the Council's oppression. But for the moment, the group is content and ready to move forward.

As the mid-afternoon pastry party is getting underway in the dining room of the Big House, the Chrysalenes from the Village of the Holy Ones are on their way over to deliver more news. They have just heard through their channels about PA, ES and SPA.

* * *

It is forlorn in the bowels of hell where total abandonment and loneliness are the ultimate torture of the human soul. The cries of the fallen are deep and mournful, lasting through all eternity.

Angie is walking on a path lined with faces appearing out of nowhere that cry out in agony and then disappear into the black nothingness. She tries desperately to hold her hands out to the hideous faces and relieve them of their suffering. But to no avail. As soon as Angie tries to touch them, they evaporate, returning to their void of despair.

The fallen one, as she calls him, said he had some business to take care of and left her alone for the time being. As soon as he left, the path she is now treading upon appeared. Walking along the agonizing road of lost souls, Angie hears very sorrowful words spoken to her heart saying, *"These are the faces of Hope Abandoned."* Her golden wings shimmer in the bleak world around her, and Angie finds herself hoping that the brilliant sight of her wings in this world of doom will give some poor soul a little respite from suffering. Her heart is truly breaking for all that she witnesses.

The Monarch Angel feels compassion pouring out of Angie's soul and speaks to her heart, *You have a loving soul, Angie creature. It is no wonder the fallen one has called out to you.*

I don't understand, Angel, says Angie. *I thought the fallen one is repelled by love that he thrives on chaos and is powered by fear.*

That is true, says Angel. *The fallen one is repelled by love and thrives on chaos and fear.*

So, what could he possibly want with a loving soul, then? But as soon as Angie asks the question, she begins to know the answer.

Angel can feel the awakening of Angie's deeper wisdom, as she says, *Yes, human creature, you are beginning to understand.*

Off in the distance, Angie sees the fallen one returning from his "business" as his familiar red glow is coming toward her in the darkness.

Finishing her thought quickly before he reaches her, she says to Angel's heart, *He must experience that which he loathes, and suffer in the same way that he dishes out to others. HE TAKES PLEASURE IN HIS OWN DISPLEASURE! That is, he thrives on ALL pain and suffering . . . including his own.*

You nailed it, sister creature! says Angel.

Wow! says Angie. *That must get rather confusing for him. But then again, he must thrive on that too; after all, confusion can lead to chaos.*

Right again! You are a smart woman creature! says Angel.

Angie laughs. *My beloved once said that to me, and he is most likely the smartest MAN creature in the whole world! Well, here comes the confused one. You know, I think I just may have figured out a strategy with him.*

I am truly looking forward to this! quips Angel.

* * *

After their pastry party the group goes out to the gardens at the invitation of the gardeners, Bem, Tafari, Nassor and Dumaka. Everyone is interested in seeing the fruits and vegetables; although, they really want to check out the whole set-up, including the huts that the gardeners live in.

"This is just great!" says Kookie.

Phil says, "This is how my people have always lived in Panamerica. I am a descendant of the Sioux nation. For a time, we were forced to live on places called *reservations*.

"But that has all changed. Now we are all equally disliked by the Council, so we are all from the same tribe, and we are all Brothers and Sisters."

"Amen, Brother!" says Kookie.

"Look!" exclaims Mimi, pointing to the Chrysalenes in the distance coming toward them.

They are walking with a bounce to their step singing their favorite song, "Siyahamba: We are marching in the Light of Love."

"Hello! We are over here!" the group calls out to the Chrysalenes.

Emeka is the first one to greet them as he calls out, "Hello, Mama Eve Zula and Papa Adam Makena! And all the rest of you!"

"Hello there, my child," Mama Eve Zula says with much joy.

"Mama, we are going to show *everybody* how to live in a garden, just like this one and your village!"

The Major interjects, "And we plan on living this way ourselves, Mama!"

"That is wonderful!" all the Chrysalenes say together as they laugh out loud.

"We have some news to bring you all," says Papa Adam Makena.

The group is listening intently to whatever the news may be that brought the whole group of Chrysalenes out to see them.

Papa continues, "We have discovered something that the UC does not themselves know, yet, but will find out very soon. They will soon learn that their leaders, PA, ES and SPA have disappeared."

"*WHAT!*" Everyone shrieks all at once before falling into a shocked silence.

Mama Eve Zula explains further, "We cannot go into details just yet, but they are apparently locked down in the underground palace at the polar location, along with their technical crew and all the High Overlord Contacts.

"The UC will have no way of knowing what happened to them, where they are, or even whether or not they are still alive. This will throw the Lords, Ladies and Masters into a state of great fear and chaos, with infighting amongst themselves. They are now left without the Council to lead them, so they will be fighting for their lives and control of the Council, no doubt."

Everyone looks at each other dumbfounded. While they are intensely excited to feel Freedom and the Garden right around the corner, they also know that the final stretch of the road to get there will be more dangerous than ever.

Eve Elli speaks up. "It's okay everybody, everything is gonna be okay. We've got Angie and Angel and the Big Daddy up in Heaven on our side! They all love us! And everything is gonna be just fine!"

All the people and Chrysalenes laugh together because they know that little Eve Elli is speaking the truth. Their hour of freedom is at hand.

Siyahamba!

* * *

That night as Kookie falls asleep, he has a dream . . .

He is walking in a beautiful garden. The sun is shining down upon a lush paradise of colorful flowers, fruits and vegetables. There is a sparkling lake with pure drinking water and a cool, refreshing waterfall for bathing and for pleasure. He can see two children, a boy and a girl, playing happily in the grass with butterflies, birds, and other friendly creatures all around. The creatures and the children are all loving on each other and having a wonderful time.

Then his beloved Angie appears out of the waterfall. She is the most beautiful and magnificent that he has ever seen her. Angie appears to be part human and part angel, with brilliant colors of orange, yellow and white, and shimmering wings of gold. The two lovers come together in a tender embrace. As Kookie holds Angie in his arms, his heart is breaking. He tells her how much he misses her and just how much he loves her.

Angie whispers to him gently: "It's alright my darling, Kookie, I love you. Hang in there my beloved and do not worry about me. I must stay here for a while and do what I can to keep the fallen one off balance. You must do what you can to help bring forth garden communities, and a world where people are free."

Angie kisses him, turns to mist, and disappears.

Kookie wakes up with his heart aching for his beloved, and says, "Thank you, Angie, my Woman, My Lady. I shall do all that I can to bring our people into a new world of Love and Freedom. I will also be here waiting for you. Please come back to me. I wish for nothing except to hold you one day in our earthly paradise."

As Kookie is falling back to sleep, he can hear a voice speaking to his heart saying, *It is already done, smart man-creature!*

The beast is growling and snarling while listening to the hopes and dreams of the two lovers.

So! You want to recreate that miserable Garden of Eden, do you?! The one where I appeared as a snake and ruined all your fun! Do you fools really think that I will

LET *you have your paradise?!* **THINK AGAIN, OH YE OF STUPID FAITH!**

The Angel of the Lord replies; *Yes. Think again, growly creature. And we'll see who the stupid one is! Hee Hee!*

Chapter 2 – Alliance

THE FULL IMPLICATIONS of PA, ES and SPA's disappearance have not quite sunk in yet. The entire group is just in a daze over the shocking news. Meanwhile, the Alliance is arriving with almost all the 36 original Lords and Ladies present now. The mansion is filling to capacity and will soon be overflowing, which creates more joy and hope among everyone.

Liling, Yakov and Kookie have been discussing the Garden Community plans with the new arrivals, and gathering ideas as folks respond with enthusiasm.

At the Trader's Market, people come from towns all over to participate, enjoying the new friends and newfound abundance that everyone gains with their free trade. Liling, Kookie and Yakov know that the Market is a great opportunity to share news with a lot of people and spread the word about their goals of a new way of life throughout One World.

The Lords and Ladies are anxious to hear from the traders and farmers about how they can all share their knowledge with each other in establishing a system of commerce, where they can trade and barter freely with one other.

Kookie knows, however, that they have not yet faced the wrath of the other members of the UC who will be angry and feel threatened by what they are doing. He is therefore, warning the UC of their fledgling Alliance to exercise caution and discretion when sharing their plans and ideas with others, whose sentiments might be unknown.

Kookie is also suggesting that each member spend time every day communing with one of the Chrysalenes at the Village of the Holy Ones, as well as the gardeners and local villagers from the Coffeehouses on what they all need to do as they move forward in laying the foundation for a true earthly paradise. The after-dinner evening gatherings are of utmost importance to get caught up with each other and share news and ideas. Kookie knows they desperately need to connect with and learn from the Chysalenes, as well as each other if they are going to make this whole new way of life happen. They must use the present moment wisely and get organized quickly before the pro-Council UC realize that they do not have leaders anymore; and all hell breaks loose.

* * *

Angie can see the red glow coming toward her accompanied by the increasing sound of growling.

"Well, Angel, here he comes. Time to throw some Light on things with the fallen one."

Whatever you say, Courageous Human Creature! I'm right here with you.

As the beast approaches Angie, his growling increases until he is howling violently. She watches him approach and notices that his appearance reminds her of a gargoyle; ugly, gnarly, grotesque-looking and angry. Although he can also appear as a large red face, red flame, or even shape shift into other creatures such as a snake, the gargoyle-look makes him seem almost comical to her.

To Angie, the ugliness of the beast is not really scary; it is just an outer manifestation of the inner, angry child who has fallen from his Father's grace.

"Now, now!" Angie admonishes him. "That's no way to have a conversation with a lady now, is it?"

AAARRRR! The beast growls in Angie's face. *I do not WISH to have a CONVERSATION with you!*

Angie looks at him and rolls her eyes, "Well then, what else do you wish to have? Without my consent, you cannot have anything because I am free to leave you at any time. And since you seem to want me here, well, things will get plenty boring if we have nothing to do or talk about for all of eternity, don't you think?

*TRICKY WOMAN! **I** . . . AM . . . TRICKSSSSSSSTER!* **NOT YOU!** the beast hisses.

Don't bet on it, trickster creature! Oops! Sorry to interrupt. Carry on, Smart Woman Creature.

"Perhaps, trickster, you are the *master* trickster, but I have learned a few things from you too, as it seems most of us humans have."

At this, the beast calms down. He is listening.

"Oh yes," Angie continues, "It was all the circumstances of Ebola that led me to the road in life that I am on now. And since you have said that the recent Ebola pandemic was *your* doing, then I have *you* to thank. For this I am truly blessed . . . and yes, even thankful to you."

The beast remains quiet. As Angie is looking at him, it seems that he has even shrunk a little bit.

"Well," she continues, "now it is your turn."

WHAT? he bellows at Angie.

"Yes, that is how you have a conversation, fallen one. First one speaks then the other. Otherwise, I am simply talking to myself."

The beast suddenly goes into an inexplicable fit of laughter. *Talk to yourself then, tricky woman, if it displeases you! And I shall take much pleasure in your DISSSpleasure!* he continues to laugh and hiss.

"So then," says Angie, "there are things which *DO give you pleasure?*"

The beast stops laughing and gives Angie an evil grin, *Oh yes, my dear, GREAT pleasure. Like what is about to happen to the people on Earth very shortly, when they realize that those buffoons are gone.*

"I believe you are referring to the Council: PA, ES and SPA," says Angie.

The beast furrows his haughty brow and says, *How did YOU ever find out about those three imbeciles?*

Angie smiles and shrugs her golden wings. "Oh, I have friends in high places, you know."

I see. Well, your friends are about to face a VERY hard time. And all because of me! he says with a sarcastic tone.

Still smiling, Angie asks, "Is that so?"

YES! THAT . . . IS . . . SO!

Angel is pleased, sensing what is going on inside of the smart woman creature. And she says to the fallen one, *Well then, trickster creature. Give it your best shot and we'll see who wins!*

* * *

Dinner is winding down and Kookie stands up at the table. He raises his glass of pure water to everyone and taps it with a spoon to get their attention.

The guests quiet down and turn their attention to Kookie as he begins.

"My friends. I am overwhelmed by the goodness and love that is around the table this evening. I am humbled and honored to be a part of it. Thank you, thank you all, for the kindness and compassion that you are bringing to this new world that we are all being asked to participate in. May we begin by joining each other in a moment of silence to honor *all* of our Brothers and Sisters of One World."

The Chrysalenes glow, radiating their love to one and all, and the rest of the people close their eyes and feel their sweet energy.

After a few moments Kookie says to the group gathered, "What we are about to do, or attempt to do, is nothing new to humankind. Throughout human history, people have been divided and pitted against each other. And perhaps throughout history we have taken it for granted that such divisiveness is inevitable; or that evil, fear and hate is just a part of who we are. Some have suggested that human beings, if left to their own devices, are basically evil and will do harm to others. Then there are others who have professed that people are basically good, and it is their fears that cause them to be mistrusting of each other, causing the divisiveness that has always existed among us.

"Dearest friends, I believe people are indeed flawed but basically good, and we would truly be happy in a world of kindness. I would say this is true for most people. It certainly includes enough people so that we *can* have our paradise here together. And our time to manifest a happy life for everyone is now."

"Here, here!" everyone cries out around the table, toasting each other and Kookie, with their glasses of purified water.

Yakov stands and says, "There is not much more for me to add to what my Brother Kookie just said, except that I too believe that it is not only possible, but that the time has come for us to have a life of unity, freedom and love for all people, including Lords and Masters, throughout One World."

Cheers and applause and glass clinking all around for Yakov.

Then Liling stands up and says, "We have much to learn from each other, as well as the Chrysalenes. They speak of *becoming love,* which I believe is what we need to learn as we move forward on our mutual path together. I think that we have been learning Courageous Love all along, and now it is time to open our hearts and give of ourselves completely, learning how to do what the Chrysalenes do. I just know that we can do this!"

"Amen, Sister!" everyone cries out.

The Major stands to say his piece. "I have already been so blessed from what the Chrysalenes have taught me about Courageous Love and the healing that they have given to me. For those of you who do not know what happened to my father recently, I will just tell you briefly.

"My father, Master Howard of Howard Pharmaceuticals, was the greediest, meanest man you could imagine, who thought nothing of the people whom he hurt. He considered them *useless eaters* and life not worthy of life. And now, he has been miraculously transformed by the same Chrysalene-love that healed me, into a totally different man; or rather, the man he truly was meant to be. Kookie always said that my father was not really a bad man inside, and now I can see that.

"I do believe that all of us in this room can learn how to use the power of love to change things in One World in a way that human beings have never done before. And I am ready, and at your service to work with all of you to make that happen."

Kookie stands up again and says, "I propose that we break up into small groups and each work with a Chrysalene to guide us and teach us the things that we will need in the coming days. I suggest we do this every day, and reach out to others, as well. There will be plenty of people coming here over the coming weeks and months, and, of course, there are also plenty of people to reach out to at the Coffeehouses.

"When we return to our homes, we can take the message of Courageous Love back to our communities and spread the energy all around. Meanwhile, I would like to suggest that for those of us who so desire, we stay together here in Johannesburg for now and gather our strength of Light and Love from each other."

There are nods of consent all around the room as everyone prepares to break up into small groups with one of the Chrysalenes.

"Oh, just one more thing!" Kookie says, "Before you all go off to your groups, this is most important."

Tapping the tips of his fingers together, Kookie says, "Um, has anyone seen that plate of chocolate chips cookies going around?"

Everyone erupts into a fit of laughter.

"Hey, Brother!" Yakov calls out to him. "Neely and I will go in the kitchen and make you some more!"

"You're on!" Kookie laughs.

* * *

The fallen one has been listening to the dinner conversation, and he is disgusted by what he hears.

Oh no, Kookie, my FRRRIEEEND! *he sneers. There is a reason why humankind has always been divided against itself. And that reason is very simple. Yes Kookie, very simple indeed. That reason is* **ME!**

It has been my greatest pleasure down through the ages, ever since I have been expelled from the paradise that you are now so eager to recreate, to keep humans mistrusting, fighting against, and hating each other.

Do you really think that I will let you, YOU, a mere mortal, High Lord Kenneth, take THAT away from me? Do not forget who I am, Lord Kenneth! I am Trickster, and I am Lucifer. And I can pull a few nasty tricks and light a few unholy fires of my own! There is one amongst the Lords and Ladies who is about to be named the new ruler of the Council. And beware, because **THAT ONE WILL ANSWER TO ME!**

Well, Kookie, my, FRRRIEEEND, *as an angel of 'you know who' said to me just a little while ago, 'Give it your best shot and we'll see who wins!'*

* * *

Phil and Doc have an idea. As everyone breaks off into groups with a Chrysalene, they go to the kitchen, bringing a little pouch that they brought with them from Lisa and Kenny's farm. They find several pots, flasks, plenty of teacups, and a serving trolly.

"This ought to do it," says Doc.

"Yep!" agrees Phil. "Let's get that water boiling."

Into each pot, Phil and Doc add Sequioa twigs and some dried flowers of Baby's Breath, Carnation, and Red Rose.

"This should get things moving in the right direction for everyone," Doc says.

The two of them go over the combined effects from the herbal formula they have just put together.

"Well, Sister, it feels to me like what we all need is the harmony and love that these here earth spirits can give us if we are going to live peacefully with everyone in our New World. And in order to do that, we must be able to let go of the pain and suffering in our own lives, learning to forgive ourselves as well as each other," says Phil.

"You bet," Doc chuckles. "Let's get some Harmony passed around to our companions here!"

Yakov and Neely are in Eve Gerda's group. As everyone comes in, they find Eve Gerda seated on the floor and they instinctively form a circle sitting on the floor around her.

She smiles at the group, bows her head, and says, "Thank you all for allowing me to be of service to you."

The Lords and Ladies respond around the circle, "The honor is all mine, ma'am. A pleasure to honor you. May I be worthy of that which I am about to receive."

Then Eve Gerda closes her eyes, holds out her hands and begins to sing an angel song, the same as if she were loving on the seedlings growing in the field.

In fact, that is exactly what she is doing. Before her sits a new crop of *human seeds*. These people have been raised with all the material wealth any human being could possibly ever need or want, just as seedlings that have plenty of good earth, water, and sunlight. Now they must be open to receive all the goodness that the heavens have been raining down upon them since the dawn of man, and face the challenges of the fallen one, who has also been around for a very long time.

Eve Gerda, along with every other Chrysalene in One World is hearing the words of an Angel of the Lord in her heart saying: *Give it your best shot, Chrysalene Creature, and we'll see who wins!*

The Major and Vi are seated around Adam Okello. The others are all listening intently as the Major shares his lifelong journey with his father, the pain and humiliation that he experienced growing up with an angry father, and how the Major always wished to be loved and accepted by him.

"It wasn't enough for me to wish for all of those things," the Major explains. "I had to *become* all of those things myself. And when I did, I was able to give to my father what I wanted so desperately from *him* all those years. I was able to give him my love without expecting anything in return. That is when the miracle with him happened."

"But wasn't that very hard to do? Isn't that easier said than done? How could any of us ever do that?" asks everyone around the room.

"Yes, we can be very knuckle-headed," the Major quips, pounding his head with his knuckles to everyone's amusement. "But our Creator knows that, and that is why He has given us so many ways of receiving the energy of Courageous Love. Because that is truly what we all need: to be open to receiving Love from all kinds of different sources."

Vi nods at him and picks up the cup in front of her. "This is what works for me," she says holding up the teacup for everyone to see. "The herbal blend that Phil and Doc have prepared and brought to us. It is the heavenly gift of nature prepared by two loving people and brought in and served to us from the heart. Weren't we all happy just to see them bring in the trolly and serve up the tea with their infectious smiles and good humor?"

Everyone nods with understanding.

Vi continues, "And that was before we even drank the herbal tea!"

"We put out what we feel inside ourselves," says the Major. "If we want Good Medicine to go out, then first we need to *be* the Good Medicine ourselves. And that involves receiving Good Medicine from the Great Herbalist in the sky, as well as from each other!"

"Ahh! Now *that* makes sense!" everyone remarks as they take another sip of their tea.

In another room, Liling, Dumaka and their group have been going over ways of helping others to receive Courageous Love.

"It seems to me," says Liling, "that the little things in life can sometimes make a big difference."

This has everyone intrigued.

"Like what? Is it really all that simple?" the Lords and Ladies say around the room.

"Actually," says Liling, "I have always believed that the answers to life's biggest questions and challenges are usually just that simple. They may not be easy, but they sure are simple!"

Everyone smiles and nods.

"So, what I am proposing is that we come up with some practical things we can do for ourselves, for each other and for the community," Liling says.

"You mean like the Trader's Market, Lady Liling?" one of the Lords asks her.

"Yes, exactly, just like the Trader's Market. Although I consider that to be a little bit more than a simple thing," she says. "Putting together an outdoor market is quite involved!"

Everyone chuckles, and someone in the circle says, "I'll bet it is, My Lady!"

"I'm sure there are even more simple, less complicated, little things we can do, especially with those we really need to reach out to; that is, those who are now left without their Council," says Liling.

The magnitude of what Liling is saying registers with the group. They all seem to be awakening to the idea that perhaps it is the simple acts of Courageous Love that are very much needed right now to heal the divide of a very broken world.

* * *

From the depths of hell, the beast is listening to the words that threaten his hold on humanity. He raises his fist and shakes it at the heavens above saying, *You know why they are divided and angry at one another; because You have given those simple sheep freewill;* **AND I HAVE NOT!** *You just open the door and invite the fools in, where I manipulate, terrify and coerce the idiots in every way that I can to* **JOIN FORCES WITH ME, OR ELSE!**

Angie listens to the fallen one ranting at the Heavenly Father, and a thought occurs to her. "Well Lucifer, if I may call you that, I think I understand now why you need to hold people's feet to the flames, so to speak, to get them to join forces with you.

Nice metaphor, Smart Woman Creature! Hee hee! Oops! Sorry to interrupt. You're doing fine. Do continue!

Lucifer laughs out loud as he says to Angie, *So, tricky woman, you think you've got it all figured out, eh?*

Angie considers it for a moment as she nods and says, "Well, yes. I believe you truly do see the Divine Light in human beings. And although we are not perfect and at times can even do bad things, we are basically born in the image of our Father. And for this, the Heavenly Father loves us and forgives us, and YOU, oh nasty beast, know this to be true; and it galls you to think that your power is actually limited, while ours, on the other hand, is not limited at all.

"If we were ever to wake up and realize that, it would be game over for you, so you have to play on our fears and imperfections to keep us from remembering who we truly are . . ."

AAAAGGGGHHHH! The beast roars and cuts Angie off as he is now in full blown rage. *YOU WICKED, TRICKY WOMAN! AND JUST EXACTLY WHO DO YOU THINK YOU TRULY ARE?!*

Angie replies, "I am, as we all are, children of our Heavenly Father. And you, my sorry little creature, are not; and never will be. And for this you hate us, and will do anything to divide us against each other, that we may suffer. And suffer we do, fallen one, in your name. But once we discover that the source of our true power, pleasure and passion is in the Light and in Love, your power over us is gone. . . for good."

The beast erupts into a screaming frenzy that echoes throughout the eternal chambers of darkness in the underworld of hell.

The Angel of the Lord is twittering with delight, and Angie is sure she can feel Angel tapping the tips of her wings together saying, *With you, human creature, we are* **all** *pleased!*

* * *

Kookie, Mimi and Ryan have been receiving some wonderful healing energy from Adam Taj, and Phil and Doc's Herbal Tea. They also love the ideas that everyone in their group has been coming up with regarding how to reach out to others in a world that has, for the time being, been left leaderless.

"I have a great idea for this evening," Kookie says to the group.

All eyes and ears are upon him.

"I say that we all go down to the Coffeehouse and talk to people; we can share some of the thoughts and plans we have been kicking around here today and see what happens."

"Yes," says Mimi, "That's a great idea! And I also want to listen to the people and hear what *they* have to say; what they consider to be a utopian world and what *they* would like to see happen as we move forward."

Kookie looks at her and smiles, "Yes, Mimi, I think that is the best idea yet!"

"Thanks, Kookie," she says, "And here is just one more thought. Since there are way too many of us to fit inside a Center Coffeehouse, I suggest that we each bring something to sit on and start a gathering outside right in front of the Center."

"Oh yeah! Sounds great! Let's do it!" everyone exclaims around the room.

"Great!" says Kookie. "Let's tell the others. We can go over there this evening right after our meal when the Coffeehouse is at its fullest." Pointing his index finger in the air he adds, "Oh, and just one more thing. I will provide all the chocolate chip cookies for everyone!"

"Ha, ha! You're on, Brother," everyone laughs, and the meeting is adjourned.

* * *

That evening, the local Center Coffeehouse near the Lord's Estate in Johannesburg is teeming with people from all over the area.

Word is getting around about Liling's weekly Trader's Market, and excitement is growing all over Johannesburg and beyond. News is also traveling to Masters who own farms, such as Master James of Judy's farm and Master Franz of Lisa and Kenny's.

The group from the Lord's Estate arrives equipped with their own folding chairs and cafe tables, ready for an outdoor evening gathering in front of the Center. Apparently Kookie spent the rest of the day in the kitchen, along with Yakov, Neely, Liling and Dumaka, baking up a storm of exquisite cookie creations.

When they enter the Coffeehouse, Liling announces to everyone, "Good evening, everyone! I recognize many faces here from our recent gathering at the Trader's Market!"

"Good evening, My Lady! Hi there, Lady Liling!" the crowd calls back to her.

"My friends and I would love to have the pleasure of your company for a little pastry feast, and good conversation, out in front of the

Coffeehouse. We are going to be talking about the Trader's Market and would love to hear your ideas on anything else we can do for you.

"Oh, and we are getting several flasks of coffee for all to share and lots of the Coffeehouse teacakes, so bring your empty cups and your appetites." With a wink and a smile, she adds, "There are plenty of exquisite cookies of all kinds, too!"

"Yes! You got it, Sister," the crowd in the Coffeehouse exclaims, as they all get up and move outside.

Everyone finds a place to get comfortable, whether it is sitting on the chairs, or the ground. And they *really* get excited when the cookie trays are passed around.

Liling gets the crowds attention and says, "Thank you for joining us, my friends! We are looking forward to seeing you all at the next Trader's Market!"

There is much cheering and applause with promises of, "I'll be there, for sure!"

Then, she smiles at the people and continues; "My friends and I who are gathered here wish to do all we can to serve you and the community, so please let us know what those needs are. We will walk around and try to reach out to each and every one of you."

The Alliance proceeds to mill about talking to and making friends with people. Of course, the Panamerican folks put on their Universal Translator pendant necklaces and turn them on.

Doc is in absolute heaven since this has always been her favorite thing to do, talking to new people and learning of their desires, passions and pleasures.

One thing they all notice is that the people seem to be yearning to have a voice and be heard; to be treated with dignity and to know that their lives count. People need to know that someone cares about them and what *they* each can contribute of their own skills and talents. And now that the Alliance has given them permission to speak up and be heard, it seems to have awakened these buried desires, which many folks did not even know that they had.

After a wonderful evening of fellowship at the Center Coffeehouse the friends get back to the Big House. The Alliance is overjoyed at the hope they feel and about what they can do to help create the life of love and freedom for One World.

Kookie takes his buddies aside: the Major, Vi, Mimi, Ryan, Yakov, Neely, Phil, Doc, Liling and Dumaka. He says, "I'm just amazed at the change I am seeing in people already and in such a short time. It gives me so much hope and—" he stops talking as he thinks of Angie and misses her terribly. He wishes desperately that he could be sharing this moment with her.

As Kookie struggles to finish his sentence while fighting back tears, he loses the battle. All his friends know what is bothering him, and they feel his pain with him. When they see Kookie break down, the rest of them are very saddened and grow quiet.

Finally, the Major says to him, "She is right here with us, bro'." Patting his chest. "Angie is here, in all of our hearts. Whatever she's saying to that guy downstairs," the Major smiles and says, "I'm *sure* Angie is giving that bad boy a *really* hard time!"

Kookie and the others have a brief chuckle. Wiping his eyes, Kookie says, "Thank you."

Vi hears a voice from another dimension saying, *You got that right, Major Creature, and I'm enjoying watching Angie make that bad boy creature squirm! Hee Hee!*

Chapter 3 – Philia[3]

IT IS THE MORNING OF the Trader's Market, and folks at the Lord's estate are preparing for a large turnout on the back field of the Big House. Bem, however, has another idea. He calls together Tafari, Nassor, Dumaka and the other gardeners on the estate to share it with them. A sizable group turns up including Doc and Phil who heard about it from Dumaka. They gather in the garden area outside Bem and Tafari's hut which is just large enough to accommodate one and all.

While everyone from the Big House now has a Universal Translator pendant necklace, Doc and Phil are learning to listen more than speak, and that listening is done more with the heart than with the ears, so the translator almost becomes unnecessary.

When she turns it on, Doc says to Phil, "We *all* speak the language of the heart, don't we?"

He touches her cheek, smiles and says, "Yes, my Sister, we certainly do."

"Thank you, my friends, for taking the time on this busy morning to stop by and share some thoughts with us," Bem says. "Let us break bread together and share our sustenance first."

He takes out two loaves of bread, and the other gardeners bring forth several jugs of water. As they pass the bread and water around, Bem invites everyone to join in.

"Please tear off a piece of bread and take a drink of the water. This is our way of honoring the trust and love among us. We ask that all who feel bound to each other in the Love and Light, eat this bread and drink this purified water in honor of our sacred friendship."

---

[3] *Friendship love*

Doc places her hands on her chest and bows humbly. Phil puts his hands together and does the same. They both graciously accept the bread and water when it comes around and thank Bem for bringing them into their circle of gardener friends.

"Here at the estate, we are most fortunate," Bem explains. "We live a simple life of growing our own food, drinking pure rainwater, and washing and bathing in the streams that run through the property. Our huts are modest and comfortable, and we can handcraft most of what we need. Though we are considered poor by the standards of the UC, I have never felt that way, with our basic needs all taken care of; our families, and our deep, enduring friendships, nurtured and supported.

"The Alliance has been talking about ways in which we can all give of ourselves to One World and help bring true freedom to the people. When our Brothers and Sisters, the Lords and Ladies, came out here the other day and showed their enthusiasm at the way we live, I just knew that we had something here worth sharing with everyone."

Bem goes quiet for a moment, inviting others to join in with thoughts or comments.

Dumaka stands up and says, "There are so many people in One World who are homeless. And even though they get points on their cards for food and basics as we all do, and the Rest Areas at the Centers give them a roof over their heads, it is not the same as having a hut of one's own and a community of friends."

He looks around the group gathered together and continues, "There is much that we can do to help others organize small communities such as ours. And I'm sure that there are other gardeners and farmers throughout all three Continental Territories of One World who feel the same way."

At this point Doc jumps to her feet, filled with excitement. She shares with the group her own farm life back home as well as her friends, Judy, Kenny, and Lisa. She describes the homing pigeons, their herbal teas, and how strongly they have all felt their whole lives about doing exactly what Bem and Dumaka are talking about.

"This is a dream come true!" Doc exclaims with her hands reaching out to everybody. "When can we get started?"

Everyone laughs and Bem says, "Actually, dear Sister, I was going to suggest getting started today."

Looking toward the area where preparations are underway for the Trader's Market he adds, "In fact, we can start just as soon as people arrive over there at the Market!"

"YEE HAA!" Doc yowls. Phil laughs with his face in his hands, shaking his head in amusement at Doc's enthusiasm.

Bem says, "One last thing I would like to mention before we go on over there and join in the preparations. I think we should use this opportunity of today's Market to ask the people if they might be interested in learning this way of life from us, either by spending some time living here or maybe even having a few of us come out to live with them. Are there any of you, my friends, who would like to be a part of this?"

Every person jumps up at the same time and cries, "Yes Brother! You bet!" and "Count me in!"

"Well then, my Brothers and Sisters, let's go on over there and get ready to make some new friends, shall we?"

With much joy and laughter, they all head over to the back field of the Lord's estate. Doc tells Phil that she has to make one quick stop first to send out a couple of birds through the Pigeons Communication Network. One is going to Judy and the other one to Kenny and Lisa. The message reads:

FARMSTEAD – GO AHEAD! – BIG DEAL

Phil sees the note that Doc is about to send out across the globe through a chain of pigeons. Once again, he smiles and shakes his head.

Doc says to him, "Judy, Lisa and I have been talking about something very similar to Bem's idea for a long time, down to every last detail, including how to handle the Master owners of the property. They will both be *very* happy to see this!

* * *

Judy has been working out in the crop fields with Adam Tate, Eve Jennie and the others all morning, and miraculously her knees and back are not sore at all. She turns to Eve Jennie and says, "You know, I just can't remember a time when I could do as much gardening as I am now, and not have to drag myself in afterwards, looking for the nearest spot to collapse in. It truly is a miracle that I can just keep on going and feel fine!"

Eve Jennie laughs and says, "Do you know why you are feeling this way, Miss Judy?"

Judy considers the idea for a moment and then it suddenly occurs to her, "Why yes! I think I *do* know! Ever since the heavy rains came and it yielded this miraculous harvest, I feel like I am about half my age! Is that possible, Eve Jennie?"

Adam Tate has been listening to the conversation and he too begins to laugh. "Well, Miss Judy," he says to her. "If that is how you are feeling then it is more than possible. It is already done."

Adam Tate and Eve Jennie are both smiling with love and compassion in their eyes. They look up and reach for the heavens and then bow their heads and say, "Thank you."

As Judy is watching them and feeling truly blessed, she sees a pigeon coming in for a landing at the coop. "*A PIGEON! YAY!*" she cries out and charges for the coop. Number 9 and #10 are making their acquaintance with the new guy as Judy reaches the coop.

"Hello, hello my new little friend! What message do you have for me today?" Judy grabs the scroll from the pigeon's leg band and reads Doc's message.

She is instantly overcome with emotion and begins to cry, dropping to her "youthful" knees. Reaching up to the heavens, Judy says, "Thank you! Thank you! Thank you, for letting me serve you in this way! I will not let you down! Thank you!"

* * *

Lisa and Kenny have been hard at work and grateful to have the new hands on deck helping them. Apart from the Chrysalenes, several homeless folks from Bear River have heard about the enormous harvest and come to help out as well. There has been much construction going on at the farm, including many more huts to accommodate all the new farmhands.

Much to the joy and gratitude of Kenny and Lisa, the Bear River Farm is slowly turning into the Bear River Garden Community, or Bear River Gardens.

Kenny is busy day and night filling orders from all over One World for new pigeons. It is all part of the Intercontinental Pigeons Communication Network, which is growing rapidly. Kenny is organizing a gathering for Masters all over One World who have heard about and expressed great interest in learning to use homing pigeons.

The Masters do not like being spied on by the Council and moles of the UC either, so they are quite happy to have a form of communication that is under the radar of the Council's surveillance system. For this, Kenny and Lisa have been receiving all kinds of goods in trade, which they have been using to further expand their new community.

Master Franz, who owns Bear River Farm, is also receiving a greater abundance than ever as Kenny and Lisa have been sharing their abundance with him too. But even more than that, the Master is also beginning to taste freedom; freedom from the controlling, watchful eyes of the Council. Lisa and Kenny have been talking about inviting him to their next Harvest Festival. They are just not sure how to approach him since friendship has always been frowned upon between the UC and the people.

"I just wish there was some way we could invite the guy, honey," Lisa says to her Man as she brings him his afternoon meal. "I mean sometimes I think he is really lonely, you know, ever since his wife, our mistress passed."

Kenny nods as he is lost in thought over this himself. Then he sees another pigeon landing in his coop. *Another request for more pigeons,* he thinks to himself, smiling. He takes the scroll and reads the message from Doc.

Turning to his Woman with joy in his eyes and laughter in his heart, he hands her the message and says, "Honey, pack up some of those scrumptious pastries of yours and a loaf of bread in one of those pretty picnic baskets. Then meet me at the autobike. We are going to call on our Master Franz!"

Lisa reads the message from Doc and she too begins to laugh and cry. "Be right there, sweetheart!" And like her friend Judy, Lisa also drops to her knees, reaches for the heavens and says, "Thank you, Father in Heaven! Thank you!"

* * *

Master Franz is out in his garden tending to the Roses and Violets. Cultivating flowers was his wife's favorite pastime, and the Roses and Violets were her favorite. He is not very good at it as Mistress Margaret was, but her dying wish was for him to take care of her "babies" as she called them. Master Franz and his Mistress Margaret never had any children, so the flowers were truly her *babies.*

Master Franz has been receiving disturbing messages lately from his Overlord. The daily Buddy transmissions of news and instructions have been "temporarily shut down," as he has been told by his Overlord, but the reasons for that are vague.

Rumors are abounding through the people and the UC about the disappearance of the Council, but no one will talk about it, either to confirm or deny.

Master Franz knows better than to come out and ask his Overlord a direct question about such a delicate matter. So, he simply says nothing and remains in the dark. It is a very gloomy place to be for a man who is already sad and lonely.

The House Servant comes out to the garden to tell Master Franz that there are two people here to see him.

"Who are they, House Servant?" asks Master Franz.

"They say that they are the Caretakers at Bear River Farm, Master. Shall I give them an audience with you, or shall I send them away?"

"Show them into my study. I shall be there momentarily."

Master Franz looks at the Roses and Violets and says to them, "Now what could those two possibly want, I wonder? From the sounds of it they had quite a harvest over there. Filled my coffers with one shot, they did!"

Looking at the flowers he says, "Do you think they are coming to gloat and boast to a lonely old man, my dear Margaret? They couldn't possibly need anything from me, now could they?"

Somewhere inside of his broken heart, Master Franz hears the gentle voice of his beloved Margaret saying one word to him, "Philia."

The House Servant escorts Kenny and Lisa into the study. "The Master will be with you shortly," he says and closes the door as he leaves.

Lisa looks around the room while they are waiting. On the mantel she sees a beautiful picture of Mistress Margaret with a vase of Roses and Violets sitting next to it.

Lisa whispers to her Man as if she is in a holy place, "He really loved her, Kenny, and he really misses her."

* * *

From the bowels of hell, the fallen one is listening to Lisa's words. They are words of compassion and tenderness, words of understanding and forgiveness, and words that are reaching out with the Heavenly Father's high and pure form of love: Friendship. Yet the words are coming from a slave to a Master!

This, the fallen one cannot bear!

STUPID WOMAN! the beast yells.

"Oh," says Angie, "I thought you said I was a *smart* woman."

NOT YOUUU! the beast shrieks at her.

Hm . . . ponders Angel, *seems like something has got his dander up, suddenly flying off the handle like that. See what you can do with this one, Sister Creature.*

Sure thing, partner, Angie says to Angel's heart.

"Well, to whom are you referring then?" Angie asks the fallen one.

She thinks she can take one of my prizes, MY PRIZES away from me! Like that other one . . . little Miss Violet did when she gave Howard that water blessed from you know who.

*WELL, IT WILL **NOT** HAPPEN AGAIN! NOT THIS TIME AND NOT THIS ONE! FRANZ IS MINE! DO YOU HEAR ME STUPID WOMAN?! ALL MINE!*

Angie and Angel have guessed what is going on up there.

"Yes," Angie says to the beast. "I can see where losing someone you thought was all yours can be irritating to you."

I SHALL NOT LOSE! I SHALL NOT LOSE! the fallen one screams.

Give it your best shot, beastie creature, and we shall see who wins!

* * *

Kenny is also gazing at the photo of Mistress Margaret. He thinks to himself, *I just can't imagine what it must be like to lose your best friend, your partner, and your lover.*

He takes a deep breath and sighs, pulling Lisa in closer to him. She puts her head on his shoulder and the door of the study opens.

Master Franz enters. He is an elderly gentleman who appears to be in his 80s. With a worn-out look on his face, Master Franz walks slowly and deliberately over to his desk next to the mantel. He pauses for a moment to look at the photo of Mistress Margaret and then sits down behind the desk.

He finally acknowledges the presence of the two other human beings in his study when he slowly looks up at Lisa and Kenny and says, "What can I do for you?"

Lisa and Kenny look at each other and then at Master Franz. Should they stand up? Should they walk over to where he is seated? Should they run out the nearest exit like a bat out of hell?

Lisa takes the plunge, standing up and cautiously walking over to him. Stopping before she reaches his desk, Lisa says, "Good day to you, Master Franz, sir." Bowing slightly and pausing for a moment, Lisa continues, "I hope that all is well with you sir."

Master Franz is looking down at nothing in particular on his desk. He appears to not be paying any attention at all to what Lisa is saying, as if he is not even aware of her presence.

Lisa becomes frightened when four words come into her head: *"Courageous Love, human creature!"*

Mustering up her courage she says to him, "I brought these for you, sir," and she holds out the picnic basket full of her pastries and bread."

He looks up at Lisa and her basket and notices that she is smiling at him.

"As you know," she continues, "We are having a most wonderful harvest, and I just wanted to share some of our blessings with you."

Master Franz looks into Lisa's eyes and sees something warm and familiar. He is reminded of his dearest Margaret's sweet soul, and the trace of a smile appears across his face.

Seeing this, Lisa carefully moves over to his desk and lifts her basket to set it down in front of Franz.

From the depths of hell, a voice suddenly screams out in agonizing fear of his imminent defeat, ***NOOO! I SHALL NOT LOSE!***

As Lisa lifts up her basket a sudden cramp takes hold in her arm. The cramp causes her to jerk her arm out of control, sending her basket flying backwards and knocking the photo of Mistress Margaret and the arranged flowers off the mantel. The picture frame and vase of Roses and Violets come crashing to the ground, shattering in a thousand tiny pieces everywhere.

Kenny jumps up, and Lisa stifles a scream; Angel say *OOPS!* and the beast yells *GOTCHA! HA!*

Master Franz beholds the shattered glass and suddenly does something he has not been able to do since he was a little boy. He breaks down and weeps.

"Oh Lord!" cries out Lisa. "I am so sorry! I got a sudden cramp in my arm! I am so sorry!"

Kenny is by her side in two seconds, and Master Franz is just sitting at his desk weeping. He says nothing, but cries for his wife and for all the suffering he has ever felt and never been allowed to express. 'Men don't cry!' he was admonished as a child and humiliated any time he did so. And now it seems, a life full of pent-up grief has been unleashed.

He puts his head down on his desk and an avalanche of tears comes pouring out of his broken soul.

Lisa and Kenny stand there feeling the Master's pain. Lisa is wanting so much to touch him that her hand starts to instinctively reach out. Master Franz senses her hand and does not flinch or pull away. Very gingerly she touches his arm and says, "I'm so sorry for your loss, Master. She was a beautiful, sweet soul, inside and out.

Then the miracle happens. Without looking at Lisa or saying a word, Master Franz puts his hand on top of Lisa's hand; he stops crying for a moment and says, "Thank you."

Kenny sees a small dust broom and dustpan next to the hearth and he starts to clean up the broken glass. Picking up the photo and flowers, he gently arranges them on the mantel, saying to Master Franz, "Mistress Margaret must have really liked flowers, sir."

The Master smiles a little and says, "Roses and Violets were her favorite."

Lisa and Kenny both look at each other and nod. Lisa says to Master Franz, "Sir, we are having another Harvest Festival Gathering tomorrow night. We would be honored if you would join us."

Master Franz stands up and looks at Lisa. He puts out both of his hands to her and Lisa puts her arms around him. Kenny pats him on the back, and a soft chuckle escapes from the Master's widening grin. He says, "Thank you both. It would be my pleasure."

When they arrive back at the farm, Lisa and Kenny are so excited they just cannot wait to share the news with everyone.

The Chrysalenes are glowing with delight, imagining all the wonderful healing that they can give to Master Franz, and everyone is very much looking forward to meeting him.

Lisa writes a message to Judy and asks Kenny to send it out immediately with #1.

WE DID IT! – THE DAM IS BROKE! – HE'S COMING TO OUR FESTIVAL TOMORROW NIGHT! – MAMA BEAR

* * *

Judy, the Chrysalene, and the other farm hands are all having their evening meal together at the tables outside. They have much to celebrate with the news that they received earlier from Johannesburg and they look forward to sharing with others their farming community way of life. They sit down and pass a loaf of bread around. As each one tears off a chunk of bread from the loaf, they give thanks for the day and the brighter days to come.

Judy gets up and says to the crowd, "My friends, I know that this is a very exciting beginning to the life we have all dreamed of, yet there will also be ups and down and obstacles on the road ahead. I believe that our biggest obstacle will be the fear created by so many years of mistrust among the UC and ourselves, as well as fear and mistrust in general. I also believe that we *will* overcome those obstacles and have One World of love and kindness. With a little faith and a lot of love, we can do it!"

Everyone cheers and Judy raises her glass of pure water. They all drink together in their strong bond of friendship.

Just as Judy sits down, they all see a pigeon heading for the coop. Adam Tate puts his hand out to #1 who flies over and lands on his shoulder. Judy retrieves the scroll from #1's leg band and reads Lisa's wonderful message to everyone. They all know that the "broken dam" is Master Franz, which means that if Lisa and Kenny can do it, so can they with their own Master James, and so can everyone.

It is the greatest gift of hope that they can receive, and everyone knows for certain that their time is at hand, and freedom is just around the corner.

* * *

Deep, down in the dimensions of hell, the fallen one cries out in unspeakable agony.

Angie just looks at him and sighs, as Angel speaks to the fallen one saying, *Sorry, beastie creature. You can't win 'em all!*

Chapter 4 – Secrets

THE BEAST IS MORE AND MORE DISTURBED by the battles of the souls that he is losing, one by one. However, he is listening keenly to the voices of those who are raging, in anger and in fear, calling out to him to give them power.

There is one in particular who has caught his attention, and for that one he has gone off to take care of urgent business.

Angel seizes the time alone with Angie and says, *Come with me, Angie Creature. Let us walk for a while in spirit through the forest. There are things that I need to show you.*

"Will anyone be able to see us?" asks Angie.

No Human Creature will see you, but every other living earth spirit will be aware of your presence.

A soft purple light is cutting through the darkness, slowly growing lighter as an underworld forest is revealed.

"Where are we, Angel?" Angie asks.

We are underneath a forest floor. I have made it just light enough so you can see what is happening here. Look closely and carefully, but not with your eyes for they will deceive you. Look with your heart, Angie Creature, for that is where the truth resides.

At first Angie notices that she is walking through what looks like a great forest of upside-down trees. Their branches appear to be hairy and without leaves. They are all dark brown and smell like earth that has just been rained upon. The trees are teeming with life, but the life is so small that Angie cannot see them; although, she is aware of occasional movement among the branches.

She turns to Angel and says, "These trees look like they are upside-down, but my heart is telling me that we are underneath the trees and walking among the roots."

Excellent! Smart-woman creature! Now you know why you must sometimes look with your heart and not with your eyes.

"I think sometimes we human creatures *want* to be deceived, Angel."

Yes, this is true, although a very strange thing about human creatures, to be sure. But then again, your hearts are fragile; they break so easily. The truth has been known to shatter the human soul, even the strongest among you. And although it will set you free, birth is never without some degree of pain.

Angie is suddenly saddened by the thought of her beloved. "Oh Angel, I miss Kookie so much. I wish I could share with him what I am seeing with my heart."

You can, gentle creature. When he is asleep you can visit him in his dreamworld.

"This is true," says Angie and feels much better. Then she looks at the large tree roots all around and opens her heart to see. "I can feel how old they are, Angel. And how they can talk to each other; yes, I see them talking through their roots. There are little sparks of light flashing as they communicate with each other."

Angie closes her eyes and feels a deep grounding within the center of her being. She knows this to be the spirit of the ancient collective soul of all the trees that ever lived upon the earth. They have been witness to everything, not only within their own individual lifetimes, but also through the spirits of trees passed. Their souls collectively pass knowledge and wisdom down to each other; wisdom of earth history as well as human history, and as such, are the wisest living beings on the planet.

With her eyes still closed Angie speaks to the tree spirits with her heart. *You have witnessed all there is to see Ancient Ones. And I feel your love to be just as deep as your wisdom.*

Angie feels a momentary shudder all around her as if the trees are taking pleasure in her revelation.

She opens her eyes and speaks out loud, "What can you show me about the secrets of the past? It has been forbidden for the people of One World to learn about anything to do with our ancestors."

She sighs for a moment and continues, "We have always been told that we are children. . . *'dear ones'*. . . and cannot deal with any knowledge from the past; that it would only frighten us, being the children that we are (she says with sarcasm) and that we must only listen to our daily news and instructions and do as we are told."

Angie feels another shudder from all around including Angel, but it is not a shudder of pleasure. "So, I ask you, loving, Wise Ones, if the truth will set me free, then please, lay it on me! I am not afraid."

Suddenly, an image appears before her, reminding Angie of Kookie's Holographic Imager. She can see many large buildings standing close together, and some of them are very tall. Going in and out of the buildings and scurrying all around them are people; lots and lots of them.

Angie has never seen so many people all in one place and all at the same time, nor has she ever seen so many large buildings either. "What kind of place is *this?!*" she asks the trees.

The image zooms in on a sign with words on it that Angie has never seen. But she spells it out and remembers that she will have to share this with Kookie. After all, history has *not* been a forbidden subject to the Lords; in fact, quite the opposite. The Council has always told them to learn from the past so that they could better understand how to control the people. If everyone else were to learn from the past, however, as the Council has taught the Lords to do, then the UC would be in big trouble.

Angie spells out the sign and memorizes it, certain that Kookie will one day be able to explain it to her. It reads:

N-E-W-Y-O-R-K-C-I-T-Y

"You know, Angel, what really amazes me is that there are so many people there. Did places like that really exist? Were there that many people in One World at one time? What happened?"

Before Angel can answer her the trees project other images. They are images of barren, scorched earth, dried-up lakes and streams, beaches littered with human trash and dead fish washing up on shore.

Angel says to Angie, *Creature of the Light. The trees are speaking to me that I may tell you what is very much weighing on their souls. At one time, human creatures were able to make lots of little human creatures. Back in those days, many people had brothers and sisters. Now it is rare for people to have more than one child in a family, if any at all. In those days, Angie creature, there were many more human creatures upon the earth than there are now.*

The trees are saying that since the time of the great, tall buildings the human creature population has been reduced by 85 percent. And the place that you have just been shown, called a city, no longer exists. Though many of the great cities still maintain their names, they have been reduced to small towns, if they exist at all.

"Oh my!" says Angie. "Kookie claims that the Council's goal is to reduce the population even further; that they feel there are still too many of us *'useless eaters,'* as we are called."

The trees are now projecting other images of human babies born with severe physical deformities, and one stillbirth after another. Angie is overcome with grief when she witnesses all those women of the past giving birth to babies who are blue and not breathing. She can feel the terrible pain of the mothers who hold the bodies of their little ones who never had a chance, and kiss them good-bye.

She turns away from the images of terrible grief, crying for all the people who have had to endure such loss.

I'm sorry, Angie of the Light.

Wiping away her tears, Angie says, "Yes, I know. We have all heard rumors about this, even though the Council has denied it. But I guess there is one bright spot to the brother and sister thing."

What is that, Angie Creature?

"When we say it now, we are referring to *everybody;* that is, everybody is a Brother or a Sister, whom I can love."

Angie feels another shudder of warm energy from the trees and Angel.

Very nice, Human Creature; very nice.

* * *

The Alliance has just had another successful day with making new friends and bringing others on board, as their fellowship continues to grow. They are especially encouraged by the UC recruits who are joining them, both Lords, Ladies and Masters. What happened with Kenny and Lisa and Master Franz is suddenly happening all over.

It seems that the last generation of Lords and Masters have been living without any real family for too long, especially after the world's population dropped so drastically. With the Council's iron rule of fear and surveillance, no one dared express their human needs for each other. Those like Kookie and the Major had to keep their dreams of a free world to themselves, as a big secret from others. The consequences were just too severe to do otherwise.

But now PA, ES and SPA are locked away in an underground polar palace. Since the Gatherings of the High Lords of the Council were always done in great secrecy, with the Lords and Ladies being picked up and taken by Council transport to the secret location, even they do not know where that location is.

Settling down for the evening after a day filled with organizing, planning, and making arrangements for local and global gatherings, Kookie and his companions at the Big House know that they have much to talk about. But they would rather just have some cookies and tea and make it an early night.

"Why don't we just get down to business tomorrow, right after our morning meal?" Kookie says.

He is beginning to like, and use, the people's words for mealtime, instead of terms like *breakfast, lunch, high tea, and dinner.* Those have always been words of the Upper Crust for as far back as anyone can remember. For the people though, there is no distinction between meals, with the fare being pretty much the same from one meal to the other. They use phrases like, *having a meal together* or *breaking bread together,* with the emphasis on the word *together.*

"Oh, that's too bad," says Liling, with Neely nodding in agreement. The two women look at each other and then at the menfolk as they hold up a plate that they have prepared.

"Neely and I have just prepared three different types of chocolate chip cookies from some new recipe ideas that she—"

"On the other hand!" Kookie interrupts, pointing his index finger in the air and then tapping the tips of his fingers together, Kookie looks at them and says, "So, what have you got, then?"

Neely says, "Oh, you mean our plans for a One World Freedom Summit which we talked about today, with over 400 brand new recruits of the Lords and Masters, bringing our new total of UC Alliance members to over 50 percent of the total UC?"

"Uh, no," says Kookie. "I mean what's this new cookie recipe?"

"HA, HA!" everyone busts out laughing, slapping Kookie on the back.

* * *

That night Kookie is preparing for bed, thinking about all the wonderful changes that are happening, and wishing so much that Angie was there to share it all with him.

Lying down in bed, Kookie has a tearful moment thinking about his beloved before he drifts off to sleep.

In a dream, Kookie is walking through a dark purple forest of ancient trees. There is soft light glowing from within the forest with something warm and familiar about the trees. He feels as if he is wrapped in a cocoon of Mother Earth herself. He sees someone coming toward him. At first, he can only make out her beautiful golden wings, but as she approaches, he sees his angel, his treasured and beloved Angie, emerging from the thicket of woods. She holds out her arms to Kookie as he receives her embrace, folding her into his chest.

"I have missed you so," he whispers tenderly into Angie's ear.

"I have missed you too, my darling. And I have come to you with something very important to share."

Kookie looks deep into Angie's large, soft brown eyes and listens to her. First, she shares with him all that she has learned from the trees about the recent history of the planet, resulting in the sudden drop in human population, the horrible stillbirths and how it has all led to the current low population. Then she tells him that the beast is gathering his own forces against the Alliance, and that they should all be cautious as they move forward.

"I will keep you informed, my darling, as his plans are revealed to me." Pausing for a moment, Angie says to Kookie, "There is one other thing which I must tell you."

Looking at him with much compassion, Angie continues, "It is to do with the origins of your birth."

"What is it Angie? Is there something you can tell me? Yakov, Liling and I have never known the truth about ourselves. We tried many times, putting our genius and intuitive skills together, but we never came up with any answers.

"Yes," says Angie, "What I have to tell you is for all three of you. Are you ready to hear the truth, my darling?"

Kookie closes his eyes for a moment and says, "Angie, I MUST know the truth, especially now."

"Okay," she says with a gentle smile. "PA, ES and SPA knew that they could never truly trust anyone because anyone might rise up and be tempted to overthrow them. So, they decided to create their own force. They made a deal with the devil that they would help arrange for him to impregnate three different women at different times. PA, ES and SPA would raise these children as their own and know that they would be born to be evil and obedient to them. That way, the Council would have three High Lord children whom they could trust, and the devil would have three children of his very own.

When his children came of age, the beast saw them as his partners in an attempt to gain his dominion over One World."

Kookie is listening and somehow this is all ringing true for him. He closes his eyes as Angie gives him the rest of it.

"But like everything else the beast puts his hand to, our Father in Heaven always has the final word. He took great pity on the three of you, and so He took the evil of your father that you all would have been born with and turned it into just the opposite.

"Somewhat like the Chrysalenes; you, Yakov and Liling have been endowed with the spirit of the Heavenly Father, rather than the spirit of the beast. That is why the Council and their world is falling apart right now.

"The beast will not take defeat lightly. He is putting together a force of the Lords, Ladies and Masters who are pro-Council and who want to take the place of PA, ES and SPA. If they do, with the help of the beast, they will be more powerful and deadly to the people than the Council ever was before. They are going to challenge you, my beloved, and the Alliance."

Angie begins to fade in Kookie's dream as she says, "Remember always that Heaven is on your side, and I am too. I love you my darling . . ."

. . . and Angie is gone.

Kookie wakes up in a cold sweat, horrified at what he has just learned.

* * *

At an undisclosed location in Euroslavica, a conference is just getting underway. Lord Igor is addressing the crowd.

"My Lords, My Ladies and Masters of the UC. I'm sure you are all well aware that our esteemed Council, PA, ES and SPA have disappeared without a trace. We have been unable to obtain their whereabouts, even with all the best of our technology. Therefore, the three of us seated before you, Lord Pavel, Lord Viktor, and I must assume command and continue with the Council's program.

All in favor, say AYE."

Several ayes are heard around the room.

"All opposed, say 'NAY'."

Several nays are also heard around the room.

Looking dismayed, Lord Igor says, "We will put it to a hand count. All in favor raise your hands."

But before Lord Igor can count hands, Lady Bella stands up. She addresses the entire room, "My Lords, My Ladies and Masters of the UC. Before you vote on whom you wish to have replace PA, ES and SPA, I would like to submit myself for your consideration."

There is some murmuring around the room as people look at Lady Bella and then at the other three Lords seated before them.

Master Mikhail stands up and says, "I nominate Lady Bella to be on our new Council, replacing PA, ES and SPA."

Several other members of the UC stand up and say aye.

"Very well," says Lord Igor. "Is there anyone else who wishes to serve on the Council?"

Lady Bella is still standing and she says to everyone, "My fellow members of the UC, let me just mention to you that while we are sitting here discussing who will or will not serve on the Council, Lord Kenneth, Lord Yakov, Lady Liling and other traitorous members of the UC are plotting against us, aligning themselves with the slaves and formulating imminent plans of insurrection."

The murmurings grow loud and angry.

"How do you know this, Lady Bella? Are you sure? This cannot be! Traitors to One World!"

"I have excellent sources of information," Lady Bella continues. "I know exactly what is going on in their camp. If you put me at the head of your Council, I will be able to help protect you. I also propose to have our esteemed Lords before you, Lord Igor, Lord Pavel, and Lord Viktor, join me as my assistants.

"With the four of us in control, *WE WILL TAKE THEM DOWN! DEATH TO KENNETH! DEATH TO YAKOV! DEATH TO LILING! DEATH TO TRAITORS!*"

The UC starts chanting and shouting:

DEATH TO KENNETH! DEATH TO YAKOV! DEATH TO LILING! DEATH TO TRAITORS!

DEATH TO KENNETH! DEATH TO YAKOV! DEATH TO LILING! DEATH TO TRAITORS!

They go on and on, working themselves into a frenzy. Before long they are shouting at the top of their lungs in a state of complete hysteria until Lady Bella holds up her hand to quieten them all down. When they finish, they look at her with exhaustion and she motions for them to sit down.

"First," Lady Bella begins, "We must call in the commandos. The Master Commandants are under direct orders from us, and they will mobilize their forces as soon as we give them the command."

"Yes! Call in the commandos! Death to traitors!" voices call out around the room, followed by clapping and cheering.

Once again Lady Bella holds up her hand to calm down the crowd and she continues, "Then we must consider what weapons we have and what will be the most effective way of taking down the greatest number of traitors, as quickly as possible. The slaves are unarmed, and the traitorous Lords and Masters of the UC will be unable to access any weaponry whatsoever from our arsenal, *once I have the power to shut them out!*" she pauses and looks around the room; then continues in a shrill cry to everyone, *"MAKE ME YOUR LEADER, AND I WILL STOP THE SLAVES! I WILL KILL THE TRAITORS!"*

With one final blast, Lady Bella wails, ***"GIVE ME THE POWER! NOW!"***

The Lords, Ladies and Masters all jump up and start cheering and applauding, "We want Bella! We want Bella! We want Bella!"

Lady Bella allows them to continue chanting on her behalf for a few moments until she finally holds up her hand and calms them down again.

Lord Igor stands up and says, "I guess you are all ready to vote now. All those in favor of Lady Bella becoming the head of the Council with myself Lord Igor, Lord Pavel and Lord Viktor as her assistants, say, aye."

In one communal voice, everyone in the room shouts, "AYE!"

"All opposed, say nay."

Not one voice is heard.

Lord Igor says, "The ayes have it." Turning to Lady Bella he says, "Congratulations my new Highest One!"

The entire room full of Lords, Ladies and Masters are on their feet chanting, "Bell-*A!* Bell-*A!* Bell-*A!*"

From the depths of hell, the beast replies, *That's my girl! I'm on my way!*

* * *

That night Lady Bella has a dream:

She is riding in her Cloudcar along a tree-lined country road, passing small houses amidst the trees. The sun is shining and the green leaves on the trees are sparkling and glittering as she passes them. Gradually the road starts to twist and turn as she finds herself on an incline. The Cloudcar disappears and she is now walking up the hill, which is getting steeper and steeper. The twists and turns are also becoming more challenging and tiresome as she goes along.

After a while Lady Bella finds it too difficult to continue and she must sit down on the side of the road. She gets frustrated because she knows that she still has a lot farther to go to get to her journey's end. But she feels the exhaustion in her whole body and knows that she cannot go on.

Irritated with herself, Lady Bella just sits there frowning and glaring at the ever-steepening and winding road ahead. Then, all at once, she sees a large snake slithering across her path.

The snake looks at her with sympathetic eyes and says, "What seems to be the trouble, ma'am? Why are you stopped here on the road along your journey?"

"I am just too tired," she says, "and I cannot go any farther."

"Well," says the snake, "I can give you a hand, if you like," with a slippery grin on his face.

"I don't see how," quips Bella, "Since you do not have a hand to give!"

The snake hisses with delight and he says, "Well, My Lady, I do have a back that you can ride on, and I can carry you the rest of the way, all the way up to the top of the hill if you like, yes indeed!"

As the snake is offering Lady Bella a ride, she notices that he begins to grow much larger, until he is indeed large enough to carry her on his back. "Well," Lady Bella says to the snake, "I accept your offer."

She climbs onto the snake and before she can say anything else, Lady Bella notices three numbers painted on his back in a bright orange hue. They are the numbers 666.

"Why, what on earth is that?" she asks the snake.

"That, My Lady is your ticket to the top of the hill. I can give it to you if you want it. All you have to do is ask me and anything you want is all yours. Do you want it from me?"

"Oh yes! Yes indeed! Take me all the way to the top and give me EVERYTHING! If you please, sir!"

The snake hisses with excitement as his voice begins to drop, turning into a deep snarling growl, "With great pleasure, My Lady Bella, with great pleasure!"

Chapter 5 – Sisters

IT IS A WARM, TRANQUIL MORNING in Johannesburg. Liling, Yakov and Neely decide to arrange the morning meal for everyone at the outdoor picnic area, which is part of the Trader's Market. Construction is now underway to make it a permanent, year-round open-air plaza. Mimi and Doc have brought the children with them from the Village of the Holy Ones for their morning meal. So, the group consists of Liling, Dumaka, Kookie, Yakov, Neely, The Major, Vi, Doc, Phil, Mimi, Ryan, Eve Elli, Emeka and little Suzie.

As the fruit of their harvest is laid out before them on the table, Liling rises to address the troops. "Good morning, everyone! I hope you all had a good night's rest since we do have very much to accomplish today!"

"Here, here!" The friends raise their glasses and clink them together with one another.

Holding up a loaf of bread Liling says, "Before we begin, let us break bread together in honor of the food and friendship that we share. And, as we move forward with our plans, may we pass onto others our love, and the fruit of this table."

"Amen, Sister!" they all say as one voice.

Liling breaks open the loaf of bread and passes it around the table, with each person breaking off a chunk and eating it.

When the bread gets to the children, little Suzie watches as everyone is eating. She simply takes the whole loaf and attempts to stuff it in her mouth.

Joyous laughter resounds around the table, and Emeka and Eve Elli help Suzie break off a toddler-sized chunk.

As they finish eating, Kookie begins the conversation by telling everyone about the dream he had last night. He omits the part about his origins with Liling and Yakov and decides to tell them later in private.

"I'm sure that the others of the UC must be fearful and in great turmoil right now, considering all that is happening," Kookie explains. "I mean think about it. PA, ES and SPA have disappeared which leaves them without leadership. That means the first order of business for them must be to establish new leadership immediately, or their ship will sink."

Everyone looks at each other and nods in agreement.

"Kookie," the Major looks at his friend searching for answers, "Do you think we can truly accomplish all that we have set out to do, fully exposed, without our usual covert concealment, and *not* get beaten to a pulp by the pro-Council UC?"

"Hey, bro'! You were always the tough guy, *Major*, like your name says. I mean, with you on our team how can we lose?" Kookie says with full confidence.

"And with three geniuses on our team, like you, Yakov and Liling, I guess I should know better than to even ask!" says the Major.

"Oh yeah! You got *that* right! Amen!" everyone exclaims.

Kookie sits back and smiles, tapping the tips of his fingers together. "Okay then," he says and turns to Liling, "So, what's on the morning's agenda, Sister?"

"First, I would like to thank Mimi and Doc for bringing all the children this morning."

Then turning to Emeka, Liling says, "Emeka, I know we have already explained to you what we are all doing here. That when your family went to Heaven, you became a ward of the state and this whole property was turned over to the Council."

Emeka nods courageously, like a little man.

The Major suddenly realizes that he is looking at himself when he was that age.

Liling continues, "And that is why I was called in by the Council to come here and help manage everything here for you."

Emeka nods.

"So now, Kookie, Yakov, Neely and I, as representatives of the UC have decided to put this whole property in your name to become fully yours and yours alone when you are 21 years old. That means you are trusting us to take care of it for you, until then."

Emeka smiles and nods vigorously in the affirmative.

"And when we get together with the other Lords and Ladies later today, we will put it forward to them and vote on it. Then I will make some nice and neat papers for you putting it all in writing and find a special place to keep the papers in the study.

"If you are happy staying where you are now, in the Village of the Holy Ones with Mama Eve Zula and Papa Adam Makena, then we are happy too. At least for now, we all feel that this is the safest place for you. But you are always welcome to come back and stay here anytime, or even stay with the gardeners if you like."

Emeka is excited about the idea of spending time with Bem and the other gardeners. "Oh boy! I sure would like to help out in the garden!"

Kookie, Yakov, Liling and Neely, get up and go over to Emeka. Kookie says, "Let's shake on it, bro'!"

Little Lord Emeka happily shakes their hands and says to them, "It's a deal!"

"Well!" says the Major. "Congratulations, my man!" and everyone, including Emeka has a good chuckle.

The Major then turns to Liling and says, "So what is next on the agenda, My Lady?"

Liling gives him a sideways look with a raised eyebrow and the Major says, "Oh, excuse me, My *Sister!*"

Liling smiles, "That's better!"

"Next, I would like to ask Doc and Phil to share an idea of theirs."

Phil gestures to Doc to go ahead and speak for them.

"Okay." Doc says, "As you already know we have been experiencing a huge interest on the part of all kinds of people, from the UC to the rest of us, to have training, offer apprenticeships and all sorts of help in setting up small, local farming villages and communities. Along those lines there is also great interest among many people wanting to learn about flowers, herbal teas, and other folk remedies. So, Phil and I talked it over and we have come up with a few ideas."

Doc lays out their vision of traveling all across One World, bringing their teachings to all who have requested it, as well as creating a real communications network to replace My Buddy, connecting all the villages with each other. The network will include the Intercontinental Pigeons Communication Network which Kenny has already started. Their first stop will be to pay Kenny and Lisa a visit, get them up to date and share their contact information of those who want to be a part of the Garden Communities and the Pigeon Network.

Doc continues to explain, "It is the beginning of a worldwide connection of small, self-sustaining communities for the people of One World, joining hands and working together with the UC. This has been the lifelong dream of many farmers and stewards of the land, and Phil and I are ready to go out and get started right away."

Everyone claps their hands and responds, "Yes! Fantastic! Let's do it!"

Liling says, "And I will do the same with my estate back in Shanghai, doing there what we are now doing here with Lord Emeka's estate. In addition to a Trader's Market, I will also establish a garden community where people can live together." Yakov and Neely love the idea and say they will do the same with their estates, too.

Kookie points his index finger in the air and all eyes are on him. "As for Kookie's Kastle," he says, "I have been thinking. All I really need of the technology from that place is in my little black box; you know,

Metatron. That and the 369-Program it contains is the whole shebang in one small hand-held device."

Kookie lowers his eyes to the ground pensively and in a soft tone of voice says, "That place has never really been much of a home for me anyway. Not until Angie came along that is. As far as I'm concerned it can go up in flames. I would like to turn the land into a true garden of paradise—that is . . ." he hesitates for a moment, collects himself, and says, "Once my Angie comes home."

The others all go quiet as they remember which Sister is *not* among them today, and where she actually is.

At the same moment a new arrival to their group comes out of the Big House. She is Liling's helper from her estate in Shanghai. Liling sees her coming toward them carrying a tray of cookies from the night before.

"Oh, I must introduce you all to someone. She came in late last night," says Liling.

The young woman brings the plate of cookies over to everyone and Liling says to her, smiling, "You can put those down on the table. Come on over and let me introduce you to all our friends.

"Everyone, this is Bi! You know, like the English word bee!" Liling adds, "And believe me, she really lives up to the English word for bee, always busy and getting so much accomplished!"

Everyone gives her a warm welcome, "Hi, Bi! Hello, Sister! Welcome to Johannesburg!"

Bi smiles sweetly at the group and says, "Thank you," and bowing to them all, "I wish to be of service to you all and to be a part of the wonderful things you are doing for the people."

"Thank you," says Mimi, "May we be of service to you, as well."

In the bowels of hell, the beast interjects, *Mimi, Mimi, dear Misss Mimi, I'm sure you will be of great serviccce to Misss Bi . . . Misss Busy Bi . . . OUR Misss Busy Bi . . .* **MY** *. . . Misssss . . . Busy . . . Bi!*

The hissing fades into the backdrop of the dark dimension.

Next up is the Major. "As you all know, my father has been through a miraculous change. Vi and I have been working with him on new product ideas for Howard Pharmaceuticals, which I would like Vi to share with you," he says, smiling at her.

"Thank you Major," Vi says as she turns to the group. "Since Master Howard's healing, he has become fascinated with the whole concept of herbal and energy medicine. He has even taken on more human help, as opposed to artificial intelligence, to learn about the healing properties of the natural world through intuiting and feeling, as many of us here have already been doing," she says gesturing to Mimi and Doc.

"Production is now underway in the creation of herbal teas and flower remedies to be mass distributed to Center Markets throughout One World. They will then be available to everyone; from everyday people to every level of the UC!"

Vi is interrupted by a huge round of applause and cheers.

"Thank you," she says smiling at everyone, and continues, "So the Major and I have been helping in those efforts over at Howard Pharmaceuticals in California and Oregon. And we are looking for folks who wish to join our team."

Mimi speaks up and says, "Ryan and I have started to work with the Chrysalenes at the Village of the Holy Ones as well as Bem and the other gardeners. The Chrysalenes are teaching us incredible things about natural healing, while Bem and the others are planting seedlings to grow all of these wonderful herbs and flowers."

Turning to Vi, Mimi says, "Well Sister, how would you all feel about collaborating with us?"

"*WHOA!*" the Major cries out. "Oops! Sorry sweetie, this is your show!" he says to Vi, as everyone laughs.

"Thank you, Mimi," Vi chuckles. "It looks like we have a consensus from Howard Pharmaceuticals. Well, I guess that is our report," she says, and the Major nods.

"Thank you Vi," Liling says. "As for the rest of us, we need to continue to expand upon the work we've been doing here, as well as continuing to reach out to others in all three Continental Territories. Today's Trader's Market will have people coming in from all over Johannesburg as well as other towns and neighboring communities. Word is really circulating through the people's news at the Coffeehouses about what we are doing here. It will be a great opportunity for us to reach out to others."

Eve Elli, Emeka and Suzie have left the table to play, as the rest are sitting around chatting about the exciting things that have just been presented.

Bi has been listening to everyone and she comes over to Liling, bowing. She is having some difficulty referring to her Ladyship as Sister and Liling understands this. So Liling does not mind when Bi says, "My Lady, I have heard about some people in the Mediterranean region who are interested in what we are doing here. If I may, I would like to take my leave of you and go and meet with them."

"Absolutely, Bi! Please feel free to take one of the Cloudtransporters and leave whenever you like!"

"Thank you, My Lady," Bi says, holding her hands against her chest and bowing.

* * *

The next day Doc and Phil are preparing to leave. They say goodbye to Mama Eve Zula, Papa Adam Makena, Mimi, Ryan, Eve Lydia, Adam Sam, Little Lord Emeka and Eve Elli.

Mimi is the first to come over to Doc and give her a great big hug.

"Well Sister," Mimi says, "We have certainly been through a lot together since that first night I came to your door back in Floraville, hungry and frightened."

The two women smile at each other. Doc says, "Yes, we sure have, haven't we!"

"You take care of yourself, my friend." Mimi continues, "And I really look forward to hearing all the new things that the flowers and trees have to tell you when you get back!"

Doc smiles at her and says, "Sure thing, my Sister. You, too!"

Then Doc and Phil pick up little Suzie of the Seashells and hold her for a long time. Doc is unable to hold back her tears.

She snuggles little Suzie close to her and says, "Now you be a good girl while we are gone. Listen to everything Mama Eve Zula and Eve Elli tell you."

Little Suzie smiles and points to Eve Elli saying, "Ee, *Eh*-yi!"

"Yes, sweet baby girl, that's Eve Elli. And Mama Doc will be back just as soon as she can. Okay?"

Doc snivels as she passes Suzie back over to Phil. He tries to think of something clever or profound to say to her but is left speechless. When he finally does open his mouth to speak, the tears begin to flow, and he just cannot make them stop. Little Suzie puts her arms around Phil's neck.

Eve Elli speaks up, "It's all right, Phil. Don't cry. Everything is gonna be okay. We all love Little Suzie very much and she is gonna be just fine."

Phil looks at Eve Elli and then at everyone else and says, "Thank you. Thank you all for everything. And thank you for taking care of the little wakanjeja until we get back. I know that she is in good hands."

And looking up to the heavens, Phil says, "We are all in good hands. Thank you, Great Spirit for bringing us all together. May each and every one of us do the sacred work that you have called us to do."

Then he hands little Suzie over to Mama Eve Zula saying, "Thank you, my Sister, and thank you one and all for the highest, most sacred love that we share between us: the love of friendship.

Phil and Doc leave the Village of the Holy Ones and head over to the Big House where a Cloudtransporter is ready and waiting for them to board. Their first stop has already been programmed in.

It is the Continental Territory of Panamerica; Bear River, Oregon.

* * *

In the Mediterranean Sea, not far off the mainland, there is a small island called the Isle of Bella, which is owned by the Lady herself. Lady Bella is preparing for a Summit Gathering. She has invited all of the Lords, Ladies and Masters who are known to be pro-Council, and some others who appear to be leaning in that direction.

Through her sources she also knows who many of the Lords, Ladies and Masters are who have become members of the Alliance, and she now has a mole planted in their organization. Lady Bella sent her mole on a recent fact-finding mission to obtain a complete list of the Alliance membership, plus any news about their activities, whereabouts, and seditious plans. She is expecting her mole to return shortly.

Lord Pavel has organized a commando force of men and women who are arriving at the Isle of Bella from all over One World. The Master Commandant in charge of the unit is Master Mikhail.

Lord Pavel is Master Commandant Mikhail's Overlord, so he knows the man well and knows that he can trust him to accomplish whatever mission he is given by her Ladyship. Lord Pavel also knows that Mikhail has a rather brutish, ruthless streak in him, which is exactly what Lady Bella told Lord Pavel she wants at the head of this mission.

In fact, her exact orders to Lord Pavel were, "You must find me a man to lead the commandos who is driven to hatred and brutality against an enemy. I want someone who has a passion to draw first blood, and who will train his unit that way. In other words, Lord Pavel," says Lady Bella, "send me a psychopath obsessed with violence."

"Yes, My Lady. I have just the man for you," says Lord Pavel. "He is Master Mikhail, and I understand that he is arriving here on the Island momentarily."

"Excellent, My Lord Pavel. Is that the same Mikhail who nominated me to be on the Council?"

"Yes, My Lady, it is."

"Good!" she replies, "I should like to be formally introduced to the gentleman. Do bring him to see me this afternoon."

"Yes, My Lady," says Lord Pavel and he goes off to the landing field to be available as soon as Mikhail arrives.

Lord Viktor has gathered technological experts from the UC with specific interest and genius in creating a new weapon. He is charging them with the task of developing a destructive laser beam capable of vaporizing anything in a long range within seconds. It is an idea the technological group of experts talked about a long time ago but never actually created. They are also on their way to the Isle of Bella.

Lord Pavel arrives at the landing field just in time to meet Master Commandant Mikhail. He is a solid-built, six-foot tall brutish barbarian in his early 30s, with thick blond, slicked back hair, and piercing blue eyes.

Besides his passionate, lust for blood, Master Commandant Mikhail has another unique qualification for this assignment. The battalion of men whom he will be leading are an elite group of top commandos, chosen from all three Continental Territories. And Master Mikhail is fluent in all three languages: Russian, English, and Chinese.

Lord Pavel goes over to greet him.

"Greetings, My Lord Pavel."

"Hello, Master Mikhail. I trust you enjoyed your trip over here in the Cloudtransporter that the UC has provided for you," Lord Pavel says.

"It was comfortable." Master Mikhail states matter-of-factly. "What would you have me do first, My Lord?"

"Well, Our Lady Bella the Most High has requested an audience with you immediately upon your arrival."

"Let us go there, immediately then," Master Mikhail replies flatly.

As they walk the short distance to Lady Bella's mansion, Lord Pavel continues the conversation with Master Mikhail. "How is your family then, sir?"

Master Mikhail responds with silence, followed by, "Hm."

"Uh, good! Good! Very good. And your health, sir? I take it that all is well with you?" asks Lord Pavel.

Mikhail is silent before responding, "Da."

"Uh, da . . ." repeats Pavel.

The two men walk the rest of the way in silence.

Lady Bella is in her study taking in the magnificent view overlooking the Mediterranean Sea, and another island off in the distance. There is an array of boats going by, from fishing vessels to small sailboats and luxurious yachts. Lady Bella lives on the island with many servants and no other family. She is in her mid-30s; a stunning beauty, as cunning and ruthless as she is beautiful. Her parents died in a mysterious boating accident when she was in her early 20s.

At the time of their death, Lady Bella's relatives never gave her any emotional support and showed no signs of sympathy for her loss. She had a sister about 10 years her junior, whom the relatives took into their care, leaving Bella on her own to fend for herself. Prior to her parents' demise, Bella discovered that the only true path to freedom is material wealth and the power that money can buy.

It has been a lesson that she learned well.

Looking out the picture window at a large yacht on the sea, Bella notices that it is bigger and more beautiful than her own. A knot forms in the pit of her stomach as she considers how to remedy that situation. A knock on the door interrupts her thoughts.

"Come in," Lady Bella says, turning around to face the "intruder," as the person wanting to enter is indeed intruding upon her private thoughts of lust and greed.

The door opens and she watches as Lord Pavel steps inside, followed by a handsome man who's piercing stare locks into her own, large brown eyes.

Lord Pavel makes the introduction. "My Lady, this is Master Mikhail. He has come here to be the Master Commandant of the commando unit—"

"You will go now, Lord Pavel," Lady Bella cuts him off.

He does.

Lady Bella and Master Mikhail are locked into each other's stare. Neither one has flinched or moved. Without breaking the stare, Lady Bella begins to move slowly over to her desk, going around behind it. She slowly opens the desk drawer and motions with her free hand for Master Mikhail to come over.

He does, slowly.

When Mikhail approaches the front of Lady Bella's desk, she motions for him to come around to the side where they stand face to face. With her hand clutching something inside of her desk, the two continue staring at each other in silence. Lady Bella gives Master Mikhail a slight grin.

Suddenly, in one deft move, Bella grabs a whip out of the drawer and cracks it hard across his face. Blood spurts out of his check and Mikhail falls to his knees wailing.

"What do you say to me!" she bellows.

There is no answer, only cries of pain from Mikhail.

"*SPEAK! NOW!*" She yells ferociously.

"Muh . . . My . . . Luh . . . Lady, Buh . . . Buh . . . Bella," he stutters trembling like a nervous puppy. "I have cuh . . . cuh . . . come to ssss . . . serve you."

"Yes," she says. "And you will serve me well, Mikhail!" she says in a somewhat softer tone.

"Yes, My Lady."

"You will stand up now, and you will look at me."

He does so, cautiously. Suddenly Mikhail is overcome with an intense burning desire for this magnificent, beautiful woman. His passion is equal to the pain that he is feeling in his burning cheek. "I will do anything for you, My Lady. Anything. What do you want from me?"

Lady Bella suddenly smiles at him with an intensity to match the luster of the Mediterranean Sea outside. In a cold-blooded, deliberate, flat tone she replies, "*I . . . WANT . . . **EVERYTHING,** FROM YOU!*"

Deep in the bowels of hell a voice growls with pleasure saying, *OOO . . . WOMAN! AND I . . . WANT . . . EVERYTHING, FROM **YOU!***

* * *

Out on the landing field another Cloudtransporter has just landed. An Overseer Attendant comes over to the craft to greet the young woman who is emerging.

"Welcome to the Isle of Bella. Is there someone you have come to see?" the Overseer Attendant asks.

"Yes. If you please, would you kindly take me to see the Lady Bella?" says the young woman.

"And whom shall I say wishes to see the Lady Bella, ma'am."

"I am Lady Bella's sister. My name is Bi."

Chapter 6 – Summit

THE INTERCONTINENTAL PIGEONS Communication Network is working overtime across the three Continental Territories of One World carrying an invitation to a new kind of gathering, to members of the UC and the general population.

The message reads:

INVITATION TO A SUMMIT – FOR FREEDOM AND A NEW WORLD – WEEKEND OF COURAGEOUS LOVE – UC AND ALL PEOPLE WELCOME – MESSAGE LORD KOOKIE, LORD YAKOV OR LADY LILING FOR MORE INFO, DATE AND LOCATION

Kookie, Yakov and Liling have left outgoing messages on their Lord's Communication Devices with further information, including contacts for those who need Cloudtransport to be arranged. Using Kookie's latest Salamander cloaking program on 369, they have been able to install a screening filter onto their communication devices. With Kookie's intuitive genius, and remnants of an old device he discovered from the past called a "lie detector," he has managed to program "Intuition" into Salamander. Therefore, only those who are truly supportive of the Alliance will be able to receive further information regarding the date and place of the Summit.

The Major and Kookie are working in the vegetable garden with Bem, Tafari and Nassor, while Kookie is smiling to himself thinking about the high-tech work that he normally does. Comparing it to the pleasure he is now receiving from the low-tech world of gardening, Kookie says, "It really is a whole new experience for me, and I'm totally enjoying the idea that what we are planting will turn into food. It makes you stop and think about what the truly important things in this world are, doesn't it Major?"

"Yes, is does," says the Major, "But I gotta hand it to you. I have seen all kinds of crazy and brilliant technical inventions of yours. But this intuitive thing, bro', is truly the crème de la crème!" he says shaking his head in disbelief.

Kookie smiles and taps the tips of his fingers together. "Thanks, bro'. It *is* rather awesome, if I must say so myself, that a computer program can detect someone's feelings and intentions. I got the idea from the old-fashioned lie-detector and simply taken it to the next level."

Vi joins the two friends out in the vegetable garden. She says, "When the two of you have finished with your newest passion of gardening, can you come on over to the Big House and help us with the Summit preparations? There are still things to be worked out, like how we are going to handle the crowds that will be here shortly. According to the latest count coming in from the invitations, there are close to a million people descending upon us soon!

"But here is the *really* exciting news. Counting the UC members only, we now have a confirmed 53% of the world's Lords, Ladies and Masters over the age of 18 on our side and coming to join us!"

"*YEE HA!*" shriek the Major and Kookie.

"Does everyone else know this? We gotta tell the others!" says the Major.

Vi laughs and says, "Liling came to tell me the good news about passing 53% a little while ago, and I told her that I would run over here and tell the two of you. I guess we should spread the word around the Big House now as well as to the folks at the Village of the Holy Ones."

"And let's not forget all of our friends at the Coffeehouse!" exclaims Kookie. "We *must* go over there tonight and let all of Johannesburg know!"

"Amen to that, Brother!" Vi exclaims.

The gardeners nearby are also listening to the good news, as they express their gratitude; "Oh, thanks be to the Kind One!" they all shout together.

"Amen to that," says Vi.

"Well, I guess we had better make arrangements for a million people, then!" says Kookie all excited. "It's kind of like back in the days when they had things called Music Festivals."

"Music Festivals!" gasps Vi. "There is just so much that we the people were never allowed to learn, and it really makes me sad sometimes to think about it."

"Yes," says Kookie, "That is something else that we are going to have to change; history, *of* the people, *by* the people and *for* the people."

"Now that sounds familiar," says the Major.

"It should," says Kookie, "But I do not wish to spoil the surprise."

"Surprise?" Vi says quizzically.

"Yes," says Kookie, "It is something I am going to introduce at the Summit."

The Major and Vi look at each other and shrug their shoulders. Whatever Kookie has planned, the Major knows is going to be most excellent.

* * *

On the Isle of Bella, the Summit is already underway. Their agenda is simple. They plan to keep the socio-political structure of One World the way it has always been for them and use military force to put down any insurrection. All the pro-Council members of the UC have been "requested" to attend the Summit meeting, and they are now about to be addressed by their new Council:

The Highest Lady Bella and her second in command Lord Igor, followed by Lord Pavel of the military and Lord Viktor of technology.

The Highest Lady Bella begins; "My Lords, My Ladies and Masters of the Upper Crust, welcome to my Island. I trust that you are all enjoying the amenities and the beautiful view of the Mediterranean Sea!" she pauses for sounds of approval.

"Let me begin by saying that there are things happening in One World that are being addressed here on my Island with those of us in command. Our intention is to maintain the life that we have always known. Therefore, we feel it imperative that you are all brought up to date on the goings-on of those who have turned against us as we discuss ways in which we can stop the insurrectionists from carrying out their treacherous plans."

A murmur has been developing slowly in the crowd, but with Lady Bella's last statement it has grown louder.

"As you all know, our most recent efforts of using bio-weaponry, neurotoxins, water poisoning and mind control through sound waves, have all been thwarted. And worse than that, the insurrectionists have developed a secret, powerful weapon that has caused people of the UC to be harmed by our own weapons instead. I have learned through a faithful servant of mine who the creators of this weapon are and where they are located. It has also been suggested that the traitors are even influencing members of the UC who are weaker minded than the rest of you, the faithful, who are gathered here."

Grumblings of disapproval travel through the crowd.

"But now, thanks to my most trusted and faithful servant, we have received information on this secret weapon; what it is and how it works. And we are preparing to send a commando unit out there to take them down!"

Loud cheers of approval resound across the crowd.

"I have decided that when this is all over and we have reestablished order in One World, those of our brethren who have gone astray, are to go through a whole program of mental deprogramming that Lord Viktor of Technology is working on."

All eyes turn to Lord Viktor whose eyes are glazed over and staring off into the distance at nothing. The crowd goes quiet.

"Lord Viktor has also been working on a long-range laser weapon that he will explain to you himself. Finally, and most important of all is what we have all learned from this experience . . ." she pauses for a moment and then says, "There are absolutely, without question, *way* too many slaves in One World. They have always been a total menace to us and now they are absolutely dangerous!"

The crowd begins to swell with voices of rage.

Lady Bella leans forward, raising both arms and pounds her fists in the air, shouting:

"THE SLAVES MUST DIE!
SLAVES MUST DIE!
SLAVES MUST DIE!"

As her furious chant reaches a crescendo, the Lords, Ladies and Masters rise to their feet and start shouting, chanting and pounding the air along with her.

"SLAVES MUST DIE!
SLAVES MUST DIE!
SLAVES MUST DIE!"

Standing in the crowd, with bandages on his face, Master Mikhail is speechless. He is staring at his object of lustful desire, feeling the pain of the bruises on his torso from their last encounter. With his passion swelling, Mikhail can hardly contain his ravenous appetite for Lady Bella's savage consumption of his flesh.

He thinks to himself, *I will die for you, My Lady. I will die a thousand deaths for you.*

In the deepest part of hell, the beast is grinning. *That's my girl!*

After the first session of the Summit has concluded, a buffet style dinner is served, consisting of roast beef, roast lamb, pasta dishes, potatoes and sauteed vegetables of every description. Dessert is a mélange of fruit and custard pies, with ice cream treats covered in sauces made from chocolate and raspberries. Of course, there is also plenty of wine flowing throughout the meal, with lots of glasses clinking, and toasts made to the hostess of the Island and great success to her mission.

Lady Bella goes off searching for her prime source of information regarding the insurrectionists and the whereabouts of their weapon. Catching Lord Pavel before he goes to the buffet spread Lady Bella ask him, "Have you seen my sister Bi anywhere?"

Thinking about it for a moment he says to her, "Why yes, My Lady. Your sister, the Lady Bi, said that she was going to spend some time poolside. I do believe you will find her either there or at the Cabana."

"Thank you, Lord Pavel. And do help yourself to the delicacies of the buffet bar, prepared by our Master Chefs," she says.

"Indeed, My Lady, I shall."

Bi is sitting in the hot tub, overlooking the glorious view of the sea and her youth spent in the Balkans. Memories come flooding back of her parents and early childhood years in Shanghai. It was the birthplace and home of her mother until she met a Lord, the love of her life, from the Balkans. They spent many happy years together in Shanghai where both of their daughters were born. Then, one day, her father was called to return to Euroslavica. Bi remembers the move when she was six years old, and her big sister Lady Chen was 16. Lady Chen was always extremely beautiful and very popular, and Lady Bi remembers how hard it was for her sister to adjust to the change, being taken away from her friends in Shanghai. It caused a rift between Chen and their mother which never healed. In fact, over the years the rift between them grew wider, while at the same time, the relationship between Bi and their mother grew closer. This caused even greater bitterness to grow in the heart of her sister Chen.

When their parents died in a boating accident, Bi was crushed, but Chen showed no outward expression of emotion. Bi was still under 18 and Chen was already an adult, so their mother's relatives from Shanghai took Bi back there to live with them, pretty much leaving Chen to go it alone. Lady Bi never heard from her sister again until only recently when Bi went in search of her. However, Bi heard years later that Lady Chen, in her bitterness, renounced her family background, changed her name to Lady Bella, and purchased an island in the Mediterranean which she named after herself.

"Hello, my sister!" Bi hears off in the distance, as she breaks out of her reminiscing.

"Oh, hi there, sister," Bi responds as Lady Bella joins her and sits down at the edge of the hot tub.

"Thank you for the reports," Lady Bella says. "I have given them to Igor, and he has gone over them with Pavel and Viktor. They are all convinced that the information you have provided is accurate and consistent with what we already know about this weapon, the ones who are using it, and most important, their hideout. The Council has been trying for a long time to uncover their identity and whereabouts. Once we have that information and the long-range laser weapons are ready to go, it will be the end of the miserable traitors of the UC, as well as any people we can take down with them."

"I see," says Bi. "You mean you *won't* be targeting the people with the laser weapons, then my sister?"

"Oh no, dear! What a waste *that* would be!" Lady Bella snorts and chuckles. "Much better to let the commandos take care of that. After all, they *do* need target practice." Lady Bella laughs.

"I see," says Bi.

"Yes dear. And they also need, shall we say, to relieve their aggressions and satisfy their bloodlust," Lady Bella says as she leans forward and gently strokes her sister's hair.

"I see," says Bi.

"Do you then?" asks Bella, "Do you *really* see, my sister . . . mother's favorite?"

There is a pause for a moment and then Lady Bella says, "Well, I must be getting back to our guests. Do come and join us shortly, dear. There's a good little sister!"

"I will," says Bi, and Lady Bella goes off to the buffet spread.

Bi is left to herself as she considers what she has done and where it all may lead. She thinks of Lady Liling and the life that she has had with her up until now.

When Lady Bi turned 18, she knew that she could never be happy in the life that she was born into, at least not without knowing what the life of the people was like. She left her relatives and her title of Ladyship behind her and went off to seek the life of a house servant. That is how she came to be in the service of Lady Liling who still knows nothing of Bi's past other than the story that Bi told her: that her parents died during the previous Ebola outbreak and how she has had to take care of herself ever since. Lady Liling took pity on her and took her in as a house servant, confidante, and best friend.

Speaking out loud, Bi says, "Hear me Liling. If things go wrong, you will hear all kinds of bad things about me. But listen to your heart, My Lady, as I know you can. I do this, out of my love for you and all the people of One World."

Lady Bi wipes her tears with a towel, gets out of the hot tub and prepares herself to join the luncheon.

At the very same moment, far south of the Isle of Bella and in the middle of rushing around getting tables, chairs, floor mats, tents, and a plethora of food ready for the Summit, Liling suddenly stops dead in her tracks. A pang of deep sadness hits her out of nowhere. It is so hard and so heavy that she must stop what she is doing and wipe her tears away with the towel she is holding.

With no time to stop and think about it, she continues to the area of the Trader's Market, getting ready for the Summit.

* * *

Early the next morning, Kookie, Liling and Yakov are putting the final touches on the preparations for the opening of the Summit of the Alliance. Arrangements have been made to accommodate over a million people, and Johannesburg is about to burst at the seams with an influx of people from every corner of all three Continental Territories. Anyone with a room is offering accommodations to the participants of the Summit, and large fields have also been set up for campsites. The Lords in attendance have made arrangements for people everywhere to hitch a ride in their Cloudtransporters, while many other folks have made a variety of other transportation arrangements.

The entire estate of Little Lord Emeka has been transformed into an event, which, as Kookie described, is reminiscent of the time when there were such things called Music Festivals. The music has already begun. Scattered throughout the grounds of the estate are musicians, singing and playing their homemade instruments. Most of the instruments are percussion, giving off an exciting energy heard all over the grounds, even down to the Village of the Holy Ones.

Folks with tents and booths are setting up their wares to trade everything imaginable under the sun. But the one that the Big House is most excited about is called, "Kookie's Cookies." Everyone on the Steering Committee of the Alliance has been in the kitchen for days, baking every kind of cookie Kookie has ever eaten, or dreamed of eating.

There is a platform set up in the center of the back field where the Steering Committee will address everyone. Kookie has set up his Lord's Communication Device so it can send an audio transmission of the Summit Conference, only to those who responded to the invitation and have been pre-screened as sympathetic to the Alliance. Each virtual participant will receive the transmission through Kookie's Universal Translator, set for the language of the persons Continental Territory. So, everyone, whether in actual attendance of not, will be tuned in and able to follow the speakers. This has put the estimated number of people attending, in person and virtual, well over several million.

Mama Eve Zula, Papa Adam Makena, and the other Chrysalenes from the Village of the Holy Ones have just arrived along with Mimi, Ryan, Eve Lydia, Adam Sam, Eve Elli, Little Lord Emeka and Suzie of the Seashells. Doc and Phil have just flown in from California with several additional passengers including Judy, Adam Tate, Kenny, Lisa, and their newest friends of all, Master Howard, Mistress Henrietta, and Reggie.

Everyone is well packed in now and the Summit Conference is about to begin. As the Alliance Steering Committee approaches the platform, a huge cry of cheers and elation goes up all around. The voices of the crowd echo on the communication devices of all who are plugged in throughout One World.

Unbeknownst to the Alliance, Lord Viktor and his techies have been partially successful in hacking into Kookie's system, so they are getting bits and pieces of the conference with much interference, and constantly losing their signal. In fact, Kookie has set it up so that if anyone uninvited, like Bella and her group, tries to pick up on them, their signal is scrambled in such a way that Bella's cronies cannot get a lock on where they are. The signal just keeps bouncing all over the planet.

Kookie expects that uninvited folks will probably get sporadic reception. So, he has already warned the speakers to exercise caution and judgement with whatever they say.

"Just pretend that the pro-Council folks are listening in on everything that we are saying, and do not say anything about where we are holding this summit. Of course, we know that we cannot hide everything from them anymore, nor should we at this point. But discretion is still advised."

They all nod in agreement.

Last but not least, Kookie points to an enormous crate that he had transported to the estate a few days ago and is now sitting next to the platform. He says to his friends, "In case you have all been wondering about my big surprise, and what is in that thing," he pauses and taps the tips of his fingers together, with everyone holding their breath in suspended animation, Kookie says, "you are about to find out!"

"KOOKIE! DOH! GIMME A BREAK" they sputter at him.

With that, Liling looks at the group and says, "We are now ready to begin."

A horn is blown and onto the platform walks nine members of the Steering Committee of the Alliance: Kookie, Liling, Dumaka, Yakov, Neely, the Major, Vi, Little Lord Emeka and Eve Elli.

Liling begins: "Hello everybody! Welcome friends! And blessings to you all. My name is Liling, and I am so grateful to all of you who are joining us today; those who are gathered here in person and those who are listening on your communication devices all over One World. Thank you so much for coming and for tuning into this Summit Conference of the Alliance of One World. May this be the beginning of a new world for all of us; for the people and the UC everywhere.

"We invite you all, people of One World, to become an equal part of our global community, as we will share ideas of a new way of living together. We will be showing you our own sustainable garden community as well as the Trader's Market we have recently established. It is to become a permanent part of our lives here and we invite all of you to join us in establishing you own Trader's Market, in your own community."

Cheers and applause go up throughout the crowd.

Liling says, "I will now introduce you to my dear friend and associate, one of our very own gardeners, Dumaka."

Everyone applauds and Dumaka goes up to speak. "Thank you Liling, and thank you everyone for being here today. My name is Dumaka, and I am a simple gardener here on this estate. I have been here for many years and my gardener friends and I are responsible for all the fruits and vegetables of our community. You will find our harvest at the booth over there," he says pointing to Bem, Tafari and Nassor. "And we are most happy to share with you how to get a garden community going."

More applause.

"And now I would like to introduce you to a very special young man."

Emeka comes forward to the communication device.

"This is our very own Lord Emeka!"

Wild cheers go up at the sight of the 5-year-old little "man" smiling away at everyone with love and joy radiating from every inch of his being.

* * *

At that moment, on the Isle of Bella, her Highest is screaming; *"AAAHHH! That's Ekene's son! The gardener said that he is on an estate! The traitors are in Johannesburg!"*

Then, with a hate-filled, snarling, guttural growl, Lady Bella turns to her advisors and says, *"Bi told us that they were in a place called WYOMING!*

I JUST SENT MASTER MIKHAIL AND ALL OF HIS FORCES OUT THERE! ***SHE TRICKED US! MY LITTLE SISTER TRICKED US!"***

* * *

Little Lord Emeka is greeted with love and warmth, as are the rest who follow . . . Neely, Yakov and Vi.

When it comes the Major's turn to speak, he looks out over the crowd and notices his father smiling proudly at him. As the Major is fighting back tears, he can hear Kookie right behind him saying, "It's okay, bro'. You got this."

The Major begins, "Hello everyone, and welcome. My name is Master John of Howard Pharmaceuticals, but people just call me the Major."

Applause and voices respond, "Hi Major!"

"Before I begin, I would like to say that there is someone very special out there in this wonderful group of people." Choking back tears, the Major says pointing, "It is that man right over there. His name is Master Howard, and he is my father. And today, I am so proud to be his son."

From where he is standing he can see his father wiping tears from his eyes, and the Major is unable to contain his emotions any longer. He begins to weep, too.

Vi comes to his rescue. "We want to tell you about the latest line of natural healing products that are now in development at Howard Pharmaceuticals. They will be out soon and on the shelves of Center Markets everywhere!"

Cheers go up from the crowd with applause, and Master Howard receives pats on the back and handshakes.

The Major finally finds his voice as he says to the crowd, "Please come over to any one of us during the Summit to ask whatever questions you may have. Or if you are an herbalist or a gardener and would like to be a part of our team, just come on over to our booth."

More applause and cheers.

The Major says, "And now, I would like to introduce you all to my dear friend, and one of the kindest human beings you will ever meet; The High Lord Kenneth, otherwise known as Kookie."

Lots of applause and cheers as Kookie takes the floor. "Thank you, Major. And thank you one and all for being here. As you have heard so far from everyone else, we are all so grateful to be here and honored to serve all of you, the people of One World."

A quiet has descended upon the crowd as if everyone seems to realize they are in the presence of a great soul.

"I would like to ask each of you, whether you are here, or listening from afar, to consider how we may best be of service to you. I have established a communication system with your devices, and either I or someone from our team will make ourselves available to you as best we can. But most of all, my good people, I will try my best to give back to you that which has been taken from you so very long ago—your freedom."

A quiet applause begins in the crowd, slowly picking up with intensity, until all are applauding strongly and cheering loudly.

Kookie looks out at the crowd of UC members and the people, and says, "I have something for you that will, I hope, light your path on the journey that we are now all embarking upon together."

As he points to the large crate next to him, everyone, including his team, is anxious to see Kookie's big surprise. He takes out his Metatron device, pushes a few buttons, and the crate opens on one side. It is large enough for people to walk into.

"With the help of my friends," Kookie says, "we will take out the contents of this crate and distribute it among you."

Yakov, Liling and the Major are bursting with anticipation as they are about to finally see Kookie's big surprise. He goes to the crate and takes out one of the objects inside. Bringing it back up to the platform Kookie raises a book in the air and shows it to one and all.

"This was once in every school throughout One World, and it was used to teach *ALL* children, not just the Lords. At some point it was considered unfit for the general population and only survival skills were taught to the children of the people after that. This special book that I am holding, and others like it, were confiscated and hidden away for a long time. Even we of the UC have had only limited access to them, as they were carefully, and cautiously, rationed out to us by the Council. Then, one day I stumbled upon a top-secret storage room that was filled with these books. I realized that I had to quietly confiscate them and give them to all of you when the time came.

"Well, my friends, the time has come, and I am giving back to you what should never have been taken *from* you: YOUR HISTORY!"

A stunned silence falls over the crowd.

"In the pages of these books you will discover our ancient civilizations and societies, as well as our more recent past. You will learn how the Council and the UC came into power, and how you the people lost your freedom."

"Oh. . . My. . . Word!" exclaims Liling.

Yakov and the rest of the friends utter their own words of shock.

"There is one passage in this book that I am holding in my hand which I would like very much to read to you, before I introduce you to our next and final speaker. The book is about the life of a great man, who came to power at a time when his people were very badly divided. He wrote a speech which begins with the following words. . ."

All eyes and hearts are upon Kookie now as if they are all experiencing a miracle.

Kookie opens the book and begins:

"Four score and seven years ago our fathers brought forth upon this continent, a new nation, conceived in Liberty, and dedicated to the proposition that all men are created equal."

"This, my friends, is where we stand now. We have a divided world with those who would like to keep the people enslaved to the Lords and Masters, and those of us who firmly believe that we are on the verge of bringing forth a new world, conceived in Love and Freedom, and dedicated to the proposition that all human beings are created equal. This is my gift to you, and my promise that I will do everything that I can, along with the Alliance, and the Courageous Love of all of you, to give birth to a free new world.

"Please, come and help yourselves; empty this crate of the many history books inside. There is actually plenty more where this came from." And finally with a few fingertip taps, Kookie concludes with, "I just couldn't carry them all!"

A bolt of laughter followed by a standing ovation and a thunderous applause bellows across the entire estate. The Steering Committee is left speechless.

Kookie holds his hand up to get the crowd's attention one more time. "In conclusion, I will have the youngest member of our team say a blessing on us. Eve Elli, please come on over here honey and tell us what you would like to say."

Everyone goes quiet one more time as they watch the three-year-old glowing child stand before them.

Eve Elli is beaming and smiling from ear to ear as she holds her hands out and says, "Don't worry, and don't be afraid; everything is gonna be okay. Everything is gonna be just fine. Our Heavenly Father loves you." With a huge grin and a little giggle, she says, "I'm Eve Elli and I love you, too."

Light radiates from the child to all who are present, as well as those who are tuned in throughout One World. Peace and joy fill everyone's hearts.

And the Summit Festival begins.

PART 2

FREEDOM RINGING

Chapter 7 – Insurrectionist

LADY BELLA IS BESIDE HERSELF WITH RAGE. *"Where is she?"* Bella yells at her advisors. *"Where is that treacherous girl? Where is Bi?"*

Lord Igor, Lord Pavel and Lord Viktor look at each other, and Lord Pavel says, "I think I saw her headed for the landing field, My Lady."

"So! She thinks she is going to get away with this, does she? STOP HER! IMMEDIATELY! DO NOT LET HER GET AWAY!" shrieks Lady Bella at the three Lords.

Lady Bi is almost to the Cloudtransporter. She is going over in her head all that she wants to tell her Lady Liling and everyone else when she gets back to Johannesburg, about her past and why she has kept everything, including her involvement with Lady Bella's Council, a secret from them. She knew that this was her burden to bear and hers alone. She felt she would only be putting the Alliance in more danger if they insisted on helping her, and that Lady Bella was *her* problem to deal with.

The Cloudtransporter is only a few yards away, and Lady Bi quickens her pace, anxious to get on board and away from her sister, the Highest Lady Bella, head of the Council and ruler of One World.

She hears a voice behind her. "Lady Bi! Lady Bi!"

She turns around and sees that the voice belongs to Lord Pavel. Lord Igor and Lord Viktor are right behind him and the three of them are flanked by several Security Overseers. Lady Bi's heart sinks to the ground, as she knows that her time left on this earth is now coming to a close. Just as the group is about to catch up with her, she closes her eyes and quietly whispers a prayer.

"Father in Heaven, please bring the Alliance through, that they may one day have their paradise here on earth. Please let My Lady Liling know the truth about me. And please, dear Lord, please, please, set the people—*all* the people—of One World, *FREE!*"

"Lady Bi," Pavel says, "I am hereby taking you into custody, on the charge of *insurrection* against the Council, the Upper Crust, and the people of One World."

A Security Overseer places shackles on Lady Bi's wrists, and she is escorted back to Lady Bella's house.

* * *

The Summit Festival in Johannesburg is well underway. Trading is going well, and the people and the UC are gathering together forming new friendships and bonds. The Howard Pharmaceuticals booth is swamped with all kinds of folks, from herbalists and gardeners to practitioners of folk medicine. Many are just curious to learn about everything, even offering themselves as apprentices to Master Howard, Vi, the Major, Mistress Henrietta and Reggie.

The Big House has a large conference room that Master Howard and the others are using in response to the great interest they are generating. Many people are curious to hear about the new line of herbs and natural pharmaceutical products that Master Howard is going to add to his inventory.

Dumaka and Liling have scheduled time in the conference room along with Bem, Tafari, Nassor, Judy, Lisa, and Kenny to discuss various aspects of gardening, farming, and organizing community gardens in towns and villages.

Kookie is hanging out with Mimi, Ryan, Doc, Phil, Lord Emeka, Eve Elli and Suzie of the Seashells in front of the giant shipping crate full of hundreds of books. He has organized the walk-in crate with layer upon layer of shelves with the books arranged by category and age group. The books for the little ones are on the bottom shelf. There is a sign posted right outside the crate that reads "KOOKIE'S LIBRARY."

This has attracted much attention, and everyone has been asking him, "What is a library?"

There has been a continuous stream of people coming over to Kookie's Library with absolute awe and wonder at what they are seeing. Kookie and his little group are there to help people navigate their way through the books and answer whatever questions they can. The friends are getting support from other Lords and Ladies about starting a library in their own communities. Kookie is arranging to have historical books of all kinds transported to all those who are wanting to start libraries for the people. Something in his heart tells him that this is probably the greatest act of insurrection and defiance that he is doing at the Summit Festival. For a moment, he thinks of Angie and how proud she would be if she were here to see his library.

Lord Emeka, Eve Elli and little Suzie are in charge of the children's books. Each child who comes to their library chooses a book to read, and one of the adults gets to read it to the group. Little Suzie is especially delighted by a children's book called Rosa, with drawings of a beautiful lady sitting on an autovehicle called a "bus." The illustrations are so inviting that she tries tasting one of them.

Everyone laughs and Eve Elli giggles saying, "Suzie, books are for *reading*, not for eating."

Little Suzie giggles too, and hands the book over to Phil, waiting for him to read it to her.

Yakov and Neely are wandering around talking to everyone and spreading around their love and happiness. They have become the official ambassadors of the Summit, making sure that everything is running smoothly, and offering their help wherever it is needed. At one point, Yakov feels a tap on his back. When he turns around, he sees two familiar faces smiling and laughing as they put their hands out to him and Neely.

"Jackson! My man! How good it is to see you!" Yakov greets them. Yakov also turns to the charming Rita standing beside him and offers her both of his hands. "And you, my dear; how wonderful it is to see you both."

"Thank you, My Lord Yakov," Rita says with much sweetness and grace.

"Yes, it is good to see you too, both of you," Lord Jackson says with a smile. "Thank you both for all the work that you are doing here. Rita and I would like very much to do our part in helping the Alliance, if you could perhaps suggest ways for us to get involved."

Yakov is truly touched. "Well, why don't we all get together later at the Coffeehouse and talk it over."

"Sounds like a great idea! Later at the Coffeehouse then!" says Jackson.

The festivities continue well into the night and the next day. The Alliance is growing as people are bonding with each other and making arrangements to move forward once they get back to their own towns or villages.

The communication devices are still transmitting all over One World, the various speakers and lectures that are going on at the festival. People everywhere are taking notes, thinking about how they too can become involved and what they can do.

This includes Lady Bella and the three Lords of the Council who are listening in, catching whatever they can with the choppy, sporadic reception.

* * *

Lord Pavel comes to Lady Bella's study and knocks gingerly on the door. There is no answer. Knowing the temperament of His Ladyship, Pavel waits to the count of five and then knocks again. Still no answer. He knows that he is in for a hard time. Slowly, Pavel turns the doorknob and walks in.

Lady Bella is staring out the window at the yachts off in the distance. Her face is expressionless with eyes staring wide open. "Where is she?" Bella says, still staring out the window.

"My Lady, she is—" he hesitates, "down below."

"Down *beLOW?*" she turns and says, still wide-eyed. Her sarcasm is slowly turning to rage.

"Yes, My Lady." Pavel looks down at the floor now, shaking. From the corner of his eye, he catches Bella opening her desk drawer and he wonders if *he* is going to "get it," or Lady Bi . . . or, first one then the other.

"Is she *shackled, My Lord Pavel?*"

"Yes, indeed she is, My Lady. As per your request."

"Very well then, Pavel, *do* take me to her." Cracking her whip loud and hard she yells, "*NOW!*"

On another part of the Isle of Bella, Lord Igor is carrying out *his* assignment from Her Ladyship. He is attempting to send out a message to Master Commandant Mikhail in Wyoming. Igor's orders are to let Master Mikhail know that he was sent there on a ruse and that the true insurrectionists are in Johannesburg. He is to bring the entire outfit of his men to Johannesburg immediately, and blow the entire estate of Lord Emeka—Big House, grounds and all—to smithereens.

They are also to kill each and every one of the insurrectionists involved in treason, beginning with those at the top: Lord Kenneth, Lord Yakov and Lady Liling. No one is to be left alive.

Lord Igor is attempting to transmit the message to Master Mikhail's communication device; however, he keeps getting a signal saying that the transmission cannot go through. He continues to try but keeps getting the same signal. Furious, he calls in Lord Viktor to see if he can figure out what is going on.

"What is happening?" asks Lord Igor in great frustration. "Why can I *not* get a signal, so I can get a message through to the Master Commandant?"

Lord Viktor says, "I do not know, Igor. Give me the coordinates that you got from Lady Bi. Let me run them by one of the techies."

"I'm going down to the lab with you," says Lord Igor.

"Very well then," Lord Viktor says.

When they arrive at the lab, Lord Viktor calls out to one of the techies, "Technician!" he says. "Tell us why we are unable to send a message to these coordinates."

The techie takes the communication device, tries it and suspecting what is wrong, shows it to the two men. "My Lords," the techie says, pulling the coordinates up on a screen in front of them. "Do you see where these coordinates are located?"

Both of them look at the map on the screen and cannot figure out what it is that they are looking at.

"It is a cave. A cave of gargantuan proportions." The techie laughs. "No wonder you cannot transmit anything there."

The two Lords look at each other and slap their heads. It seems Lady Bi has really duped them in a bad way.

"In fact," continues the techie, "I can't even get an exact lock on the location of the device that you are trying to find. There must be a 500-mile radius of small caverns with nooks and crannies. Whoever is down there, I sure hope they know their way out. Otherwise, they are all in big trouble. Mind telling me who *is* down there?"

In a shaky voice, Lord Viktor responds, "Master Commandant Mikhail and an entire battalion of commandos."

* * *

The message Lord Igor was trying to send to Master Commandant Mikhail, did *not* go unnoticed. The vibrations of the message bounced off the walls of the enormous cave with such a force that it is still ringing in every hollow across the globe. The message is heard by every creature, every flower, and every tree on the planet.

The message is also heard by the seven Monarch Butterflies that Angel left in charge when she descended into the bowels of hell with Angie. A battalion of Monarchs are now ready for action.

The pigeons also hear the message vibrations, including #3 and #4. Angie's pigeon buddies cry out to all the other doves on earth, and they all tune in to the signals sent to the cave of Wyoming.

With all of nature behind the Alliance, and the Monarchs rising to their defense, the vibrations of Igor's message are about to become the sound of freedom ringing for the people of One World.

* * *

In an underground chamber inside the mansion on the Isle of Bella, Lady Bi is lying on the cold, hard ground in a pool of blood. She is behind bars and shackled to the wall. After whipping and beating her close to death, Lady Bella suddenly stopped because she decided that death would be too easy for Bi. It is not so much Bi's body that has been broken, but the words that her sister said when leaving her alone in the dark, and in pain.

"I am sending word to your *frrriend*," Bella sneered with sarcasm, "this very day! Your *ever-sooo-kind* Lady Liling will know that you came here to betray the Alliance and that now you are with us! Ha!"

With those cruel words, Lady Bella left Bi alone in a pool of blood and torturous pain; physical and emotional. But the worst pain that Bi simply cannot bear is the thought that her dear Lady Liling will think that she has betrayed her.

Bi cries out in despair, "Please My Lady Liling, please do not listen to the words of vicious lies. I love you, as I love all the people you want to help, and everything you stand for. Please listen with your heart and not with your ears. Listen for the truth, my kind friend." Bi breaks down in tears. "Oh, please my Sister, Lady Liling, listen with your heart that you may know the truth."

* * *

The doves follow the vibrations to the cave in Wyoming. When they get to the mouth of the cave, they see several Cloudtransporters parked on the ground. Although the vehicles are empty, the doves feel an energy of anger and destruction from within the aircraft. As they circle around the Cloudtransporters, they come across various openings with vent screens covering them. The negative energy seems to be the highest around the openings, so the doves do what all birds do. They sit on all the vent openings and proceed to have a glorious potty party. Poo is hitting the fans, belts, and assorted machinery beneath their butts.

After filling the vents with enough of their sticky business to gum up the workings of the aircraft, the doves can now feel a peaceful energy radiating from within the Cloudtransporters. With their mission accomplished, the birds are ready and waiting for their next assignment from #3 and #4.

* * *

The Monarch Butterflies hear Lady Bi's passionate cry. Their love and compassion for all human creatures is deep, but they have a particular soft spot for those who would sacrifice themselves for the lives of others. So, the prayer of Lady Bi goes directly to the hearts of the seven

Monarchs in Angel's flutter. They know what they must do, as they head straight for Bella's communication device.

Her Ladyship begins to send a message to Liling, but all she is getting on her communication device is a dropped signal. She tries again and to no avail.

"What's going on here?" Bella yells in frustration. Going over to the door of her private suite, she yells for Lord Igor who is just down the hallway.

"*EEEGOR!*" Lady Bella yells.

He quickly comes to her door, "What is it My Lady?"

"I can't get this stupid thing to work!" she says, irritated.

"Dear me!" says Lord Igor, "Let me see what I can do for you."

Igor fusses with Bella's device for a little while, but he cannot get it to send a transmission either. All they continue to see on the screen is the dropped signal.

Lady Bella sighs with resignation and says, "I guess we'll have to take this to Lord Viktor and his techie crew tomorrow. Meanwhile, Igor, give me some *good* news before I retire for the evening."

"Yes, My Lady," he says a little bit worried about what is coming.

Lady Bella continues, "While I was down there, *disciplining* my baby sister I trust that you and Lord Pavel took care of the other business for today? And I expect that you were able to reach Master Mikhail to get him out of that ridiculous situation my sister got him into, and that he and his commandos are now almost in Johannesburg. Yes?"

There is a pause as Igor does not answer.

"*Yes?*" Lady Bella repeats herself.

Still no answer from Igor.

"*YES?*" she yells at him in frustration. "What's the matter, Igor, cat got your tongue?"

The Monarchs are sitting on the window just outside of Lady Bella's suite. They are proud of themselves for jamming the transmission signals of her Ladyship's communication device, and when they hear those last words from her, they all respond, *Hee Hee!*

* * *

The Summit Festival in Johannesburg is coming to a close. People are beginning to leave, taking with them a taste of true freedom and a whole new way of life. The UC is taking knowledge, information, and newly formed connections with them back to their homes, and all the people are feeling a hope that they have never felt before.

For all, this new freedom is about living a life of their own choosing in a way that gives them meaning, purpose and a deeper bond with others; the highest bond of all being the friendship between them. Everyone knows that they will be taking with them a very precious gift: the inner connection and support that comes from a loving community, and the power to spread it around to others.

The Chrysalenes from the Village of the Holy Ones are happy at what they have witnessed at the Summit Festival, learning all the new ways that they can be of service to others. Liling and Dumaka are as happy as can be, sharing gardening tips with others. And they are most anxious to put what they have learned into practice. Liling is especially amazed at all the varieties of fruits and vegetables there are as well as all the health benefits they each provide. She thinks about her cherished Brothers, Kookie and Yakov, and how she just cannot wait to get caught up with them on everything wonderful that has happened at the summit.

She stops suddenly in her thoughts and pauses. Turning to Dumaka, she says to him: "Honey, have you seen Bi lately?"

* * *

Footsteps stomp down the dark hallway leading to the underground cell of Lady Bi. Lying on the cold ground in extreme pain with no food or water in her body since the day before, Bi is very weak. She recognizes the footsteps of her sister getting closer to her cell, and Bi closes her eyes in sadness and fear.

Suddenly, she becomes aware of another presence. Lifting her head to the stream of pale light that is coming in from the small window at the top of the cell, Bi can barely make something out through her blurry vision. Coming toward her are seven Monarch Butterflies, and perched on the window ledge just behind them are two doves.

The Monarchs flutter over to her gently and alight on her broken body. As soon as they touch her, Bi notices that her body has gone numb; she is feeling no more pain.

The Monarchs whisper to her heart, *Fear not, gentle creature, for we are with you. Your friend Liling will know the truth and will never hear anything else.*

The pain in Bi's soul is now gone as she releases tears of joy. Then the door opens and in walks Lady Bella.

"You little witch!" Bella says, in a low growl. "It wasn't enough for you just to send our men on a wild goose chase. Oh no! You had to send them to a place where they will be lost in the dark for who knows how long, *and* incommunicado from the rest of the world! **WITCH!"** Bella screams in a violent rage and slams her foot into her sister's side.

There is no response from Bi; she simply stares through bleary eyes at Bella.

Getting down on the ground so she is eye level with her sister, Bella grabs a hold of her chin and says, "What makes you so special anyway, huh?" Tears of anger start to well up in Bella's eyes. "Why did mother love *you* and not me? *HUH? Answer me **that** you little witch! WHY?"*

Bi is staring through her puffy, swollen eyes straight into the wrath of her sister's tortured soul. The only words that come to her are the last words that she will ever speak upon this earth. Bi says to Bella, "But, *I* love you, my sister."

Bi suddenly becomes aware of the light coming into her cell. It is becoming brighter and stronger. The seven Monarchs grow larger and even more beautiful in their colors of radiant, shimmering yellow, orange and gold. Their wings have turned into beautiful wings of angels with arms outstretched to Bi, beckoning her to leave her earthly body behind.

She holds her arms out to the Monarch angels who gently raise her ethereal body up, turning her to the Light. A tunnel has formed around the Light with the doves dancing inside. They are overjoyed that a Sister of Love is about to come home. The Light is brilliant now, and Bi can see her mother and father at the end of the tunnel. They are both smiling at her with arms reaching out to bring their daughter home.

The seven angels rise, gently holding the spirit of Bi, pouring love and peace into her soul. They carry their Sister up the sparkling tunnel, to the Light at her journey's end.

Bi has gone home.

Chapter 8 – Veritas[4]

DUMAKA PONDERS HER QUESTION for a moment when Liling asks if he has seen Bi. "Actually, no I haven't. Didn't she say that she had some business to attend to elsewhere?"

"Yes," says Liling, "And she also said that she would be right back."

They look at each other and a feeling of foreboding settles into the pit of their stomachs, as they start heading for the evening meal at the Big House.

Yakov and Neely have prepared an exquisite meal of freshly picked garden vegetables made into wonderful salads and veggie pastries. Quiche seems to be quite popular as are the veggie wraps made with grilled cheese.

Yakov sees Liling and Dumaka approaching and calls out to them, "Hey there you two, come on over. Everyone else should be here shortly."

"Hello, Yakov," says Liling. Looking at all the scrumptious dishes that he and Neely are bringing to the table, she says to him, "You just seem to be getting better and better at this!"

"Well thank you, thank you," Yakov says quite pleased with himself.

"Oh good," he says with a nod towards the Big House. "Here comes everyone else. Looks like the group from the Village of the Holy Ones are also with them. That's really good, you know, we could all use a break; maybe relax at the Coffeehouse this evening."

Liling and Dumaka smile and nod, but it is not with the enthusiasm that Yakov expects. He knows his Sister too well and can see something is bothering her. "What's wrong?" he asks.

---

[4] *Latin for Truth*

"Have you seen Bi lately, Brother?" she asks without a moment's hesitation.

"Uh, no, I haven't. Do you think there is something wrong?" Yakov says.

"Well, um, I don't know. I–," she pauses, looks him in the eyes and says, "Yes."

"Hey there!" yells Kookie as the others have all arrived at the table.

The Major and Vi are looking at the interesting spread of vegetable dishes, and Vi is bursting at the seams to try her first ever grilled cheese sandwich. "My! Don't those things look absolutely divine!" she exclaims. But when Vi looks up at everyone, she notices that all is not well.

Everyone gathers around the table and takes a seat. The three children are also present along with Mimi, Ryan, Doc and Phil. Kookie also feels that something is amiss as a feeling of discomfort is settling into the pit of his stomach, too.

With everyone looking at each other and the ill-at-ease feeling growing stronger, Kookie finally breaks the ice. "Okay folks, what's going on here? Am I the only one feeling like I have suddenly lost my appetite?"

Everyone looks around the table at each other and nods; they all appear to be in the same boat.

Suddenly, Liling jumps up, staring upwards, and is hit with a hard jab in her guts. She doubles over in pain and cries out, *"Bi! My Sister!"*

Eve Elli comes over to her and takes Liling's hand. "Don't worry Liling. Lady Bi is not in pain anymore. The Monarchs are waiting for her. She will be ready any minute now. She will be just fine."

Everyone turns to Eve Elli with a sudden realization of what is happening.

And Liling breaks down and cries, "Oh No! Great Mother Kwan Yin! No!" and a very faint voice comes into her head saying: *But **I** love you, my Sister.*

All goes quiet. A stillness fills the air and the stomachs of everyone around the table relax. Liling sits down quietly with tears streaming down her face.

Eve Elli says to her, "It's okay, Liling. Lady Bi loves you, and she is very happy now. . . She has gone home." And then with a soft voice and gentle smile, Eve Elli says to Liling, "You will see her again one day. But it's okay to cry when you are sad."

Liling takes Eve Elli in her arms and in her great sorrow, breaks down crying.

* * *

That evening the group takes a somber walk together to the Coffeehouse. They walk in silence, stopping several times along the way, to pick flowers, or just to feel the spirit moving through their hearts. There are many questions going through Liling's head, like why Eve Elli referred to Bi as *Lady* Bi, but she knows that the answers to so many of her questions will come in time.

Kookie is thinking about what Angie told him in his recent visit with her, regarding the origins of Liling, Yakov, and himself, and he knows that the time has come for him to share the truth with the other two.

Eve Elli is holding hands with Little Lord Emeka and thinking about all the things she cannot tell the others. The Monarchs have told her that the human creatures must learn their own lessons, each in his or her own time and own way; and that is why they are sometimes allowed to hurt and suffer so much. Mama Eve Zula has explained to Eve Elli that it is a great blessing and time for rejoicing whenever someone has learned a soul lesson. It means they now have that much more compassion in their hearts and will be able to love and serve others even better. And this, in turn, brings them closer to the Heavenly Father.

Eve Elli likes this line of reasoning, but she still wishes she could tell the grown-ups more things sometimes, especially her Gramma Mimi, whom she loves dearly.

The Coffeehouse is now in view. They are all looking forward to relaxing on the outdoor patio and talking to some of the locals. But for Kookie, there is another agenda that he will have to reveal.

Phil, Doc, Mimi, Ryan, Vi and the Major are well into their conversations with folks who are now a regular part of the Trader's Market. Doc and Phil have hooked up with some local herbalists who are interested in working together with the Major and Vi.

Master Howard and Mistress Henrietta are staying at the Big House and will be going back to California in the next few days. They were exhausted after the Summit and decided not to join the group at the Coffeehouse this evening and just retire early, but they have all talked about opening a Howard Pharmaceutical plant in Johannesburg. The plant will focus on creating herbal products from the region and working together with local herbalists and healers. The Major is talking to the new people who will be working for them, with an actual remuneration for their services.

Walking around to the tables where all his friends are seated, and engaged in conversations with their new local friends, Kookie asks if he can have a word with them whenever they are ready.

"Sure thing, bro'!" says the Major and the rest of them.

As they all come together seated at the café tables under Johannesburg's warm, evening sky, Kookie begins to share his news. "First, I would like to beg your pardon and ask if Liling and Yakov can sit here next to me. What I am about to share with you all is about the three of us."

They all look around a bit curious while Liling and Yakov change seats so that they are sitting right next to Kookie.

"As I have already told you about the visit that I recently had with my beloved Angie, there was one detail of her revelation to me that I have not yet shared. I felt I needed to wait for the right time." Looking at Yakov and Liling, Kookie says, "It is about our origins."

Their eyes go wide, and Yakov says, "Angie told you about our origins?!"

"Oh, my goodness!" exclaims Liling.

"Yes, she did." Kookie proceeds to share with everyone the whole story; beginning with the pact that PA, ES and SPA made with the devil for wealth and power, and their fears that others would come along to challenge them and their leadership. For this, they wanted to have three children to raise as their own, one from each Continental Territory, to be their High Lords. These High Lords would be conceived in evil, by their father, the devil himself, and raised under the total control and domination of the Council and the lord of the underworld.

"WHOA, BRO'! OH MY GOODNESS! GOOD GRIEF! GOOD LORD . . . NOT YOU!"

"And that," Kookie says, pointing his index finger in the air and looking at Yakov and Liling, "is what the three of us were born and bred to be."

"So, what happened?" asks Liling, completely dumbfounded. "I mean it seems obvious that we are not exactly the devil's disciples."

Kookie looks up to the heavens and says, "The Lord happened." Turning to the Major and smiling, he says, "Not me. The one up there!" he quips.

The Major rolls his eyes and Kookie says, "Sorry! Heh, heh." Then he clears his throat and continues. "According to Angie, our Heavenly Father took pity on us, and did a genetic switch, you know like what we did with the Ebola bioweapon. So, we ended up with, well, you know, more of the characteristics of our Father in Heaven, rather than the other guy."

"You mean like the Chrysalenes?" Yakov asks.

"Not quite," says Kookie. "But similar. We received the intellectual and intuitive gifts, though, and I guess you could say, a kind heart."

"Wow!" says Liling, "That certainly does explain a lot, my Brothers."

"Yes," says Kookie, "And I think it also explains why the beast wanted and took my Angie."

They all look down and sadly nod their heads.

"Yep," says Kookie, "I think that big bad beastie boy wants to have some bad boy company. You know, like maybe wanting me to make some kind of deal with him and trade places with Angie."

Eve Elli chimes in, "But, Angel is with Angie now. So that big bad beastie boy has to do what *Angel* says!"

Everyone chuckles at Eve Elli and Mimi says, "Come on over here you! It's time for a great big Gramma hug!"

"Hee, hee, hee!" Eve Elli giggles giving her Gramma a great big cherub hug.

* * *

Lady Bella calls for a meeting with her Council Advisors. She arranges to meet them in one of the offices near the lab where the techies are at work. Lord Igor, Lord Pavel and Lord Viktor arrive and are seated and waiting when Bella arrives.

"My Lords," Lady Bella begins. "We have a most urgent matter to discuss. I'm sure you all know by now what is happening with Master Commandant Mikhail and his commando battalion. It is most unfortunate that we had an insurrectionist right here among us who led us astray in such a despicable manner. But that matter has already been taken care of."

The Lords look at each other with much fidgeting and sideways glances. Considering what their High Lady just did to her own sister, they are more than a bit fearful for their own lives should they displease her Ladyship.

"While we are waiting to hear from Master Commandant Mikhail, after he and his battalion find their way out of the cave, we must aggressively move forward with our plans."

She pauses and waits for a comment from the others, but none is forthcoming. Lady Bella continues, "Our real offensive plan of attack is not with the men in the field anyway. Our enemy is too scattered, and our numbers are too few. That has always been the concern of the former Council and why they have been trying so hard to drastically reduce the slave population for so many years. And why we need to use more effective forms of aggression to eliminate them."

The Lords seem to have relaxed their fear of her Ladyship as they are leaning forward and looking directly at her. Lord Viktor even ventures a comment.

"My Lady," he says, "I believe that you are referring to the long-range laser weapon that we now have in development.

"Yes, Lord Viktor, that is exactly what I am referring to. And I take it that when you say *'in development'* you mean the thing is still not *ready*?!" Lady Bella raises her voice with the last few words, causing the fear to return to all three Lords in her presence.

Lord Viktor swallows hard and says, "Yes, My Lady, or, um . . . No, My Lady, that is, it is still not ready . . . High Lady Bella. . . ma'am."

Dead silence hangs in the room like thick mud. Lady Bella is clicking the end of her pen; click, click, click. With an ice-cold stare slicing into the very heart of Lord Viktor, Lady Bella says, "And why is the weapon not ready *YET,* Lord Viktor?"

Shaking in his shoes and trying with every ounce of power in him *not* to stutter, Lord Viktor says, "My Lady, the techies are perfecting the accuracy of the long-range fire power on the laser beam. The farther out it can go, the more slaves we can destroy with greater speed and accuracy."

Bella stops clicking her pen.

To the Lords this is a good sign, and they relax again. . . a little.

"I see," she says. "Why don't we go over to the techies and you can show me how your progress is going, and what kind of timetable we can expect for our strike."

Lady Bella starts clicking her pen again as three nervous Lords take her over to one of the techies.

* * *

The hour is getting late at the Coffeehouse and Eve Elli needs to get back to the Village of the Holy Ones. Gramma Mimi says to her, "I think it's time to take you back now, honey. It's already past your bedtime."

"Okay Gramma, tomorrow is another day!" Eve Elli says. She takes Lord Emeka by the hand, and smiling sweetly at him says, "Ready?"

"I'm ready. Let's go," Emeka says.

Mimi turns to everyone and says, "Thank you again for allowing us to be a part of this journey with you."

"The pleasure and honor are ours," says Liling.

They all say goodnight and the group from the Village of the Holy Ones heads for home.

Liling turns to Kookie, Yakov and the rest of them and says, "There are a few other things that we need to discuss. I know that we are all feeling well protected and supported, and loving the progress we are making for the people of One World. But, my friends, there is another reality that we must also face."

They all know what is coming and that Liling is right. It is time to face the *whole* truth of what is happening.

Liling continues, "I don't know all the details of what happened to Bi, but I believe it is time to look into the world of the pro-Council UC and see what we are dealing with."

Kookie, Yakov, Neely, Dumaka, the Major and Vi all look at her and nod in agreement.

Yakov says, "What we need to know first is where did Bi go. And that should be easy enough for us to figure out with our surveillance tracking system."

"Can you do that?" asks Dumaka, who is new to all of the Lords' surveillance capabilities.

"We sure can, honey," Liling says. "That has been our job, so to speak, all of our lives."

"Gracious me!" Dumaka exclaims.

"Don't worry Dumaka, you'll get used to it!" says Vi.

They all have a chuckle and Kookie and Yakov take out their Metatron devices.

"Now that we have these," Kookie says, showing Dumaka his device, "we don't need the other tracking equipment anymore.

Kookie and Yakov enter the tracking information of the Cloudtransporter that Bi took when she left Johannesburg. Within minutes they have it. They both look down with sadness and frustration.

"I might have known," says Kookie.

"Known what, you guys?" says the Major, "Mind letting the rest of us in on it?"

Kookie sighs, with a sorrowful half-smile and says, "The current location of the Cloudtransporter that Bi took when she left here is an Island in the Mediterranean Sea. It is called the Isle of Bella and is the home of Lady Bella, a pro-Council Lady who presented aggressive genocide ideas to the Council, along with Lord Ekene. I would bet anything that she is one of the top advisors of the Lords now, if not *the* top Lady of the Council," says Kookie.

Suddenly Liling is gripped with a searing pain across her cheek as if someone sashed her face open with a knife. She yelps in pain as Dumaka holds her and the others instantly come to her side.

"What is happening, Liling? What can we do for you? Is it Bi?" they ask her.

Liling is caught breathless from the pain, holding her face. The pain suddenly disappears as fast as it hit. She closes her eyes and sees a whip cracking hard against Bi's face and Liling begins to sob. She knows that this kind woman, who was her dearest friend for so many years, suffered terribly before leaving this earth. This is one truth that Liling is just not ready to deal with yet. She turns to Dumaka and says softly, "Let's go home now."

The group reaches the Big House and they all go to the living room. Reggie is milling about in the kitchen enjoying some leftover grilled veggie and cheese sandwiches that were put aside. Appetites were not exactly up to par when everyone sat down to eat and then, suddenly, experienced the passing of Bi.

When Reggie sees everyone has returned, he peeks into the living room. "Good evening, everyone. Sorry about what happened earlier. Would any of you care for a bite to eat?" Reggie says while holding up a sandwich.

They all look at Liling who sighs and says, "I guess that wouldn't be such a bad idea."

She starts to get up out of the soft loveseat that she and Dumaka just settled down into.

"Stay where you are, My Lady," offers Reggie, "I would be happy to bring some of the leftovers from the meal in here and serve you."

He rushes off to the kitchen, and Neely and Yakov follow him in there to offer their help.

The Major turns to Kookie and says, "So what about this Lady Bella, bro'? You say she came up with some genocide ideas at the last Council Gathering. What's the deal with her?"

Kookie takes a deep breath and says, "The deal with Lady Bella is that she is basically a sociopath. I got to know her somewhat as we were growing up, and if she is at the helm of the Council now, we really need to be prepared."

Reggie, Yakov and Neely come in with a plate of sandwiches and a flask of purified water.

Yakov just caught Kookie's last sentence and chimes in, "Sociopath, indeed! I got to know her family when I was younger. I remember when her folks died. It was a terrible boating accident that was shrouded in mystery, but rumors were flying all over with the Lords and Ladies of Euroslavica. They believed that their daughter might have had something to do with it. Back then her name was Chen."

Suddenly, there is a familiarity to all this for Liling.

Yakov continues, "After her folks died, Lady Chen decided to change her name, and that was when she became Lady Bella. We all thought that was kind of strange. I mean normally when people you love and care about die, you want to honor them and their memory, not bury everything about them completely. She also had a younger sister, as I recall, whom their relatives took, probably for the poor girl's safety, to raise in Shanghai." says Yakov. Pausing for a moment he adds, "and come to think of it, her name was Bi."

Everyone freezes in place and stares at Yakov. He says, "Whoa, wait a second! I know what you all must be thinking, but I do believe that Bi is a common girl's name in Sinopacifica. Isn't that right Liling?"

He looks at Liling who is now on her feet and staring wide-eyed, with her hands holding her face.

"Yes!" Liling says, "It is a very common name. But when Eve Elli was telling us what was happening as Bi was leaving this world, she referred to her as *Lady* Bi!"

Everything comes rushing into Liling's heart. She closes her eyes and sees what Lady Bi's life was like after her family brought her back to Shanghai; how she decided to leave her Ladyship heritage behind her, becoming a simple woman of the people. Liling then sees how Bi came to be a servant in her house.

She shares all of this with everyone as well as her vision of Bi's last mission here on earth; convincing Lady Bella of her fealty to her while sending an entire battalion of commandos to a cave in Wyoming. For a moment Liling smiles and says, "And that is where they are all stuck at the moment."

Looking up to the heavens she adds, "Nice touch, Bi!"

Then Liling closes her eyes and puts her hands on her chest saying, "Thank you for all of your love and service to the people of One World, my true Sister, Lady Bi."

A voice of gratitude breathes down from Heaven into the heart of Liling saying, *Thank YOU, most gracious Lady Liling, my true heavenly sister.*

Liling weeps tears of sadness mixed with joy, sitting back down in the loveseat, and resting in Dumaka's arms.

There is a long silence in the group while everyone processes what they have just heard.

The Major finally speaks up. "Well, I guess we now know what we are dealing with."

"Not quite," says Kookie. Staring down at the floor, Kookie has been receiving voices in his own heart. He says, "You asked me a while back, Major, which High Lord I am; the one of Reason or Intuition, or Reason *and* Intuition. At the time I told you that I would share it with you another time."

The Major looks up at Kookie with raised eyebrows, drawn to the edge of his seat.

"I was once very good with my intuitive skills, similar to Liling," Kookie says.

"Better!" she chimes in.

"Yeah well, whatever," Kookie says, still staring at the floor. "I was only a young child, about the same age as Emeka, and I started to see things that really frightened me. That is why I always had such a hard time relating to other young people when I was younger," Kookie says, now looking up at the Major, "and what *really* caused me to run off that day at camp, you know when you all found me playing my tuba alone at the lake."

Every eye in the room is glued to Kookie, but none as intensely as the Major's. "I had the gift of vision then and could see all of these terrible things happening to people. And I could never say anything, because I knew that no one would ever believe me." Staring back at the floor, he says, "It is a very painful thing to hold the truth inside of your heart, to see so much pain and suffering and know there is nothing you can even *say* about it, much less *do* about it.

"That day, when I ran off to the lake with my tuba, a vision came into my heart and filled me with more compassion than ever. It was about a world of harmony and love where we all lived together, the UC and the people. Words came to me saying, *One World under God, indivisible, with freedom and love for all.* Then the words said that I was to go out and share this message with the world. I knew that this would make a total freak out of me, and that I wanted nothing to do with it. So, I ran to the lake, to my tuba, to my gadgets and devices and flashing red lights, and to anything that would shut the voices and the visions down inside of me. Which eventually they did."

Everyone is as still and silent as stone statues, staring at Kookie, who finally says, "Now the voices have come back through my beloved Angie, who has been speaking to me from the underworld."

Kookie looks up and says directly to his friends, "I will not let One World, or my Angie down. Liling, let's get those intuitive powers going, Sister! We've got work to do!"

* * *

Early in the morning near a cave in Wyoming, a group of farmers are out picking their fruits and vegetables. Several days ago, they had noticed a fleet of Cloudtransporters off in the distance that appeared to be abandoned. They asked around in the local Coffeehouse, but no one had any idea who they belonged to or what was going on, so the farmers paid no attention to the aircraft and went back about their business.

This morning, however, as they are out filling their baskets, one farmer notices several people emerging from the mouth of the nearby cave.

"Hey Jim, get a load of that!" he says to one of the other men.

They all look up and see a steady stream of men emerging from the cave wearing commando uniforms and back packs. They are carrying automatic weapons.

Chapter 9 – Uprising

MASTER COMMANDANT MIKHAIL has rounded up all his men. They are frustrated and angry after days spent searching the cave that Lady Bi said was harboring the insurrectionists and their secret deadly weapon. He did not want to stop searching until they had looked in every nook and cranny they could find. But they turned up nothing.

Now that they have emerged from the cave, Mikhail messages Lady Bella, thinking, *Perhaps the swine were tipped off and they made a run for it!*

Lady Bella accepts the incoming message from Mikhail and appears on the screen.

"My Lady!" Master Mikhail says with irritation. "We—"

"*QUIET!*" Lady Bella cuts him off sharply. "Listen to me, Master Commandant. We have been tricked. The traitors are in *Johannesburg! At the Estate of the late Lord Ekene!*"

"*WHAT?*" he yells.

"Just get your men over there! Now! The coordinates for their location are being sent to your Cloudtransporters. And when you get there, Master Commandant, *TEAR THEM ALL TO PIECES!*" As an afterthought she says, "Except for Kookie, Yakov and Liling. I've changed my mind. I want those three captured *ALIVE!*"

Bella is licking her lips thinking about which whip she will use on each one of them

"Ma'am! Yes, Ma'am!" he shouts at her, and their connection is terminated.

The Master Commandant shouts at his men, "They're in Johannesburg! We're moving out now!"

They race for the Cloudtransporters. Master Mikhail uses his communication device to activate the portal and open it for them. But when he gives the voice command, 'Portal Open," nothing happens. He tries again, and still nothing happens. He tries a third time to no avail. One more failed attempt at opening the doors of the Cloudtransporters and Master Commandant Mikhail loses it. *"WHAT THE BLEEP* IS GOING ON?"* howls Mikhail at the top of his lungs.

Raging at his communication device and ready to smash it to pieces, Master Mikhail is unaware of two pairs of eyes watching him from within his device.

* * *

"Well," Kookie says to Yakov, "that oughta keep him tied up for a while."

"But how did you know they would have a problem opening their doors?" Dumaka asks Kookie.

He is baffled and amazed at the high-tech surveillance stuff.

With #3 and #4 snuggled in against both sides of his neck, Kookie looks at them both affectionately and scratches their little heads. In response to Dumaka's question he says, "Well, my friend, let's just say that a little birdie told me!"

The friends sitting around the living room laugh, and the Major rolls his eyes. Shaking his head he says, "I think I liked you better *without* the intuition, bro'!"

Vi says, "Seriously, you guys. To quote Master Mikhail, *what the heck is going on?*"

"Oh, it is all quite simple," says Kookie, tapping the tips of his fingers together. "And to be fair, none of us can really take any credit for this one." Nuzzling #3 and #4 with his cheeks he says, "Yep! These here are the creative geniuses for this master-minded, brilliantly executed, poo ploy of the pigeons."

Yakov and Liling both shake their heads and laugh.

Kookie says, "In fact, it seems that we have all kinds of 'natural events' on our side. If you all want the exact order of things, the Monarchs heard it from the wind, who heard it from the mouth of one very nasty Lady on her island in the Mediterranean Sea. The Monarchs then sent word to the pigeons who went and unloaded their nasty business right into the heart of the Cloudtransporters, firing away at the machinery and gumming up the works of the aircraft, of said Lady Sociopath."

Watching everyone laugh out loud, Kookie finishes his spiel with, "So it looks like our buddies in Wyoming will be grounded for a bit. Does that answer everyone's question?"

"Oh, and just one more thing," says Yakov. "Just now, we disarmed and disabled their entire battalion through Metatron, connecting to Master Mikhail's communication device. So, they will be unable to fire an automatic weapon, or send or receive a message.

"Wow!" says Master Howard, who has joined the group with Mistress Henrietta. "I am truly impressed! Sounds to me like this whole thing is about who outmaneuvers whom."

"In a sense, yes," says Liling. "Strategy is important. But don't forget. They too, have brilliant minds with access to higher technology. That is why Kookie, Yakov and I are going to connect with each other's minds as well as with the pigeons, and the Seven Monarchs of Angel, to see what we are up against with them.

"We *must* find out what technology they are working on. I have no doubt, or I do not know my people, that they are planning something big. Master Mikhail and his commandos are no more than a mere drop in the bucket for them, a *warning shot* if you want to call it that."

"So, when do you plan on connecting with the butterflies?" Vi asks, "And, um, can I . . . you know, join you guys? That is, I'm pretty well connected with the Monarchs myself."

Liling laughs, "Well of course, you are. And we would be honored to have you join us."

"Yes? Thanks!" Vi exclaims.

"We are expecting the Seven shortly," Liling says to everyone. "Please feel free to connect with us, and if anyone gets any heart messages, do come right out and share them."

* * *

Master Commandant Mikhail looks at his men. He considers the consequences of messaging Lady Bella again, and not just the obvious ones of inciting her rage. He knows that if he cannot deal with this one on his own, then he risks looking weak in her eyes. Lady Bella will probably lose interest in him as an object of desire if she feels that he is incapable of taking a good beating. His passion for her and for her whip has taken on an addictive quality for the Commandant, and he knows that as soon as he gets back to the Isle of Bella, he *must have both:* the Lady *and* her whip! Therefore, he chooses not to contact her for assistance with the malfunctioning Cloudtransporters; not yet anyway.

He thinks to himself, *If I can tell My Lady that I have killed a few insurrectionists while being stuck here, perhaps she will be satisfied.*

With that in mind, the Commandant turns to his men and says, "I have just heard from our Lady, and she says that the town nearby is full of insurrectionists. We are to go there at once and take care of them!"

"Sir! Yes, sir!" the commandos yell out grabbing their automatic firearms and heading for the nearby village.

The folks of the small farming community of Cavern Village, Wyoming are gathering their corn harvest. They are strong and healthy people of the earth who have plowed the fields and done hard physical labor their whole lives. Like other farmers all over One World, they too have been able to fill the Masters' coffers quickly with the abundance of the harvest. Thanks to the Summit Festival transmission coming out of Johannesburg, which they all listened to, the folks here have also organized a community Trader's Market.

The couple who has been directly responsible for organizing the Trader's Market is Lester and Barb, the caretaker overseers of Master Sam's farm. Master Sam and Mistress Sheila, who were also tuned into the Summit Festival, couldn't be happier to have free trade, happy people, and an abundant harvest for everyone. They have both developed very close and caring relationships with the farmhands and their families over the years. Master Sam and Mistress Sheila are pleased to see everyone prospering, not just themselves.

Lester and Jim are about to take a break from their morning's labor when they look up and see the commandos coming towards them.

"Say," says Lester. "It's those guys down yonder over by the cave; they're coming this way. Wonder who they are and what they want?

"Beats me," says Jim, "But they don't seem very friendly like, now do they."

The two men see the commandos carrying automatic weapons, and suddenly a bad feeling comes over them. All the farmers wear a loud, high-pitched whistle around their necks, which they keep for emergencies, like if one of them should suddenly fall ill out in the field and need immediate attention. Jim and Lester look at the commandos, and then they look at each other. All at once, both men take off their whistles and start blowing just as hard as they can.

All across the field, the farmers hear the whistles. They look up and see the commandos coming onto their land with automatic firearms, and they too start blowing their whistles loud and hard. Pretty soon high-pitched whistles are crying out a distress signal throughout Cavern Village.

Master Commandant Mikhail is within several yards of Lester and Jim now, and he orders his men to stop. He puts his hand up in the air, and all the commandos raise their weapons.

The farmers are unarmed, with only their shovels and hoes in hand.

Master Commandant Mikhail, looking straight into the faces of unarmed, peaceful people of the land, drops his hand, giving the command to open fire. Every single one of the computerized, automatic weapons jams and will not fire. Not since Kookie and Yakov disconnected them.

The commandos panic, not knowing what happened, and Mikhail goes into a maniacal rage screaming at his men, in Russian, Chinese and English, *"STRELYAT! SHEJI! SHOOT!"*

The sound of the whistles, followed by the multi-lingual, maniacal screaming of Mikhail has drawn the entire farming village to Master Sam's fields. Pandemonium ensues as Jim, Lester and several other farmhands start to yell, and charge the commandos with their shovels and hoes. The commandos start hitting the farmers with their otherwise useless guns, but the shovels, courage, and sheer determination of the men of the earth are very strong. They are outnumbered by the commandos, but not for long, as other farmers are arriving with picks, axes, shovels, and rakes. Even the women pick up whatever they can find and charge onto the battlefield.

On a cornfield in Cavern Village, Wyoming, first blood has been spilled.

The uprising of One World has begun.

* * *

Kookie has turned on the Metatron's Salamander program to connect with the Monarchs and his friends. They all know that privacy is of the utmost importance and the tools of surveillance that Lady Bella is privy to is almost as good as theirs; almost, but not quite. Everyone is in place for their gathering with the Seven Monarch Butterflies of Angel, including everyone from the Big House. From the Village of the Holy Ones there is Mimi, Ryan, Doc, Phil, Eve Elli, Suzie, Lord Emeka, Mama Eve Zula and Papa Adam Makena. They are all awaiting the arrival of the Monarchs.

They do not have to wait long. Eve Elli is the first one to spot the flutter at the large picture window in the living room.

"There you are!" Eve Elli says, going over to the window to let them in.

Thank you, little human creature, she can hear them saying to her heart, as they all alight on her hair.

Little Suzie giggles at the sight of seven butterflies perched on top of Eve Elli's head, and Mimi just smiles with pure gramma pleasure.

Kookie, Yakov and Liling are seated together on the floor in a close circle. Number 3 and #4 are perched on Kookie's shoulders and Eve Elli comes into the center of the circle and sits down, with the Seven Monarchs of Angel snuggled comfortably in her hair. Everyone else is asked to sit on the floor as well, in a circular formation surrounding the little group in the middle. Mama Eve Zula and Papa Adam Makena are facing each other from either side of the outer circle.

The group is ready to begin.

Mama Eve Zula asks everyone to close their eyes as they feel the loving energy that is connecting them. She then asks them to direct their love to the center of the circle, focusing on Eve Elli and the Monarchs. Next, Mama instructs everyone to widen the circle of love and focus on Kookie, Yakov and Liling. And finally, she has them send loving energy to all in the outer circle.

After a few minutes of quiet meditation, Eve Elli is glowing and speaks with a soft, angelic voice, that is not her own:

". . . And the spirit of the Lord shall rest upon him, the spirit of wisdom and understanding, the spirit of counsel and might . . ."[5]

The Seven Monarchs of Angel start to glow along with Eve Elli, as they are nestled in her hair. Mama Eve Zula and Papa Adam Makena are glowing with compassion, sending their energy around the circle, and the Monarchs are fluttering gently as the incoming signal from the Isle of Bella is reaching their antennae.

Eve Elli describes to everyone what she is seeing with her heart: "There's a very big house," she says, "just like this house. Only there is water all around it with lots of pretty boats on the water." She pauses for a moment and says, "There is another house next to the very big house, and a room downstairs with lots and lots of big computers. There are lots of buttons and lots of people pushing the buttons."

Kookie, Yakov and Liling are connecting with the Monarchs and Eve Elli so they are also seeing with their hearts what Eve Elli is seeing. Kookie says to her, "Honey, can you show us the people who are pushing the buttons and ask if there is any one of them who would be willing to connect his or her heart with ours?"

"Okay," says Eve Elli.

She begins to scan the folks in the room. The butterflies antennae are going furiously now, assisting her in finding someone in the lab whose heart is really aligned with the Alliance and not with Lady Bella and her agenda. Then they all see him; a young boy seated in front of a computer.

"Oh my!" exclaims Eve Elli, "That boy's heart is *not* happy! *Sheesh!*"

Everyone seated around the circle looks at each other, and Kookie says, "Can you ask him if we have his permission to talk to his heart?"

She pauses, and then says, "His heart says, *okay*. His name is Rudolpho."

---

5 *Isaiah 11:2, KJV*

A 12-year-old prodigy, Rudolpho was being groomed by PA, ES and SPA to become another High Lord upon coming of age. Before Kookie, Yakov and Liling went rogue, Rudolpho was to be their apprentice, and a full-fledged High Lord, when he reached 18 years of age. However, once PA, ES and SPA began to suspect what Kookie, Yakov and Liling were up to, they passed him off to Lady Bella instead.

The Monarchs and Eve Elli help to strengthen the connection between Kookie, Yakov, Liling and Rudolpho.

Liling speaks to his heart, *"I hear that you are not happy, Rudolpho. I am sorry."*

"Thank you, ma'am. You are Lady Liling?" Rudolpho responds from his heart.

"Yes, and I am here with others, and we all care about you."

Liling, Kookie and Yakov can feel a heavy sadness in Rudolpho's weary, overburdened soul.

Yakov reaches out to the sad young boy and speaks to his heart, *"Would you like to come here and help us? Would you like to join us, son?"*

* * *

Lady Bella and Lord Viktor are walking around the lab. She is arguing with him. "No, Lord Viktor, I do *NOT* understand why the **bleep** this is taking so long! While we are messing around here with your unfinished piece of technology, the masses could be preparing for an uprising!"

Lord Viktor looks down and shrugs his shoulders.

"And besides," Lady Bella continues griping, "What is that so-called boy genius doing over there just staring off into space like that?"

She shouts out loud across the lab, *"HEY, GENIUS! RUDOLPHO! Taking a mental coffee break, are we, kid?"*

Rudolpho shakes himself back into his present reality, putting his hands back on the keyboard.

Lady Bella comes over to him and says, "Well? So, what was *that* all about?"

"Oh, uh n—n—nothing, My Lady," Rudolpho stammers. "I was just trying to figure something out with the program."

"I see. Well? So? Did you figure it out then? Huh?"

"May*be,*" says Rudolpho. "Just have a few adjustments to make here," he says, fiddling with a few buttons in front of him.

Bella turns to Viktor and resumes reprimanding him, "Now that's exactly what I'm talking about. Why is everyone still making adjustments to this thing? Why isn't it ready?"

She turns to everyone in the lab and yells at the top of her lungs, *"HEY! LISTEN UP! THIS PROJECT HAS TO BE COMPLETED! AND IT HAS TO BE DONE **NOW!** DO YOU ALL UNDERSTAND THAT?"*

"Ma'am, yes Ma'am!" they all reply in unison.

Lady Bella takes the whip she has been holding in her hand and cracks it loud and hard on the stone floor of the lab while screaming, *"**NOW!!**"*

Everyone, including Lord Viktor suddenly flinches.

Even the butterflies on Eve Elli's hair jump.

With that, Lady Bella huffs out of the lab followed by a very nervous Lord Viktor.

* * *

Eve Elli, Kookie, Yakov, and Liling have been following the altercation, when Eve Elli pipes up, "That boy needs to get out of there!"

"I couldn't agree more," says Kookie. "Let's see what we can do to help him."

Several others in the circle have also been following everything, including Mama Eve Zula and Papa Adam Makena, and they all nod in agreement.

Eve Elli can now feel Rudolpho reaching out to them, and she tells the others.

Liling starts speaking to his heart again. *"Rudolpho, if you want to come here and be with us, just says 'yes.'"*

They all feel a sad little voice saying, *"Yes, PLEASE!"*

Kookie looks at everyone else, gets their consent and proceeds to get right to work with Metatron. First, he activates the Salamander cloaking program and begins to transmit it to the terminal that Rudolpho is working in. Then he nods at Liling who speaks to the youngster's heart and says, *"Rudolpho, we have you covered. No one will notice you. Get up and go to the landing field right now. "*

Rudolpho looks around and sees that everyone is anxiously glued to their work in front of them. He quietly removes something from the computer and sticks it in his pocket as he slowly backs away with his eye on the exit door.

So far so good, he thinks to himself.

Walking slowly and with great caution, Rudolpho reaches the door, opens it and steps outside. Closing the door behind him, he can see the landing field straight ahead. Then another voice comes into his head that says, *"Go to the Cloudtransporter marked #21 and #22."*

Rudolpho sees the aircraft and starts walking towards it. There are people milling about on the landing field, but sure enough, no one seems to notice him at all. As he gets to the portal entry of the Cloudtransporter the voice in his head says, *"We are opening the portal. Go inside."*

The portal opens and he wastes no time embarking on the Cloudtransporter that was left behind by Lady Bi. The portal closes behind him, and Rudolpho is on his way to freedom.

* * *

Kookie remotely sets the coordinates of Liling's Cloudtransporter for Johannesburg, and grinning away, proudly announces to everyone, "Rudolpho is in the air! He should be here in the next couple of hours!"

Everyone who has been following the communication with their hearts lets out a big cheer. And for the benefit of those, like Master Howard and Mistress Henrietta, who were *not* able to tune in and follow along, Vi and some of the others fill them in on the soon-to-be new member of their team who is now inbound.

Master Howard chuckles, shakes his head and says, "No wonder you guys beat the crud out of PA, ES and SPA!"

While everyone is chatting away about the wonderful thing that has just happened, taking this young lad out of the clutches of the evil Lady Bella, and the information that they will soon gain access to, no one notices that Eve Elli is staring off into space. The Monarchs in her hair are going full tilt at transmitting from the Continental Territory of Panamerica, in the small farming community of Cavern Village, Wyoming.

* * *

Master Sam hears shouting coming from the fields. He runs outside and sees a multitude of men and women running towards the skirmish, carrying whatever farming tools they have. Sam sees the commandos and the fighting that has broken out. Without a moment's hesitation, he picks up the largest shovel he can find, and joins the farmers, his people, in their fight.

The news of the battle spreads like wildfire throughout Cavern Village and into neighboring communities. When the word gets out that Master Sam is fighting alongside his people, a fire is lit in each and every heart of the farmers and other townsfolk across the region. They come in droves, descending upon Mikhail and his diminishing battalion until, finally, the remaining commandos surrender in defeat.

They look around for their Master Commandant and find Mikhail's body near a stream, partially decapitated. The shovel marks under the base of his skull tell the whole story of his struggle and his suffering in the end.

There are many casualties on both sides, and that is when the Monarchs start their transmission through Eve Elli.

* * *

Vi is the first to notice the butterfly's frantic activity and Eve Elli's glazed over expression. She calls out to Kookie, Yakov and Liling that something is going on. Suddenly all eyes are on Eve Elli.

Liling turns to her and says, "What is it? What can you see, sweetie?"

Eve Elli says, in a faraway voice, "Very sad, very sad! Oh, Mama Eve Zula! I want to cry!"

"What? What is it, honey? What do you see? What is happening?" they all say softly to her and instantly reconnect their heart energy with Eve Elli and the Monarchs.

A mournful silence overcomes the group around the circle as they hear what has just happened in Cavern Village, Wyoming. They listen to the sounds of anguish and tears from folks who are mourning the sudden, unprovoked, violent slaughter of their loved ones.

Mama Eve Zula comes over and sits down with Eve Elli. She holds the little child against her chest and starts to rock her gently saying, "So many people have gone to Heaven all at the same time. Their relatives are crying because they are going to miss them. But they will see them again one day."

Eve Elli is crying. "But they are all crying, Mama. They are crying very hard," she sniffs. "They are very, very sad. And it is making *me* very, very sad."

Mama Eve Zula says, "I know, precious child. It makes me feel very sad too. But there is something we can do that will make us feel better."

"What is it Mama?" Eve Elli cries, "Please tell me so I can feel better."

All eyes are on Mama Eve Zula, waiting for her response. They too want to know what they can do to feel better.

"We can go over there and serve the people who are suffering."

"Oh yes! Yes! I want to do that!" Eve Elli cries out.

A collective sigh of agreement is heard around the circle.

Mimi says to Eve Elli, while looking at everyone else, "I would like to go there with you, sweetie."

"Oh Gramma, can we go there?"

Kookie looks at Eve Elli and then at the rest of the group, and he sends out a message on Metatron. "Let's see who I can reach in Wyoming, if someone there has got a communication device. I'm sure they will welcome whoever among us wants to go. But first, I must send Cloudambulances to them."

Kookie contacts the paramedics nearest to Cavern Village and several Cloudambulances are on their way to the scene.

Meanwhile, Yakov has been searching the files on his Metatron device for the Master of the farm, and he comes up with the names of Master Sam and Mistress Sheila. Kookie sends a message out to Master Sam, hoping that he is alright, and Master Sam receives and accepts Kookie's incoming message.

"Master Sam!" Kookie says, "This is Kookie! We just received word that there has been a skirmish over there. Are you okay, sir?"

"Thank you, Kookie, and bless you sir," says Master Sam. "Yes, I am all right. But many others are not."

"I have sent the paramedics to you; they should be there at any moment."

"Yes!" says Sam, "I can see them coming now! Oh, bless you, Kookie, bless you!"

"We would also like to send some of our people over to you to help out in any way that we can, if you would like that, sir," says Kookie.

"Oh, My Lord Kenneth!" exclaims Master Sam almost in tears. "Your presence here would be most welcome, sir, most welcome."

"Very well," says Kookie, "I will send a team out to you right away. You just hang in there, Sam. And let your people know that help is on the way."

"Thank you, sir, thank you."

The transmission ends.

Kookie looks at everyone and says, "Some of us will have to stay here, to receive Rudolpho. But for those who want to go with Eve Elli and her team that can be arranged."

"Oh, thank you, Kookie!" exclaims Eve Elli, throwing her arms around his neck and giving him a big kiss on the cheek.

He smiles at her, and the butterflies in Eve Elli's hair start dancing around Kookie's head.

"Well," says Kookie, tapping the tips of his fingers together. "So, who else will be going with us to Wyoming?"

Chapter 10 – Mercy

LILING SAYS TO THE GROUP seated in a circle around Eve Elli, "I propose that we get up and stretch, take a break, and consider where each one of us can best be of service right now."

They all agree that this is an excellent idea, and Yakov, Neely, Reggie and Liling head to the kitchen, followed by Mistress Henrietta. The rest go off into the dining room.

Dumaka, the Major and Master Howard are particularly touched by Rudolpho and express their desire to be available when the youngster arrives.

Yakov feels the same, except he is also intrigued at the thought of going to Wyoming. After all, he almost ended up there a while back himself, when he threw his unit of commandos off course in their search for Kookie, in Bear River, Oregon. *Must be something about that place,* he thinks to himself, *like Johannesburg, or we wouldn't all keep getting sent there!*

The kitchen crew comes out with platters full of pastries, fruit, and tea, along with their new apprentice baker, Mistress Henrietta. She has been learning all the secrets of gourmet baking from Yakov and Neely since arriving at Lord Emeka's Estate. Henrietta is particularly fond of the sweet fruit cookies and has made a batch for her husband to try.

Master Howard takes one bite out of his wife's cookie and declares his undying passion for both his wife and her cookies. "Oh, but this is scrumptious," Master Howard exclaims staring at the cookie in his hand, "my sweet little peach cookie!"

Shaking his head, the Major is wondering whether his father is referring to the cookie or his mother.

Mistress Henrietta covers her mouth in dainty, lady-like fashion, and chuckles. "Oh Howard," and she smiles at him affectionately.

Mama Eve Zula says to the group, "Papa Adam Makena and I have decided that the need for us to go to Wyoming is great. We have also reached out to the other Chrysalenes in the Village of the Holy Ones and they wish to join us as well."

"Well, Mama," says Kookie, "I am thinking of leaving just as soon as we finish our snacks. You might want to communicate to the others at the Village to start heading on over here."

"Yes, sir," says Mama Eve Zula and Papa Adam Makena at the same time, with big smiles on their faces.

Liling says to everyone, "I feel I need to be here when Rudolpho arrives, since it was I who communicated with him."

"And I wish to be here for him too," says Dumaka, gently touching Liling's cheek and smiling at her.

Yakov says to Kookie, "Once Rudolpho arrives, I can get started immediately, analyzing Lady Bella's plans. I think it will be important to stay in touch with you, my Brother. I will let you know right away whatever I find out from Rudolpho."

"Okay," says Kookie. "We shall leave as soon as the Chrysalenes from the Village get here. I will message Master Sam and let him know as soon as we are on our way."

* * *

Everyone gathers outside near the back field of the Big House where all the Cloudtransporters are parked. Rudolpho is about an hour away from his arrival, and Kookie and company are about to take off for Wyoming. His group consists of Eve Elli, Lord Emeka, Mimi, Ryan, and all the Chrysalenes from the Village of the Holy Ones. They are acutely aware of the seriousness of what lies before them, and they are also deeply honored to be of service to the people of One World.

Kookie gets down on his knees along with Eve Elli and Little Lord Emeka. As they join hands, the others also drop to their knees and Eve Elli leads them in prayer:

"Heavenly Father, please make the people all over One World happy. Please let all the very sad people in Wyoming know that You love them so much. Please let the very sad people know that Emeka loves them so much, and Kookie loves them so much, and my Gramma and Ryan love them so much, and all the Chrysalenes love them so much, and I love them very, very, very much!"

Then Eve Elli remembers that the Monarch Butterflies, who are still nestled in her hair, are also going to Wyoming. She adds, *"And the butterflies love them very, very, very much, too!"*

Everyone says, "Amen," and they all hear the voice of the Monarchs speaking inside their hearts saying, *Amen, little human creature!*

Deep down in the bowels of hell another voice hisses, *And I am ALREADY in Wyoming, awaiting your arrival, LORD KENNETH!*

Kookie and company board the Cloudtransporter and are on their way. Eve Elli curls up for a nap on Gramma Mimi's lap and the others settle in for the three-and-a-half-hour flight.

Kookie looks out over the ocean and projects his heart to the depths below. He can see his beloved Angie's face in the water as he whispers softly to her, "I love you, Angie. I wish you were here with me."

Angie whispers back to Kookie from the darkness below, *"I love you too, My Beloved. And I AM there with you!"*

* * *

Liling and Yakov's group remain at the landing area near the back field of the Big House waiting for their recruit to arrive. It is late in the evening and the Cloudtransporter carrying Rudolpho is expected any minute. They are all watching the dark sky with great anticipation. Then an approaching light appears coming from the north.

When Phil heard from the Chrysalenes about the arrival of Rudolpho, he decided to join the welcoming party, and take Little Suzie of the Seashells with him. Suzie has fallen asleep on Phil's shoulder and wakes up as the Cloudtransporter approaches. Looking up at the light quickly coming toward them in its descent, little Suzie catches everyone's excitement. She points up and calls out, "Da Light! Da Light!"

"Yes! It's the light! The light!" they all join in joyously with Suzie.

"OOO!" she exclaims with wide eyes, watching the aircraft land right in front of her.

Yakov opens the portal with his Metatron Device, and they wait for Rudolpho to emerge. . . but nothing happens. Liling and Dumaka look at each other, as well as Yakov, and the Major. They begin to worry if everything is okay.

Finally, Liling calls out to him: "Rudolpho? Honey? This is Liling. Is everything okay? Are you alright, sweetie?"

Little Suzie is fidgeting so Phil puts her down. As soon as her little feet hit the ground, she does a quick-toddle-waddle-dash to the ramp leading up to the open portal. Suzie squeals with delight, "Weeee!" toddle-waddling at breakneck speed right up to the portal.

Everyone holds their breath while Phil darts after her. But just as little Suzie gets to the opening of the Cloudtransporter, Phil stops short. A young person appears in the doorway. Everyone can see from his puffy eyes that he has been crying and is probably very frightened. But when he sees little Suzie, the youngster looks at her and starts smiling. She goes right up to him all smiles and giggles, putting her arms, out expecting a great big hug. The boy is obliging and reaches out to accept the little one's welcome.

Suzie then takes her new friend by the hand and leads him down the ramp of the Cloudtransporter to greet his new family. Liling puts her hand out to him and says in Russian, "Hi there, I'm Liling. You must be Rudolpho!"

The youngster smiles and nods his head.

Liling proceeds to place a Universal Translator pendant necklace on Rudolpho. Having seen all the Lords and Ladies wearing a UT, he knows exactly what it is, and Rudolpho is now very proud and honored to have one of his own.

The Major walks over and shakes his hand. "Hey there, buddy, I'm the Major. Welcome to Johannesburg. We are really happy to have you here."

Each person goes around introducing him or herself to Rudolpho and finally Liling says to him, "I'll bet you must be hungry."

Rudolpho nods.

"Well, why don't we all go inside, and you can have cookies and pastries, if you like them."

Rudolpho nods more vigorously this time, and Liling continues, "This is little Miss Suzie of the Seashells. She really seems to like you! Would you like to hold her hand as we all go to the Big House?"

"Ladno," Rudolpho says in Russian, which everyone hears in their own language as "okay."

They all start walking to the house, but Rudolpho stops for a moment remembering something. He reaches into his pocket and takes out what looks like a USB flash drive and gives it to Liling. As soon as Liling takes it in her hand she can feel strong energy coming off the device and hands it immediately to Yakov. He takes one look at it and inserts it into his Metatron. The screen on Yakov's device opens and he nearly faints dead away on the spot. A document opens to a title page that reads:

Project Laser Beam –
Plans for Long-Range Laser Weaponry.
In Development – Phase 3.

Yakov's eyes pop out of his head as he holds up the screen for everyone else to see. They all hold up their Universal Translators to Yakov's Metatron device, which gives them the translation.

Looking at their new 12-year-old rogue companion Yakov clears his throat, collects himself and says with an air of pseudo-casualness: "Uh, heh-heh, well there, young man. Um, let's see. This here thing says *Phase 3*. Hm. Okay, so how many phases *are* there of this, um, you know, laser thing? You know, before it is ready for (he clears his throat one more time) *use?*"

Rudolpho looks up at him with round, sad eyes and holds up four fingers.

Everyone in the group understands what's happening as Yakov says, "Hm. Well. Thank you, my man." And looking at the others he says, "Why don't we all get to the Big House and contact Kookie, through Salamander . . . *now!*"

* * *

Kookie and company are about mid-way to their destination when he gets an incoming message from Yakov.

"What's up, bro'?" Kookie says. "Did everything go okay with Rudolpho's arrival?"

Kookie and Yakov are looking at each other on their Metatron screens so Kookie can see clearly from the look in Yakov's eyes that everything it most definitely *NOT* okay. He holds up his index finger and says to Kookie, "I have something to send you." He proceeds to send Kookie the file from Rudolpho's USB flash drive, through the cloaking protection of Salamander.

Kookie receives the file and opens it. Seeing the title page, he sits back and closes his eyes. "Have you opened the file yet, bro'?" asks Kookie.

"No," says Yakov. "I wanted to show it to you first, and open it together."

"Yes, well, let's do that. And remember the two things we want to discern quickly are, one: how serious is the damage they can inflict from this type of weaponry, and two: how much time have we got to try to stop them."

"Okay, bratan,[6] let's get to work." Kookie and Yakov open the document together marked "Project Laser Beam."

From the depths of hell a snickering, growling voice says, *The damage is VERY serious, bratan, and your time has already run out.*

Angel responds, *We shall see, evil creature; we shall see.*

* * *

Cloudambulances have arrived in Cavern Village, Wyoming. The AI paramedics quickly gather all men and women who are injured and attend to their needs. As for the fatalities, the AI collect the bodies and dig large trenches on a nearby hillside to serve as a mass grave.

By the end of the day, the AI paramedics have the entire battle scene cleared of all that remains of the carnage. The survivors from both sides are either grief-stricken, in shock, or both.

Master Sam is doing his best to comfort all the surviving victims and their families. He is also looking out at the remaining commandos on the field. They are without a leader, without transportation, out in the middle of nowhere, in a strange land, and with no place to go.

Although he cannot understand why the farmers were attacked in the first place, Master Sam feels a strong desire to go over to them and ask one big question: "Why? Why did you attack peaceful people in cold-blood and for no reason?"

---

[6] *Russian slang terms for bro'.*

He is thinking about this but does not really know quite how to go over and ask. Then he sees a Cloudtransporter coming in for a landing right next to the cornfield. Recognizing the insignia on the craft, Master Sam looks up to thank the Heavenly Father for the help that they are about to receive.

Kookie, his companions and the Chrysalenes have arrived.

There are no physical injuries left to deal with as the AI paramedics have already healed the wounded, but what *is* left is a mass of traumatized human beings. Master Sam, Mistress Sheila and a few others run over to Kookie and his crew, and they all embrace each other with tender hugs.

"I am so sorry," says Kookie, as he holds one grief-stricken person after another.

The Chrysalenes and all the others walk around from one person to the other, holding them and saying the same thing: "I am sorry. I am so very sorry."

Kookie's group open their hearts to everyone, offering healing and comfort to each person.

Eve Elli and Emeka go to all the children, many of whom have lost one or both parents on this day, witnessing their violent deaths. As Eve Elli holds each child in her arms, she begins to glow with a light from the heavens pouring down through her soul into the hearts of the stricken little ones. She says: "I am so sorry that you are sad, so sorry. I know that your mommy and daddy are in Heaven now. They are looking down on you and will always be right here in your heart. And one day, you will be with them again."

Eve Elli and Emeka hold each child, offering comfort, love, and healing to so many.

But their healing and love are not limited to the children of Cavern Village. Eve Elli and Emeka are also comforting and offering healing and love to the adults. Many begin to come over to them because they are attracted to the soothing energy of the heavenly light that radiates from both children.

Mimi and Ryan are also offering hugs and words of comfort to all, and Mimi is placing Rose petals in people's hands. She has brought with her all the Rose petals that she had in Johannesburg. Ryan's quiet, gentle spirit has a very soothing quality, though he speaks no more than a few simple words to each grief-stricken soul.

Master Sam feels relieved just from the presence of Kookie and his companions. He seeks Kookie's advice on what to do with the surviving commandos, most of whom are stunned and wandering around aimlessly. But most of all, he wants Kookie's insight on why all this has happened.

"My Lord," Sam says to Kookie. "I do not understand any of this. Why would these men come here unprovoked in any way and try to murder us all? Why My Lord, why?"

Kookie looks down and shakes his head. He cannot understand it either. Although, he knows that a leader who is filled with hatred and obsessed with violence, Lady Bella, is behind it all, he too does not understand how anyone could blindly follow such hatred to commit atrocities against innocent, unarmed civilians.

However, there is someone watching who *does* know the answers to all those questions. It is the same someone who puts fear into the hearts of people, and who makes folks mistrust those who think, act, or look different from themselves. It is a someone who is himself miserable in his dark world of hell, and, as the saying goes, "misery loves company."

Kookie sighs and finally says to Master Sam, "Oh I don't know, sir. Sometimes I have to wonder myself why the Heavenly Father, who I know loves us very much, allows such things to happen."

Then the two men see something else which they cannot explain. A young child who does not understand the difference between the uniform of a commando and the clothing of a farmer is offering comfort to the commandos.

Eve Elli is walking over to the men in uniform whose spirits seem to her to be just as broken as the farmers. She does not ask the sad men in uniform why they are there, what they have done, or what they are feeling. Eve Elli does not understand what it means to be an aggressor or even to kill people. Although she has seen such things in her short life, she is now a Chrysalene and can only see things through the heart of the Heavenly Father.

Eve Elli sees a man in uniform who is sitting on the ground all by himself, staring at the earth, surrounded by a mass of scattered, broken corn stalks. She approaches him and says, "I'm sorry you are sad."

The commando looks at her and does not say anything. But Kookie, Master Sam and everyone else nearby suddenly stop everything and turn to Eve Elli and the commando.

"I'm sorry you are hurting," she continues, reaching her arms out to him. "I am Eve Elli and I love you. Can I hug you?"

The commando looks at her, and an unseen presence from the bowels of hell also turns his full attention to them. The dark lord reaches into the man's mind growling: *You will let this unruly child make a fool of you? You are a warrior, and this child is a child of the enemy. Kill her, commando! KILL HER! Take that little neck into your hands and snap it in half. DO IT!*

The commando slowly raises his hands to Eve Elli who is holding her hands out to him, waiting to give him a hug. *DO IT!* He keeps hearing a voice hissing and howling in his head. *She is a useless eater! Life unworthy of life!* His hands wrap around Eve Elli's neck. *DO IT!*

As he begins to apply pressure to her neck, the commando suddenly has a vision. It is of his own little daughter who died not too long ago of Ebola. He sees his daughter's eyes in the eyes of this loving child standing before him, and he relaxes his hands from her neck.

Eve Elli smiles at him, stretching her hands out even further. The commando stares at her with a growing sadness welling up inside of him, thinking about the death of his own little girl.

The evil voice wails from the bowels of hell: *YOU ARE MINE! YOUR SOUL BELONGS TO ME! YOU WILL DO AS **I** SAY, AND I SAY **KILL HER! DO IT NOW!***

Kookie suddenly hears the hissing voice from hell and realizes what is going on. He moves quickly to the commando and Eve Elli, saying, "My good man, you are free. Free to listen to the voice of love which resides in your heart."

At that moment, Eve Elli gives the commando a big hug. With tears in his eyes, the man suddenly sees the spirit of his deceased daughter standing before him. He hugs Eve Elli back and says, "Thank you child, thank you."

Eve Elli smiles at him and asks, "What is your name?"

"I am Tom," the man says, looking intently at this precious child.

A circle has started to form around Eve Elli and Tom. No one moves as they silently witness the scene of mercy and grace unfolding before them.

Eve Elli is all aglow sitting on the ground with Tom. "Hi Tom," she says to him, and he smiles at her angelic face. He looks around at the broken ears of corn lying everywhere and a partially filled wheelbarrow close to where he is sitting.

For a while Tom does nothing, not knowing what to do next. Then, he hears Kookie's voice in his heart saying, *My good man, you are free.* The words *good man* and *free* echo in the deepest chambers of his heart, and he slowly crawls over to a corncob lying on the ground.

Tom picks up the corn and holds it for a few moments. He can see where the butt of a gun smashed into it, breaking off a piece.

Was it my gun? he wonders, looking at his blood-stained weapon lying on the ground nearby.

Tom takes the corn and gently tries to straighten it out, but to no avail. For some reason, which he himself cannot understand, Tom finds himself fighting back tears. He looks at the blood-stained butt of his gun and back at the corn. Then he looks at Eve Elli, patiently sitting there, and Kookie who is calmly standing nearby, and a crowd of people who are anxiously holding their breath, while the commando is stuck in his own personal stalemate.

Tom is causing the beast great irritation, as the dark lord yells out to his mind one last time: *WHAT KIND OF A MAN ARE YOU? YOU SLOBBERING WHIMP! YOU WILL LET A LITTLE CHILD DEFEAT YOU?!* ***WHAT KIND OF A MAN ARE YOU?!***

Hearing the voice of the beast in his head, and the voice of Kookie in his heart, Tom replies, "I am a *free* man!"

He stands up on his feet with the cob of corn in his hands and proudly walks over to the wheelbarrow, gently placing the corn into it.

The beast is beside himself with rage as he screams into Kookie's head: *YOU WILL **NOT** WIN, LORD KENNETH! TOM IS **MINE!***

Walking back over to Eve Ellie and smiling, Tom reaches out to give her another hug. But it is more than the beast can bear. He throws a rock in Tom's path, which causes him to trip just as he is about to reach her. The commando falls, twists his ankle and comes down hard, head-first onto the butt of his weapon.

Instantly Kookie and the entire crowd of farmers rush over to Tom, who is lying motionless on the ground.

Eve Elli goes over to him and looks up. Pointing up at the sky she says to everyone, "Look! It's Tom's little girl, Anna!" She waves to the spirit of little Anna and says to Kookie, "She has come to take her daddy home!"

Kookie picks her up and smiles sadly at her. "Anna is happy now, Kookie. And her daddy Tom is happy too!"

Kookie holds Eve Elli with his face buried on her little shoulder and the farmers slowly come over to them. Without saying a word, the farmers gently touch Kookie and Eve Elli, and then they go over to where Tom has fallen. One of the women takes off her shawl and carefully places it over his body. They all offer a few words of kindness to him.

Across the cornfield the lost commandos have been watching the scene unfold. And one at a time, they begin to follow Tom's lead, picking up the fallen corncobs and placing them in the nearest wheelbarrow. The surviving farmers from the battle as well as their friends and neighbors are all witnessing the actions of the commandos, as are Master Sam and Mistress Sheila.

When the wheelbarrows are full, the commandos who can speak English ask the farmers who are standing nearest to them, "Where do these go?" and "Where can we put these?" and "What shall we do with these?"

The farmers look at each other, and then reply to the men, "Here, this way. Let us show you."

And Master Sam, Mistress Sheila, the farmers, and the commandos, take the wheelbarrows over to the silos, and together, they fill them.

The people of Cavern Village, Wyoming have all stepped into a new world of Courageous Love, and freedom.

Chapter 11 – Mine

EARLY THE NEXT MORNING in Johannesburg, the Garden Community Committee is preparing for a gathering of the Alliance at Lord Emeka's Estate. They will be sharing many ideas with others, including the reopening, and reorganizing of the Centers that have been shut down, as well as healthy lifestyles for the people of One World. During the Ebola pandemic, many of the Centers were left abandoned.

The UC members who are a part of the Alliance now see a great opportunity to build up whole farming communities around them, owned and operated jointly, by the people and the UC. Since Kookie opened his Library, books have been discovered that talk about businesses of the past that were based on such a system. It was called a "Worker's Cooperative."

Neely and Henrietta are going to lead an open forum on healthy eating and tasty recipes. Bem, Nassor and Tafari are preparing a hands-on presentation of gardening for a large community. Dumaka, Phil and Doc will be discussing the medicinal and healing properties of herbs and flowers, which Master Howard and the Major will be sitting in on to learn all they can.

The Major will also be organizing a group with other UC members who wish to find out how they can contribute their resources for a newly integrated world of the people and the UC.

Phil and Doc, as well as many others, have traumatic memories of some of the Centers that were abandoned during the pandemic. For Phil, it was hearing about the brutal way in which little Suzie's mother was gunned down, and for Doc it was witnessing such brutality; the horrific massacre of hundreds of Chrysalenes. They would both love to have a hand in helping the Centers reopen and creating Garden Communities in these spaces as a way of sanctifying the sacred ground.

In fact, Phil and Doc have already decided they want to live in one of the reopened Centers, turning it into a garden community and helping to build it from the ground up. They want to honor the memory of the original little two-year-old Suzie who died of Ebola, back in Floraville, calling it Suzie's Garden.

* * *

Liling, Yakov and Rudolpho get together in the study of the Big House, to open the file of Project Laser Beam. Before Kookie landed in Wyoming, he helped Yakov connect the file to the 369-Program of Metatron, which will not only allow them to read it, but also to see beneath the surface into the deeper intentions of the architects of Project Laser Beam. They hope this will help them analyze a weakness in the project with enough time to figure out a means of stopping its destruction of possibly, millions of people.

"How much has Lady Bella told you about this, Rudolpho?" asks Yakov.

"I don't know sir, she is always so angry; always yelling at everybody," Rudolpho says forlornly.

"Did she say anything to you about *us* in particular?" asks Liling.

Rudolpho looks down at his feet. He cannot look Liling or Yakov in the face when he nods in the affirmative to her question.

Liling leans forward and asks just as gently as she can, "Is she planning on using laser weaponry to destroy Emeka's Estate?"

He nods, yes.

Yakov also leans forward in his seat and speaks to Rudolpho in a kind, fatherly voice: "Is she planning on attacking other strongholds of the Alliance?"

Again, Rudolpho nods in the affirmative.

Yakov continues, "This is very important, son. The plans say that a laser weapon system is being developed. And our 369 analysis says that the system is to have long-range power, which can theoretically be fired from the Isle of Bella, hitting a target anywhere in One World. Is this true?"

In a meek voice, still looking at his shoes, Rudolpho says, "Yes, sir. The beam of light is to bounce off reflectors, from one to the other. The reflectors are being built onto Cloudtransporters that will be placed in hover positions around the world. This is phase 4, the phase currently in development, and the final phase before the laser weapon is ready to launch."

Liling and Yakov are now the ones who are forlorn and looking down at the carpet.

Rudolpho continues, "Once the light bounces off the reflectors it will set off a chain reaction causing a blinding flash of light followed by a powerful beam that will incinerate everything within its radius."

Yakov asks, "And what is the light beam radius, my man?"

"That is what I was working on, when I, um, heard your voices in my head. So far, after bouncing off 1000 reflectors it is about 1 mile across. But Lady Bella wants it to hit many more than 1000 targets."

Rudolpho's voice becomes shaky, and he begins to fidget, clearly becoming more upset as he describes the details of the project.

Liling asks, "So, how many reflectors and beams of light does Lady Bella want to hit, um, that is, how many targets does she want to destroy all at the same time, with one push of a button (she clears her throat) in a manner of speaking?"

"That is what they are working on in the lab now," says Rudolpho. "When I left, the last count was over a thousand, but Lady Bella wants to at least double that number."

Liling and Yakov both clear their throats and sputter.

Yakov says, "So, let's be very clear about this. You are saying that with one push of one button, over a thousand Cloudtransporters, or more, will reflect a beam of light in such a manner that the light will bounce off them, hitting all thousand or more targets with dead accurate precision, totally incinerating everything within a 1-mile radius of each target?"

"Um . . . Yes."

There is a silent pause in the room as Liling and Yakov stare at each other considering the consequences of what they've just learned.

"Kookie! We've got to get Kookie back. Now!" says Yakov.

Liling replies, "Something is telling me to turn on Salamander and make it look like none of us are here. At least until we can figure out how to protect ourselves and not be sitting ducks for Lady Bella.

"Agreed," says Yakov.

"We have also got to get that gathering of the Garden Community Committee away from here. We need to send Neely, Henrietta, and the entire group to the Village of the Holy Ones immediately. They will be able to continue with their conference without anyone being able to spy on them. We can even cloak the Cloudtransporters parked on our back field with Salamander once all of the guests arrive."

"Yes," says Yakov, "Everyone is much too open to Lady Bella and her Council's surveillance system here.

* * *

On the Isle of Bella, tension is high. Her Ladyship has not heard back from Master Commandant Mikhail, who was supposed to be on his way to Johannesburg to deal with Kookie and his fellow traitors of the Alliance. Mikhail is long overdue in returning to the Isle of Bella with the announcement of his mission accomplished.

Lady Bella calls together her Lords Igor, Pavel and Viktor and grills them. "So where is he? Where is Master Commandant Mikhail? Should he not have been back by now, bringing me excellent news?!"

Lord Viktor speaks on behalf of the three of them as he says, "My Lady, we have been focusing our efforts day and night on Phase 4. We have tried a few times to reach Master Commandant Mikhail, but he has not accepted our messages. If your Ladyship would like, we can put a tracer on the Master Commandant's communication device and see where he is."

"You mean to tell me," Lady Bella shouts at the three of them while gripping her whip tightly and slamming it down on the ground with a load crack, "*YOU HAVEN'T DONE THAT YET?!*"

Lord Igor, Lord Pavel and Lord Viktor are trembling with fear. They have all seen the repeated acts of savagery which Lady Bella has lashed out with that whip.

In a soft, trepidatious voice Lord Viktor says, "My Lady, we have almost completed Phase 4 of Laser Beam. It is at a critical point in development requiring our full attention; even Lord Pavel and Lord Igor have been helping in our efforts to secure rapid success. Once it is ready to be fired, the entire Alliance will be crushed.

"If you like, I can—"

"Yes, yes, yes!" she cuts him off, "Of course the completion of Phase 4 is most important."

Quickly finishing his thought, Lord Viktor continues, "And we *did* leave a message for Master Commandant Mikhail and checked to see if it was received. It *was* received, My Lady, several hours ago."

"Fine, fine, fine," Lady Bella says impatiently. "Perhaps he has already completed the mission then and we should be hearing from him soon."

"If you please, Your Ladyship, we should like to get back to the lab and the mission at hand," ventures Lord Pavel.

"Yes, you do that."

She is about to dismiss them when the thought occurs to her that if Master Commandant Mikhail has indeed accomplished his mission, it would be satisfying for her to look in on Lord Emeka's Estate to see her enemies' broken bodies lying around in pieces.

"My Lords!" Lady Bella calls out to them as they are already making haste back to the lab. "I should like very much to see if Master Commandant Mikhail has indeed been successful in slaughtering the enemy. Let's go to the lab together and look in on the Johannesburg estate through our surveillance system."

* * *

Kookie has just gotten word from Liling and Yakov. He has gathered up his troops and they are all getting ready to board the Cloudtransporter heading back to Johannesburg. Master Sam, Mistress Sheila, and several farmers and commandos have come to see them off.

"Thank you, My Lord Kookie," says Master Sam. "Thank you for giving us something we have all so desperately needed; the hope of a better world for all of us."

Turning to the rest of Kookie's little group, Master Sam says, "Thank you *All*, my Brothers and Sisters."

"It has been our honor to serve you, sir," says Kookie "and give you whatever we can. Please call for help anytime you need us."

One of the commandos steps forward. He has been holding onto a Master's Communication Device which he hands over to Kookie. "I found this in the field, My Lord. It was lying next to the body of Master Commandant Mikhail. I read the messages on it, and I thought you should have it. You will want to know what Lady Bella is up to."

He smiles meekly and lowers his head.

Kookie looks at him and says, "Thank you, my Brother. We are all one people of One World. There is no real enemy among us, only the evil one that lives in the underworld. As long as we know that and stay true to each other, we will always win in the end. The one who likes to invade the minds of people will always fall, living up to his name as the fallen one."

The commando smiles and nods in understanding.

Kookie and company leave Wyoming. On the trip back to Johannesburg, he is thinking about the show down with the dark lord of the underworld which he knows is coming . . . soon.

* * *

Angie is sitting on a soft earthen floor, deep beneath the roots of a very old forest. The mellow, purple light casts a somber shadow across the thicket of woods. There are occasional patches of light on the ground, which come from the sparkles of thoughts at the very deepest part of the tree roots. It has been Angie's connection to the Light source as it nourishes the trees above and filters down to her lonely world below.

She is listening to the echoes beneath her of hissing, snarling and growling. The beast has been restless lately, losing one battle after another to his arch enemies of the Alliance.

She can hear his footsteps coming towards her. Boom . . . boom . . . boom. A red glow appears out of the darkness below. The growling is getting louder, and the footsteps are booming faster.

Angie smiles to herself. *I wonder what Kookie did to tick him off so bad this time.*

As he gets closer, she hears his voice muttering through the hissing and snarling . . . *and they call ME trickster! It is YOU who are the trickiest trickster of all! Oh yes, my deeear Kookie, niiice Kookie, goood Kookie!*

The booming is very loud now, and Angie can see the beast's face appearing and disappearing in the thicket of woods.

Angel is also listening to the angry grumblings of the beast. She says to Angie. *Your time has come, gentle human creature. It is time for you to do what you came down here to do. I can help a little, but it is really up to you now.*

"I don't understand, Angel. What am I supposed to do?" Angie asks the Monarch.

I cannot tell you. I can only guide you. For now, I must be quiet and listen. I have faith in you and the One who is guiding us both. Give it your best shot, human creature, and we shall see who wins!

All at once the beast grows quiet, and an unsettling feeling comes over Angie. The purple begins to fade until it goes out altogether, and the only light in the underground world is that which is glowing from Angie and Angel's body. The angelic glow is casting an eerie shadow in the underground forest. And the beast suddenly appears right in Angie's face. He is oozing venom and snarling at her saying, *He was mine! Mine! I created him in the likeness of ME! HE – WAS – MY – **SON!***

Angie looks at the fallen one and says to him in a casual manner, "Oh, I'm sorry. Are you referring to my husband?"

Husband? HUSBAND?! Are YOU referring to that foolish nonsensical thing he did with a rose in front of your party guests? The beast snorts and snickers. *And what exactly makes you think that gives you the right to call him your husband?!*

"And what makes *YOU* think that simply contributing your seed gives *YOU* the right to refer to him as your son?" Angie shoots back.

The beast screams with rage in Angie's face: ***AAAAAAHH!*** *HE **IS** MY SON! **MY** SON! **MINE! MINE! MINE!***

The evil one is jumping up and down, shaking his fist at the heavens, looking up to the Father and screaming, *MY SON! NOT YOURS! **MINE!***

Angie rolls her eyes, waiting for the evil one to stop screaming, jumping, and flailing about. Then she says, "Well, from the looks of things and what *MY* husband is doing up there, I'd say he is nothing at *all* like his dad, if that is who you claim to be."

The evil one snorts and snickers some more: *That's because I was tricked! Fooled! Lied to!*

Angie asks, "How is that, fallen one?"

Spewing venom, the beast replies, *As the favorite archangel of. . . HIM. . . I thought I was going to have all kinds of power over people. And then HE went and changed all that! Just because I was SSSOOO beautiful, SSSOOO wise, and SSSSSSOOO perfect! He punished me! He took my power! Took it all back! And He send me away! And when I created a son of my own, with two others as his disciples, HE TOOK THEM TOO! And THAT my DEAR Angie is why I have taken YOU! An eye for an eye and a child for a child. And I shall take back MY child, Lord Kenneth, through YOU, Angie dear!*

* * *

Lady Bella and the three Lords are in the lab. Lord Viktor has gone over to one of the monitors and opened the surveillance program, and in a matter of seconds, he has Lord Emeka's Estate on the screen. They are searching the place inside and out including every room of the Big House and every square foot of the outside grounds. From what they can see, it looks deserted, and Lady Bella is not sure what to make of that.

"Well, My Lords," she says, "it appears that Master Commandant Mikhail has accomplished his mission. The AI clean-up crew is always so efficient in cleaning up the mess afterwards."

Turning to Pavel, Igor, and Viktor, she says, "Do you not agree with that, My Lords?"

"Oh yes, yes! Indeed! They are truly most efficient, Your Ladyship! Yes, indeed they are!" they all tweet back at her, sounding like baby chicks in a chicken coop.

Lady Bella thinks for a moment and says, "Still, I should have heard from him by now. Lord Victor, I want you to check the whereabouts of Mikhail's communication device."

"Yes, My Lady, right away. The surveillance program should make it very easy to pinpoint an exact location, Ah! Here it is, My Lady. Seems like the device is on a Cloudtransporter sitting on the grounds of Lord Emeka's Estate. Of course, I cannot tell if the craft has just arrived or if it is about to take off, but considering that the Estate appears to be deserted, I would have to concur with your deduction, My Lady.

"It does appear that Master Commandant Mikhail has successfully completed his mission and is preparing to leave Johannesburg. In that case, we should probably be seeing him within the next couple of hours."

"Excellent!" exclaims Lady Bella. "Now the three of you get back to work on Phase 4!"

"Yes, Your Ladyship!" they all chirp, as Lady Bella goes back to her mansion, looking forward to the return of Mikhail.

Wearing her whip around her neck, she thinks about the collection she has back in her boudoir and contemplates which whip to wear for Mikhail upon his arrival. Going through her wardrobe, Lady Bella thinks, *he really did like this brown braided one last time.*

In the lab, when Lord Viktor is quite sure that Lady Bella has gone, he turns to Lord Pavel and Lord Igor. Putting his index finger against his lips, letting them know to keep quiet, he motions for them to follow him. They go to an area in the lab which Lord Viktor has secured for privacy. In a hushed voice he says, "There is something you both should know about the communication device of Master Commandant Mikhail."

"What is it, My Lord" says Lord Igor a bit anxiously. "Is it not in the Cloudtransporter like you said?"

"Oh, indeed it is," says Lord Viktor, "only it is not in a Cloudtransporter belonging to Lady Bella."

Lord Igor and Lord Pavel look at each other with raised eyebrows. They are both completely puzzled.

"Well, whose craft is it then?" Lord Pavel asks.

Lord Viktor huddles in closer and whispers, "It is a Cloudtransporter belonging to Lord Kenneth."

* * *

Kookie and his crew have arrived back in Johannesburg. Eve Elli, Emeka, Mimi, Ryan and the Chrysalenes have all gone off to the Village of the Holy Ones, where the gathering of the Garden Community Committee is well underway. When Liling had asked them all to move their conference from the grounds of the estate to the Village of the Holy Ones for security reasons, not a question was asked.

Kookie heads straight for the study where Liling, Yakov and Rudolpho are waiting for him. They all look at each other with sorrowful expressions, and an old instinct kicks in for the three of them. Before saying a word, they come together, join hands, hold them up in their air and do their childhood greeting:

"Ni hao, Privyet, Hey!"

They laugh for a moment, but the laughter turns instantly to sorrow. And the sorrow is followed by hugs.

Finally, Kookie turns to the new kid in the room and says, "Hey there, bro'! Didn't mean to ignore you!" Putting his hand out to Rudolpho and his other hand on the young man's back, Kookie says, "Hi! I'm Kookie. And you must be Rudolpho!"

Rudolpho smiles, nods, and shakes Kookie's hand.

"Before we get started with our business," Kookie says to Rudolpho in a gentle, fatherly voice, "how would you like to join me for some of my best-ever chocolate chip cookies and tea?"

Yakov and Liling shake their heads and smile as Rudolpho vigorously shakes his head *yes*.

"Sounds like a plan, my man!" says Kookie.

* * *

The evil one is pacing back and forth, grumbling, snarling, and hissing.

I SHALL TAKE HIM BACK!

KENNETH IS MINE!

MINE! ALL MINE!

Angie is listening and watching as the beast rants and raves. She thinks about how much she loves and misses her Kookie and how the sacrifice that she is making, being in the underworld kingdom of the dark lord, has been keeping her beloved out of the clutches of the beast. She watches and listens and thinks of all that has happened to her and to Kookie since they have known each other.

The beast continues pacing and muttering to himself, *Mine, I say! Mine! Mine, all mine!*

Angie remembers how she felt when she opened the door and first saw Kookie, at Kenny and Lisa's cottage at Bear River Farm. How those golden eyes of his took her breath away. How he melted her heart when he first played his tuba for her in Kookie's Kastle. How she felt when they were almost killed by Lord Ekene, which was the first time he called her My Woman, and . . .

Mine! *Mine! I shall take him back! Mine!* ***My*** *son! Mine!*

Watching and listening to the beast as he continues to pace and carry on, a slow realization is coming into Angie's heart as she thinks to herself, *Mine . . . My Man . . . Mine!*

Suddenly, she looks at the beast and sees nothing more than a master manipulator; an angry, frustrated fallen angel, who was once held up high. She also comes to realize that Kookie and the others of the Alliance have a great advantage over the lord of the underworld. And that advantage is love.

Suddenly a ray of Light filters through the darkness from above. And in the Light, a Voice from Heaven, speaks to Angie saying:

With LOVE all things are possible,[7] my daughter.

Angie begins to weep with tears of joy.

Angel says to her, *What is it, Angie Creature? Why do you weep?*

"Because," Angie cries to the Monarch, "It is now time to go back to my Beloved!"

Amen, Angie creature! Amen!

Angie looks up to the ray of Light from Heaven and says to Angel, "I wonder if we can ride this Light beam back to the other world."

Yes, we can, sweet Angie creature, yes, we can. LET'S GO!

---

[7] *Matt 19:26. Actual verse says "With God all things are possible."*

Chapter 12 – Beloved

Hold up your arms to the Light of Heaven, Angie creature. Let your heart see the Creator, let your soul connect with Him, and then reach out with all the love in your heart to your Beloved.

Angie holds her arms up to the Light and sees in her heart the beautiful face of the Divine. She connects to His Spirit, as a child who is holding onto the hand of her father. And then, Angie also connects to the heart of her beloved, Kookie.

Slowly her feet lift off the soft earthen ground of the purple forest, and Angie begins her gradual ascent.

Angel's wings are sparkling with their beautiful colors of orange, yellow and gold as Angie's heart sings the words to her lover, over and over:

My beloved Kookie,
Your Woman loves you so.
Hold on Darling, Wait for me,
For I am coming home.

* * *

The four pigeons are splashing around in the bird bath by their coop, and the Seven Monarchs of Angel are fluttering happily by a patch of wildflowers.

Kookie, Liling, Yakov and Rudolpho have just finished their cookies and tea and are back in the study ready to dive into their analyses of Phase 4 of Lady Bella's Project Laser Beam.

Suddenly, the butterflies come to full attention, receiving an incoming signal and the pigeons are receiving the same message.

Number 3, #4, #21 and #22 jump out of the bird bath, shake their feathers dry and are in the air instantly, with the Monarchs fluttering right behind them. They fly into the study through an open window, where the four human creatures are bent over a couple of hand-held devices.

The pigeons and the butterflies know that when human creatures are lost in deep concentration as these four are, it takes a major blow to the top of the head to get their attention. So, while the Monarchs start fluttering around the hand-held devices to break the human creatures' concentration, the four birds each pick a head to start smacking, pecking and whacking upon.

"*OW!*" the four human creatures all cry out together.

"What the—? Hey, wait a second!" exclaims Kookie while rubbing the top of his head.

Number 4 perches on his shoulder staring straight at him, as if she is saying, *You know the drill, man, follow me!*

Kookie is too heartbroken over the loss of Angie to believe what he thinks #4 is trying to tell him. Still, he must know. He takes #4 and holds her against his chest, listening to the heart of the dove.

The others see what he is doing and they each follow suit. The doves send them all the same beautiful vision: Angie rising up from the underworld, singing her love song to Kookie.

When Kookie hears her voice singing, "For I am coming home," he closes his eyes tight, and a stream of tears flow down his cheeks. "Dear Lord! Is it true? Angie! My Angie!"

He looks at the others, and they all shout at the same time: *"TO THE BEDROOM!"*

* * *

Angie is in the tunnel of Light, but it is not the swirling tempest that she experienced on her descent into hell. This time the journey is peaceful and filled with the voices of angels singing. It is also filled with sparkling colors of the rainbow, as if she were in a kaleidoscope. Only this kaleidoscope has a brilliant White Light at the end of it, radiating a warm, loving energy.

A part of Angie wants to continue on to the Heavenly Father and stay there, and that is why Angel is there to help.

Remember, sweet Angie creature, your work is not yet finished on earth. I cannot tell you more at this time, but when you are ready you will come to understand.

"Oh yes," says Angie, "When I *do* go to that beautiful, loving place at the end of the kaleidoscope one day, it *must* be with my beloved, my Kookie, my Man."

Angie and Angel smile at each other from within as one being, one soul.

And now, Angie creature, it is time for me to leave your body and reconnect with my Seven Monarch friends. They are very near to us now and awaiting our return.

"Oh, my goodness!" exclaims Angie. "How can I ever thank you Angel, for being with me. I shall miss being so close to you, that is, having a Monarch Butterfly connected to my spirit."

I will always be connected to your spirit, Angie creature. You will see.

With that, the Monarch rises out of Angie's back, diminishing to her normal size and appearance of a butterfly.

I will see you soon on the other side, Angel says as she fades and disappears.

* * *

The miraculous news has been transmitted to the Chrysalenes of the Village of the Holy Ones that Angie is returning from the underworld. They proclaim the great news and make an announcement to everyone at the Village, including the conference guests. Everyone is overwhelmed with excitement.

Eve Elli, Mama Eve Zula, and Little Lord Emeka want to be there for Angie's arrival, so the three of them are on their way to the Big House.

Kookie, Yakov, Liling, and Rudolpho are gathered around the bed where Angie left them. They are holding hands and praying as they can feel Angie's energy getting closer to them.

Suddenly, they see something small and ethereal materialize out of nowhere right over Angie's pillow. The form takes shape and begins to solidify; Kookie, Yakov and Liling recognize it at once.

"*ANGEL!*" the three of them cry out.

The Seven Monarchs of Angel are overcome with joy to see her again, fluttering around Angel in an ecstatic dance of the butterflies. The pigeons are very happy to see Angel too, and Rudolpho is totally amazed at what he is witnessing.

* * *

MINE! MINE! MINE!

*I **SHALL** HAVE HIM! I SHALL **TAKE** HIM!*

Looking up to the Light the beast shakes his fist and cries out:

YOU ALREADY HAVE A SON!

*LORD KENNETH IS **MY** SON!*

MINE! MINE! MINE!

*I **SHALL** HAVE . . .*

The beast suddenly stops ranting and howling. He stops dead in his tracks, and looks up again, realizing what he has just seen. The Light!

*What? Where did **that** come from?!*

He looks around some more and begins to panic, yelling, *AND WHERE IS THAT **WOMAN?***

Then the beast glances up one more time and notices a figure near the top of the tunnel. Instantly, he realizes what is happening and lets out a terrifying, blood curdling scream.

AAANGIEEE!

* * *

Kookie and his friends are all happy to see Angel again.

Then, #4 becomes excited and starts flapping her wings right over Angie's pillow, heralding the return of her beloved human friend.

An ethereal mist begins to materialize on top of the bed, with definite features of Angie's face forming on the pillow.

Kookie is feeling more anxious than ever and sheds new tears upon seeing the face of his beloved. *She is almost home now!* he thinks to himself.

Suddenly, Angie's face and ethereal form vanish altogether.

Kookie stops breathing for a moment, looking at Angel, and says to her: "Angel! What happened! Where did Angie go?! What happened!"

The others are all stunned into silence.

* * *

Angie is almost through to the other side when she hears the terrific bellowing of the evil one, screaming her name. In a moment of fear, she realizes that her protection from Angel is gone, and she hears the dark lord's thunderous footsteps raging towards her.

The kaleidoscopic tunnel suddenly turns blood red.

* * *

The eight Monarchs and four pigeons stop dancing and perch themselves on the empty space where Angie's ethereal body was forming only moments ago.

Angel listens in to what is happening with Angie, and she speaks to the hearts of everyone in the room:

Do not fear, human creatures; Angie still has one more test to pass and one great lesson to learn. And for this she needs all our help. You must send her loving energy, all that is in your heart to give. Let her know that she is loved and how much you want her to come home.

Kookie gets down on his knees at the foot of their bed and stretches his arms out in front of him. With his face down, he begins to pray, "Dear Lord, please bring my Angie back to me." He pauses for a moment and then says, "Angie, if you can hear me, my Woman, I love you so much. My beloved, please come back to me. Please Angie, I love you, my darling angel. I love you so much. Please hear me. Please come home. Your Man needs you so much. I love you. Please come home."

* * *

Angie hears the booming footsteps getting louder and coming closer, with the beast screaming her name:

*ANGIE! ANGIE! YOU WILL **NOT** ESCAPE!*
*THIS MOMENT IS **MINE!***
*LORD KENNETH IS **MINE!***
AND NOW, SWEET ANGIE,
YOU ARE MINE!!

Angie can now see the beast closing in on her. She turns her face up to the Light above and says, "Father in Heaven, Help me! Please! Help me!"

Suddenly the Light grows strong, blinding the beast with its intensity and slowing down his pursuit. The thunderous sound of his footsteps become a distant echo, so now, Angie can hear several other voices coming to her in the tunnel of Light:

We all love you, Angie, our sweet angel.
You got this, Angie! Come on back now!
I love you Angie, my soul Sister creature.
Have no fear; just take that last step and come on home.
My Woman, I love you so much. My beloved, please come back to me.

Angie raises her tearful eyes to the Light of Heaven and cries out with passion. "Heavenly Father, I now know why I was brought here, and why you allow the evil one to roam the earth in the hearts of humankind. I have learned that the fallen angel is no match for You, and therefore, we truly have nothing to fear. For You are Love, and with You, all things are possible."

Angie sees two figures appearing in the Light. They are her mother and father, and they are smiling with great happiness and waving to her. Angie can hear them saying to her heart, *We love you, Angela, and we are so proud of you! Kenneth is a good man. We love him, too.*

Angie is overcome with emotion. She cries and waves back to her parents saying, "Thank you, Mom and Dad! I love you too!"

The Light begins to fade, and her vision becomes a darkening blur. As Angie closes her eyes, everything goes black. She can hear Kookie's voice off in the distance whispering tenderly to her, "I love you, Angie. Please come back to me."

* * *

Kookie's arms are still stretched out on the foot of their bed. He is weeping softly while listening to the gentle murmur of the loving words coming from the others. Suddenly, he feels a fullness underneath his arms and he sits up. The fullness is rapidly taking form as his beloved fully materializes in front of his very eyes. Kookie lets out a cry, "*ANGIE!*"

Slowly opening her eyes, Angie looks around at everyone. They are all on their knees, laughing and crying, and Angie begins to laugh and cry too.

Her Man takes her in his arms, and they hold each other close, knowing that they will never, ever let go.

Liling says to everyone, "Perhaps we should leave these two alone for a while. Would anyone care to join me in the kitchen? Seems like we could all break some bread together!"

"Amen to that! You got it Sister!" and they all go down to the kitchen.

Their beloved Angie has come home.

* * *

Word has gotten back to the Village of the Holy Ones of Angie's return, and everyone is overjoyed. The guests of the conference have heard about her descent into hell for the good of the people, and it has made Angie into a legendary folk heroine. Those who are visiting are all excited to meet her, and of course, the Chrysalenes and all of Angie's friends are filled with ecstasy over seeing her again. The love and respect that Angie has generated amongst everyone extends far and wide, along with the stories about her acts of courageous love and support of the Alliance. Her relationship with Kookie has also become a source of emotional strength and spiritual courage for all who have gotten to know them both.

It is a great relief to one and all to have Angie back home. And apart from Kookie, no one is happier to have her back than #3 and #4.

Kookie and Angie are on their way over to the Village of the Holy Ones to greet everyone, along with Liling, Yakov, and Rudolpho. Of course, #3 and #4 are snuggled softly against Angie's neck.

The Garden Community Committee and all the guests in attendance are lined up, waiting at the entrance of the Village. And when Angie arrives everyone starts to cheer and applaud. As she walks in and greets everyone there are members of the UC who are meeting her for the first time. The men bow and the women curtsy to Angie, which is an honor rarely given to anyone, even in the UC. The Chrysalenes cross their hands on their chests, lower their eyes and bow humbly before Angie as she passes them.

Number 3 and #4 have forgotten that they are mere pigeons and are just as proud as two peacocks can be.

At the center of the Village of the Holy Ones there is a water well. It often serves as a gathering place for special events, and today the whole conference will take place around the well. Angie is invited to be the keynote speaker.

Kookie, Liling and Yakov have not yet disclosed to the Alliance the most recent findings given to them by Rudolpho, regarding Project Laser Beam and Phase 4. They have decided to do so with those of their inner circle after the conference is over. Kookie has decided that today is for celebrating and rejoicing, as well as giving Angie the opportunity to share her good news with the crowd.

The bad news of Project Laser Beam can wait until the next day.

With everyone seated around the well, Lady Neely and Mistress Henrietta bring out several loaves of bread and flasks of well water.

Lady Neely begins. "Welcome everyone to our final day of the Garden Community Conference. We have learned so many wonderful things from each other these past few days, about how to bring people, *all* people, together in community with each other. We have talked about farming, nutrition, free trade and barter, and an environment for our families and loved ones where everyone is loved and cared for. We have talked about the need to treat every human being with dignity and respect, encouraging everyone, from the smallest child to the oldest adult to awaken to their gifts and talents, and start living their dreams.

"We have also talked at length about the importance of starting libraries in our communities and how we might even network with each other offering educational services for all ages, including higher education. Basically, we have talked about what our lives are about to become, now that the former Council is gone, and freedom is ringing in our ears!"

There are lots of cheers and applause, by one and all. Lady Neely passes the flasks of water and loaves of bread around, as she continues, "May we all break bread together on this most auspicious day, after which Mistress Henrietta will introduce our special, and pleasantly unexpected keynote speaker!"

More cheers and applause, as everyone eats of the common loaf and drinks the water of the pure, sacred well.

Mistress Henrietta gets up and addresses the crowd. "My, what a lovely time this has been together with all of you! Thank you all *so* much for coming!"

She extends her arms and applauds to everyone, as they applaud her.

A very proud Master Howard, sitting in the front row turns to the Major and Vi and says, "Yep, that's my little Sugar Cookie!" Blowing kisses at Sugar Cookie he calls out to her, "You tell 'em, my little Peach Cupcake!"

Vi raises her eyebrows and whispers to the Major, "I guess we know what's on the dessert menu this evening!"

The Major rolls his eyes, shakes his head and smiles.

"Thank you honey," Henrietta says sweetly, noticing that old 'charging rhino' look in his eyes. Back to the crowd, she says, "Without further ado, allow me to introduce to you a very special young woman. She has quite a story to tell you all, I'm sure. Please welcome our very own, Angie."

Cheers, thunderous applause, and a standing ovation greet Angie as she rises and stands before the crowd of the Garden Community Committee. Putting her hands up to her lips in prayer style, Angie lowers her eyes and bows her head to everyone. They all do the same to her and then sit down.

Angie looks adoringly at all the people seated before her and begins to share. "Thank you, good people of the Village of the Holy Ones, Chrysalenes, cherished friends, and all the new, dear friends gathered here today. Thank you for such a kind, warm welcome. I know that many of you have traveled a long way to be here, which lets us all know how important this gathering is.

"My friends, as I believe most of you already know, I have just returned from a life-altering encounter with, what is said to be, the darkest force of the universe. My original intention was to protect my precious Man, my Kookie, who is sitting right here, as well as all my cherished friends, and the rest of you, the people of One World. But as it turned out, there was another purpose to that encounter, which I have come here today to share with all of you."

The attendees of the conference are all on the edge of their seats waiting to hear her story.

She begins by telling them everything that happened to her, starting with the dreams that she and the others were having, to the moment she knew that she was the one to go down to the underworld of hell. Angie does not divulge the specifics about Kookie, Yakov, and Liling's origins but focuses on how the beast was using her to get to Kookie, hoping that Kookie would join forces with him as an evil force incarnate, here on earth.

"Kookie has always emphasized that there is nothing to fear but fear itself. And the Chrysalenes, as well as the forces of the natural world, like the Monarch Butterflies, have also been telling us the same thing. In fact, we have been told by all of them that the opposite of fear is Love, and that Love is more powerful than fear. And, my friends, from the moment I chose to enter his unholy world, I also chose to believe that *NOT* fearing the beast would take away his power over me."

Angie pauses for a moment and looks around smiling at everyone, as she says, "and that is exactly what happened. His growling, snarling, stomping, and hissing were reduced to nothing more than the childish tantrums of an overgrown brat not getting his way."

Everyone laughs and cheers: *"Yes! You tell him, Sister!"*

"In fact," Angie continues, "I believe that the dark lord is most dangerous when he uses his trickery, lies and deceit to turn people against one another. I believe, *it is the **influence** of the evil one, not the evil one himself, that is the real danger to humankind.* By himself, he is nothing. He is an angry creature making a lot of noise. When we stop listening to his lies and stop being afraid, his power is *greatly* diminished. Yes, good people, *WE* are the ones who can disempower the fallen one! And, it really made him furious when he saw that he could not frighten me."

More cheers and laugher; Kookie smiles and says, "That's my Woman!"

Angie continues, "But his evil doing is very real, and it is up to us to understand what we can do about it." Turning to the Chrysalenes Angie says, "We have been greatly blessed by the gifts of wisdom, knowledge, and all things holy given to us by those whose only desire is to serve. They are great guides for us, but there is only so much they can do. The rest are the lessons which each one of us came into this world to learn for ourselves. Some lessons we all have in common, and some are specific to our individual calling. The Chrysalenes cannot tell us what to do, but they *are* here to help and guide us."

"Why is that?" asks Mimi, who is sitting up front. "Why can't they just tell us what to do in a given situation?"

"Because," Angie replies, "the challenges are *our* lessons to learn; ours alone. As a dear friend of mine tells me, we *human creatures* can be very stubborn and hard-headed. Sometimes we have to get whacked on top of the head by a charging pigeon before we get the message!"

Kookie restrains a guffaw, and everyone nods in agreement.

"But then, once we come to understand whatever the lesson is, it seems to stick better when we learn it through experience, rather than merely being told. Each one of us will have different lessons to learn, different callings in life. And once we learn them and answer the call, we are then able to pass the knowledge and wisdom on to others.

"Which brings me to the big lesson that I was meant to learn from my visit with the unholy one. My lesson has been that regardless of how hopeless all things may seem to be, there is *always* hope because with love all things are possible. It is love that brought me back to all of you, and to my beloved Kookie."

Everyone smiles gazing at Kookie and Angie, who are locked into each other's gaze in lovers' heaven.

Mimi speaks up again, "Angie, I have just one more question for you. It seems to me that bad things keep on happening to good people, and I have never quite understood why. Although now, I think you have partially answered that question already, you know, about learning lessons, and so on.

"But I still do not understand why so much evil is allowed to exist in the world. Why life has to be so much harder for some than it is for others. Why some people are hated and treated shamefully while others seem to have a life of ease. Is it really necessary for some people to have such hard, and even brutal encounters with the disciples of the dark lord, and if so, why?"

Angie sees the expressions on everyone's faces reflecting the suffering and hardships many of them have been through, as well as the compassion they are *all* feeling, somewhere in their unconscious, collective human soul, for persecuted people throughout human history. She knows deep in her heart that these are the voices of the broken spirits of children crying, whose sorrow she is now feeling, all the way down through the ages.

Angie walks to the center of the crowd, where everyone is seated and opens her arms as if she is wanting to take them all into a motherly embrace. With much tenderness and compassion, she says: "Our Heavenly Father allows the dark lord to exist and for bad things to happen to good people because that is how we are drawn closer to him. It is in those dark times when we reach out to him with passion, like little children seeking parental comfort and love. And that is also when we learn our greatest lessons.

"Some have an easier life because they have chosen to learn and to serve less. Others have chosen a life of deep and meaningful service to their fellow humans, and in so doing, have accepted the suffering that goes along with such a life. The fire that is lit by Lucifer, allows us to become grist for the mill for our Creator. We become pliable so that our Heavenly Father can bend and mold us to His will. We then become His sharp sword, ready and able to usher in something much better than the world has ever known. *It is an honor to be His holy grist for the mill. Through our suffering, may we become his sharpest sword.*"

* * *

An Angel of the Lord is looking down upon the crowd in the Village of the Holy Ones. With all the love in her heart, she says to her soul Sister:

Bless you, Sister Angie, creature. Bless you.

PART 3

ONE WORLD

Chapter 13 – Trickster

LORD VIKTOR, LORD IGOR, AND LORD PAVEL have hacked into Master Commandant Mikhail's communication device located on Kookie's Cloudtransporter in Johannesburg. They can see everything that happened to Master Commandant Mikhail right up to his demise. The three lords know that they will have to come up with a story for Lady Bella that will satisfy her Ladyship while they continue with their covert plans. The three of them go back into the lab and run the communication device through the surveillance system's data analysis. They can see everything that happened to Master Commandant Mikhail right up to his demise.

Viktor, Pavel, and Igor realize that they must buy some time in order to move forward with their plan, by crafting a story about Mikhail for Lady Bella. So, the three Lords tell her that they spoke to him and he was detained; that is, he found another Alliance base to destroy. She is happy with that for the moment.

Viktor, Pavel, and Igor, have been quietly speaking with others on the island, waiting for an opportunity to meet with them, and talk about their scheme. Lady Bella just announced to Lord Pavel that she will be on the mainland for a little while, attending to some personal business. He knows her absence is the opportunity they have been waiting for, so he quickly rounds up their comrades. There is an area on the other end of the island that is hardly ever used, and the three Lords decide that this will be a good spot for their rendezvous. So, they send word to everyone to go there immediately for an urgent meeting.

The group of men and women, assembled at the designated location, consists of 15 Lords and Ladies and three Master technicians from Lord Viktor's lab. Although they are basically pro-Council, they are most definitely *not* pro Bella. The group fears that the cruelty of their sociopathic leader is a threat to all the people of One World, including the UC, leaving them feeling uncertain and vulnerable about their future.

The techies have also analyzed a weakness in Phase 4 of Project Laser Beam, with the possibility of Kookie and his team coming up with a way to outsmart them. So, they have agreed that there is only once course of action that they can take: to play for time and get away from Lady Bella just as soon, and as safely as they can.

Lord Viktor begins, "My Lords, My Ladies and Masters. Thank you all for coming here on such short notice. The business that we need to discuss here today is urgent. We really have to take immediate action and move forward."

Then he proceeds to share the data analysis with every one of the last days and moments of Master Commandant Mikhail's life, including his ultimate decapitation. They all sit there stunned as one of the Ladies present, Lady Nita, says, "So are we to understand, My Lords, that Lady Bella knows nothing of Master Commandant Mikhail's death?"

"That is correct," says Lord Pavel.

"Whatever did you tell her then, man?" inquires Lord Jonah.

Lord Igor says, "We told her that he was on his way back from Johannesburg when he got word of yet another group of insurrectionists in Benghazi. He decided to land there first. Using various methods of torture, he is allegedly extracting much useful information from the traitors, gathering an extensive list of enemies from every corner of One World. We then told her that he said his communication device was not operating at full capacity, with many more blackouts than usual, since the exposure to high earth frequencies in the cave in Wyoming. So, when he was able to reach Lord Viktor on the lab's computer, Mikhail asked him to pass this information on to her as he knew that she would want to hear it."

The Lords, Ladies and techies all look at Viktor, Pavel, and Igor, and give a nod of approval. "Very clever, very ingenious, most excellent!" they all concur.

"Well," says Lady Nita, "So what do we do now?"

In a yacht filled with high-tech equipment, just off the coast of Benghazi, a voice that is not heard by the group says, "Yes. So, what *will* you do now?"

* * *

The Garden Community Conference is over and everyone is returning to their homes, from the locals to the UC, all across One World. They will be taking back with them to their local regions, townships and communities, many great ideas, and blueprints for ushering forth a free new world. They also have a strengthening bond of love amongst them all.

Master Howard, Mistress Henrietta and their group of people will be convening today to discuss their new line of natural healing products. They plan to leave shortly afterwards for California, along with their new team. The staff from the main location of Howard Pharmaceuticals in California now includes the Major, Vi, Reggie, Bem, Nassor, and Tafari. The Johannesburg staff includes Neely, Dumaka, Phil, Doc, Mimi, and their young apprentice Emeka. In fact, little Lord Emeka has announced that he wants to donate a portion of his mansion to Howard Pharmaceuticals, creating the new Johannesburg plant right there. And he also wants to create a garden community with the entire estate.

The Garden Community Committee has also created a special branch of the Alliance to support the planting of new garden communities in all three Continental Territories throughout One World. It is called the Garden Alliance of One World. Among the global members of the advisory committee are Judy, Lisa, and Kenny, who have a vast array of knowledge and experience with sustainable, community farming and living.

Kenny also has an expanded training and breeding program underway for the Intercontinental Pigeons Communication Network, so that all community gardens across One World will be connected by carrier pigeon.

Ryan has been captivated by the whole technological thing and is apprenticing himself to Yakov, Liling and Rudolpho. Inspired by his time as a mole, he wants very much to learn everything he can from his brilliant mentors, so he can offer his services for the greater good through advanced technology.

The Lords and Ladies who are part of the Alliance are becoming more and more enthused over the idea of doing exactly what little Lord Emeka is doing. They are inspired by him to turn their vast estates into garden communities, with schools of higher learning for the people, libraries, and trader markets.

Lord Yakov and Lady Neely already have such plans underway at their estates, while Lady Liling is doing the same with hers in Shanghai. She has decided to transform her entire estate into a garden community, calling it "The Garden of Bi" to honor her late friend. Word is getting around about naming the garden communities after those who have died serving the cause, or in some other tragic way, and everyone seems to love the idea.

As for Kookie and Angie, they want to do the same with Kookie's Kastle. For the time being though they have other business to attend to. Right now, they need to be a constant support to all who need them, while also staying on high alert to Lady Bella and associates . . . and the dark lord below.

Their focus must be on protecting One World's incoming sacred child. That child is a new world; a Wakanjeja called One Garden. The

Wakanjeja, has already begun its descent down the birth canal, about to be born, and is vulnerable to the vultures stalking in the shadows.

* * *

On the far end of the Isle of Bella, Lord Viktor is about to answer Lady Nita's question about 'what happens next.' As he opens his mouth to speak, all three of his techies suddenly bolt upright.

One of the techies starts to cough and sputter, saying, "Excuse me . . . choking on spit . . . wrong pipe . . ." as he eyeballs Lord Viktor with their pre-arranged signal.

Lord Viktor catches the eye of everyone else sitting there and he discreetly puts his index finger to his lips. He is tapping his lips and glancing sideways, thinking about how he is going to answer the question.

"Yes, well, what happens next? Now *that* is the question!" he says, putting his index finger in the air and then quickly back in front of his lips.

There seems to be confusion among the group, so he holds his index finger firmly in place against his lips while raising his eyebrows and staring at each person one at a time. This time, they realize that something has just happened, and they all sit still and follow Lord Viktor's lead.

"Something just came into my head," he finally says, "And I will need to check it out. If you all would just bear with me for a moment and follow me."

Quietly, they all stand up and follow Lord Viktor. Not one word is spoken among anyone, which has the techies concerned. They do *not* want to rouse any suspicion with the one who, they have just come to realize, is eavesdropping and possibly even observing their every move. They were alerted to the security breach when the "voice from

Benghazi" triggered a vibration alarm on the devices in their pockets. So, they start up a "casual conversation" with each other.

"Isn't it a lovely day!"

"Well yes, it is, a most lovely day!"

"My goodness, it certainly is, a very lovely day!"

"Oh, and do look at that *exquisite* yacht!"

"Well yes, it is, a *most* exquisite yacht!

"My goodness, it certainly is, a *very* exquisite yacht!"

The mood lightens among the group, with eye rolls, head shakes, chuckles, and smiles, while Lord Viktor leads them down the beach toward the mansion.

The voice from the yacht off the coast of Benghazi snickers and says, *"WEIRDOS!"* which is exactly the effect the "weirdos" were hoping to achieve.

Lord Viktor arrives with everyone back in the vicinity of the mansion. He suddenly stops, turns around and faces the group. He is standing in front of the lab building with the landing field and Cloudtransporters nearby. With his eyes fixed on the techies, he looks at them, looks at the lab building, and then, looks at a Cloudtransporter.

He is asking his three techies, with his eyes, to make a decision for all 18 of them that will affect the rest of their lives.

Looking at the lab building and then looking at the Cloudtranporter, Lord Viktor also searches his own heart and asks himself, *Can we make a run for it now? Would it be safe? Will Lady Bella find out and hurt our families as she has already threatened to do if we were ever to betray her?*

Looking at the techies and then at the Cloudtransporter one last time, Viktor's eyes ask them, *Should we return to the lab and wait for a safer time to leave, or should we run like hell. . . RIGHT NOW?!*

* * *

Lady Bella is sitting on her yacht, off the coast of Benghazi. She lays back in her captain's chair watching and listening to the group of conspirators making their decision. She sees everything, hears everything, and misses nothing.

"So," she says out loud, to the three monitors she is watching, "Will you chicken-scratch morons make a run for it?"

She is sipping on a bottle of wine while stroking a whip that is lying across her lap. Bella looks down at the whip with a moment of sadness and says, "This was to have been for our wedding night, my darling Mikhail. I was going to propose as soon as you got back." She then holds up the whip and the bottle of wine together, tapping the bottle against the whip. "Here's to you, my love."

Lady Bella then proceeds to polish off the bottle of wine and passes out in her captain's chair.

Everything goes black, and dead silent. Gradually, Lady Bella notices a pale red light coming from deep down below. It is pulsating gently, softly, whispering her name, 'Bella, Bella, my beautiful Lady Bella. Come to me and be my bride. And I will let you whip me for all of eternity.'

The voice is getting closer and louder as the red light throbs with intense passion. 'Come to me, my Beautiful Bella, come to me. I will give you everything and anything that your heart desires.'

Bella responds, "Will you give me the firepower I desire for Phase 4 of Project Laser Beam?"

'OH YEEEESSS' the voice hisses. . . yeeeessss. . . anything, anything your heart desires. It will be the biggest blast the world has ever seen!'

"Then I shall come to you and be your bride," says Bella, "When this is all over and One World is MY World!" As an afterthought she says, "And don't forget your promise about the whip!"

'Oh no, my bride-to-be, I shall never forget THAT. I've got a veeery big one, my love, and it is waiting here just for you.'

Bella smiles and the beast snickers. He begins to fade as she begins to come out of her drunken stupor.

Suddenly Lady Bella comes to and looks at the three monitors. She does not know how much time has passed, but the group of eighteen conspirators are not showing anywhere on the screens. She looks at the Cloudtransporters, but cannot remember how many there were or if any one of them is missing.

Bella realizes that she had better get home in a hurry.

* * *

Kookie, Yakov, Liling and Rudolpho have reconvened in the study. Angie has now joined them with #3 and #4, resting snuggly against her neck. Ryan is also joining them now as a new member of the team. Kookie has given Rudolpho a Metatron device of his own, and Ryan is using the device that the Major gave Mimi way back in Floraville.

Turning to Angie and Ryan, Kookie says, "Just to let you know where things are at right now with Lady Bella and company, they are developing a laser weapon. Their goal is to launch a large-scale attack against the Alliance from the Isle of Bella, to points all over One World. The points will be marked by Cloudtransporters hovering over specific targets with weaponized reflectors ready to receive and reflect the laser beam.

"If Lady Bella has her way, she will be able to fire from several thousand Cloudtransporters all at once. According to Rudolpho, she now has over a thousand of them, functioning and ready to go. The last phase of this project, which is still in development, is called Phase 4. When completed, it will determine exactly how many targets can be hit, all at the same time."

Looking at everyone with a grave expression and tone in his voice, Kookie continues, "She means to use this, just as soon as she gets her largest number of reflectors ready to go."

Angie is not at all surprised or afraid. Ryan, on the other hand, goes pale.

Angie sees this and pats Ryan on the hand saying, "Don't worry my friend, we've got some firepower of our own."

She points up to the heavens and then turns to Kookie and the rest of them with a warm, smile of confidence.

Kookie softly smiles back at Angie as he continues, "So our job now is to figure out a way of hacking into their program and stopping the attack."

Ryan now looks at everyone with complete amazement. "You guys can really do that?" he says.

They all look at each other and Yakov says, "Um, well, would you mind turning off your Universal Translator for a moment?"

Ryan does so.

Yakov gets right in Ryan's face and says one word to him in Russian, with enough force to power a rocket, ***"DA!"***

Kookie and Liling laugh at their old familiar childhood antics with each other.

Then Kookie turns to Ryan and says, "Welcome to the family, bro'!"

Angie just shakes her head and smiles at all of them as she says to Ryan, "Feeling better?"

Ryan just looks down and chuckles saying, "Yeah, I guess so."

* * *

Lady Bella has been going full throttle to get home as fast as possible. Her island has now come into view and her anxiety is mounting. She thinks to herself, *What have those treacherous snakes done? Who have they talked to? And where the blazes are they?!*

She is going over all the possible scenarios in her head including how she is going to handle them. . . and their families now that they have betrayed her. Assuming they have not decided to make a run for it, Lady Bella really wants to allow them to play out their little scheme with her and see where it all leads. The thought of having her way with them in a kind of public scenario is just too delicious. If she allows them to play it out as far as possible and then act like she is catching them red-handed, it will be a great opportunity for her to dole out some truly heinous corporal punishment.

But where are they?

Lady Bella has just finished docking her yacht and is making a mad dash for the lab. She gets to the front door of the building and yanks it open with a fury. *Where are they! I'll bet those chicken scratchers ran for the hills!*

Lady Bella bursts through the lab door and everyone stops what they are doing. They look at her wondering what the sudden burst of energy is all about and she just looks around.

The office door next to the lab opens and out walks Lord Igor. Seeing Lady Bella he says, "Oh, hello Lady Bella, I see you are back."

"Yes," she says with an ice-cold voice, throwing daggers at him with her eyes. "I am back."

Lord Igor continues with his work in a casual, nonchalant manner, going over to one of the techies and discussing something that they are looking at on the screen in front of them. Lady Bella recognizes the techie at once as one of the "three weirdos" on the beach. She begins to walk around as if she is performing an inspection, at which point everyone knows to just get back to work. No one there is really all that anxious to talk to her. Then the door to the side office opens again and Lady Nita steps out.

"Oh hello, Your Ladyship," she says. "My, but we *are* making progress here today."

Lady Bella looks at her with suspicion and then notices Lord Pavel and Lord Viktor also coming out of the side office along with the other two "weirdo" techies from the beach. When they all see Lady Bella standing there glaring at them, the two Lords come over to her and the two techies go back to their terminals.

Lady Bella thinks *that seems a bit rehearsed, almost like they were choreographing a dance. What the devil are they all up to?*

Lord Viktor says, with great enthusiasm, "My Lady, I do believe that we have reached maximum potential for firepower of Project Laser Beam. Once the construction is all finished, Phase 4 will be completed. You will be able to hit 5000 targets all at once!"

Lady Bella starts to get excited about this, forgetting her anger at them for the moment. Then she asks them about the chemicals for the reflectors, "Did you also figure out how to come up with enough chemical solution to create the needed effect when sprayed onto 5000, concave mirrors with a six-foot diameter? And then, how to attach them to the Cloudtransporters? And how much time all that will take, Lord Viktor?"

"Oh, it's all very simple, My Lady," exclaims Lord Viktor.

"Yes indeed," says Lord Pavel.

In her excitement, Lady Bella is thrown off her guard and does not notice all the faces in the lab whom she was looking at only a little while ago, on the far end of her island. They, however, are on hyper alert with *her*, pretending to be busily involved in their terminals in front of them, when in fact, they are completely tuned in to her reactions and comments.

She is also not remembering the fact that there is a small, sliding panel in the side office which reveals a glimpse of the lab to those who are inside the office. And the remainder of the 18 people who she was spying on earlier are all in that side room right now, spying on *her* through the sliding panel.

"My dearest Lady," says Lord Pavel, just as sweetly as he can, "As you know, Howard Pharmaceuticals has quite the capabilities of producing all sorts of magnificent little chemical goodies in all sorts of humongous quantities, and at breakneck speed. Besides, Master Howard was always so loyal to PA, ES and SPA. Why should he not do the same for us? Hm?"

"Hm, indeed!" Lady Bella snorts, as she is definitely finding it hard to control her excitement. "I shall contact Master Howard directly myself and make all the necessary arrangements."

She leaves the lab and runs to her mansion office.

* * *

Kookie and company are intensely studying the file on Project Laser Beam, specifically focused on Phase 4. Rudolpho is a great help in explaining all the specifics about the convex mirrors and chemicals, as well as the suspected targets.

Yakov asks him, "Have they perfected the chemical formula yet?"

"Yes sir," Rudolpho says. "That was Phase 3. Here, let me show you."

He proceeds to pull up the document which contains the chemical formula for the aerosol to be used on the reflector mirrors.

"This formula," Rudolpho explains "should give the reflectors enough power to attract and receive the laser light from a great distance in the atmosphere and transmit it to a specific earth target. It should also create a sudden flash of bright light with a super-intense heat that will instantly, and totally, incinerate the target, and everything else within a 1-mile radius."

As Rudolpho says this, he looks down with a sad expression and starts shuffling his feet.

Kookie, Yakov and Ryan all look at him with great compassion.

Yakov touches his shoulder and says, "It's okay, son. You did what you were told to do. And now you are here with us."

Kookie touches his other shoulder and says, "What you are doing now is going to help us save all the lives of those who are being targeted. And we are all proud of you for that."

Ryan is seated in front of Rudolpho and says, "I think you are the biggest hero ever. And I just want to thank you for what you are doing."

Ryan puts his hand out to shake his hero's hand, and Rudolpho goes in for a hug, crying in Ryan's arms.

Liling and Angie look on with compassion, feeling the weight of the world on this 12-year-old boy's shoulders.

Kookie looks at everyone and says, "You know, I think I may have just figured something out here."

They all look at him with curiosity. Tapping the tips of his fingers together, Kookie suddenly stops, looks at Yakov, points his index finger in the air and exclaims, "That's it! I've got it!"

"What! What have you got! What is it, Kookie?!" everyone suddenly bursts out with great excitement.

"It's Phase 3!" Kookie cries out. "That's how we're going to stop them!"

"*Huh?*" howls everyone.

Kookie takes a deep breath, composes himself, and explains, "Chemicals! That's the ticket! You know, for every action there is an equal and opposite *re*action! With this formula staring us right here in the face, we can play around with it and do all *kinds* of things with those aerosols!"

"Yes but, how do you propose to gain access to it, bro'?" says Yakov, "I mean, how do you expect us to put our own variation of this formula into Lady Bella's baby bottles? Oops! I mean her *aerosol* bottles?" he says with a smirk.

"*Aha!*" hails Kookie with his index finger in the air. "Put yourself in the shoes of Lady Bella and her companions for a moment. If you needed so many gazillion gallons of a chemical formula, enough to wipe out an absolutely massive portion of the population, in a hurry, and by someone who has done much of that sort of the thing in the past, totally complicit with the Council, who would you . . ."

"*MASTER HOWARD!*" they all shout together.

"*WOO HOO! WOOF! WHOA!*" they all exclaim.

Kookie sits back and smiles. Tapping the tips of his fingers together he says, "I rest my case."

Chapter 14 – Farma-ceuticals

LADY BELLA RUSHES TO HER STUDY and closes the door. Sitting down at her terminal with the large monitor in front of her, and no one standing around, she sends out a message to Master Howard.

The message is picked up and accepted by Reggie, whose face appears on her screen. "Who the devil are *you?*" she says abruptly, "and where is Master Howard?"

"Well, hello there! I am Reggie, Master Howard's lab Overseer. I am afraid that he is busy at the moment. Is there something that I can help you with, madam?"

Lady Bella is in no mood for a "nice guy," and she says to him sharply, "You just go on over to Master Howard and tell him that Lady Bella needs to speak to him immediately. You got that?"

"Oh, hello, Lady Bella, darling! I am so sorry that I did not recognize you. My goodness what a lovely Lady you are, indeed!"

That is as much "nice" as she can handle. Lady Bella snaps at him and says, "Look, chicken brain, first of all I do not care if you recognize me or not, I am *not* a *Lovely Lady* as anyone in my service can tell you, and apparently you do not seem to understand what the word *IMMEDIATELY* means! So go and fetch your Master and put him on the screen with me *IMMEDIATELY!* You got that straight?!"

"Oh yes, My Lady, yes indeed!" Reggie says.

He approaches Master Howard's office suite. *Dear me!* Reggie muses, *Master Howard said he was not to be disturbed. Something about an urgent message from Kookie.*

He sighs and knocks on the door. Opening it slowly he says to Master Howard, "My deepest apologies for disturbing you, sir. But Lady Bella is trying to reach you. She sounds like it is most urgent and insists on speaking to you immediately."

Master Howard raises his eyebrows and motions for Reggie to come in. "Come on over here, my good man, and repeat what you just said to Kookie here on the monitor."

"Yes, sir."

Turning to the monitor he says to Kookie, "Hello there, Kookie, I *am* frightfully sorry to interrupt your conversation with Master Howard."

"That's okay, bro', what's up?" says Kookie.

"I just accepted an incoming message from Lady Bella on Master Howard's behalf. She said that she needed to speak with him immediately! So here I am, and there she waits," he says pointing to a flashing button on Master Howard's terminal.

Master Howard and Kookie smile at each other, and Kookie sits back, tapping the tips of his fingers together.

"Well," Kookie says, "This is quite the opportunity Master Howard, wouldn't you say?"

"It sure is, sir!" says Master Howard grinning away. "What would you like me to do with her?"

"I suggest that you speak to our Lady Bella, see what she has to say for herself, and well, you know, leave the line open. After you disconnect with her, we can finish our conversation."

"Sounds like a plan," says Master Howard, who turns to Reggie and says, "Why don't you stand behind the screen, my good man. I would like for you to hear all of this too, but without Lady Bella's knowledge of anyone else's presence."

"Sure thing," says Reggie as he steps behind the screen.

Master Howard then presses a button and Lady Bella appears on the screen. "Well, hello, My Lady Bella. I am told that you wish to speak with me and that it is urgent, yes?"

"Yes," Bella says, "It is urgent. And most profitable for both of us."

"Oh! Well! I do like the sound of *profitable,*" he says with a chuckle. "So how can I help you, My Lady?"

"I need a chemical formula to be processed by you and put into aerosol tanks. I will then need to have them sent here to my Island. It is highly flammable, so you will need to take great care in the processing and shipping. Of course, you will be compensated handsomely, by the usual method.

"And there is one more thing, Master Howard." she pauses for a moment.

"Yes, My Lady, I am listening."

Lady Bella lowers her voice and says in a serious tone, "This is top secret. When you see what the formula is, you are not to breathe a word of this to anyone. Or that word will be your last."

Again, she pauses, and Master Howard is silent, but does not take his eyes off of hers. "And finally, there are to be no questions asked. Do we have an agreement, Master Howard?"

He holds her gaze for a while and says nothing, knowing that Lady Bella will be suspicious of him if he agrees to her terms too easily. Master Howard knows the drill well when dealing with the dark side of the Upper Crust.

Lady Bella finally breaks the silence and the staring contest.

"There are two more things for you to consider, Master Howard. One is that we are aware of your, *dealings* with the Alliance; that is, you appear to have joined forces with them. Do not kid yourself, sir. You belong to *US!* I can make things very hard for you, you know; even dangerous," she says with an evil grin. "Remember who we are. The Lords are the surveillance people."

Then she leans in close to him and continues with a sultry voice and jiggle of her shoulders. "Do you think that your peach cupcake and sugar cookie would be interested in hearing about your, how shall I say, indiscretions? Or does Mistress Henrietta think that she is the only one who gets an after dinner rose from her charging rhinoceros?"

Master Howard glares into Lady Bella's eyes with an anger that is smoldering under the surface. Without batting an eyelash, he says to her, "Don't worry, My Lady, you will have your chemical formula, as fast as we can make it. I shall put you through now to our order department. Just leave all the information with them."

Lady Bella smiles at him and says, "Thank you, Master Howard. It is a pleasure doing business with you."

Kookie is now back on the screen and he says, "I'm sorry, sir. We are dealing with a sociopath in Lady Bella. Cruelty to others is what gives her pleasure."

Master Howard looks down in shame as he says to Kookie, "It was a long time ago, the indiscretion that she is referring to."

"I understand, sir," Kookie says.

Reggie doesn't say a word. Both he and Kookie give Master Howard a moment to recover from the encounter.

Then he looks at Kookie and says, "What do you want me to do, My Lord Kenneth?"

Kookie just smiles gently at him and says, "It's Kookie, sir."

Master Howard manages a trace of a grin as he says, "Thank you, Kookie, my friend."

Reggie smiles at Master Howard and says, "Is there anything you need from me now, sir?"

"Actually, my son and his good woman are planning to go to Judy's farm later today. I have just decided that I would like to go with them; there's something that I need to attend to there. Would you take over here while we are gone? And especially see to it that our new staff members are all settled in and have everything that they need."

"Absolutely, sir. I shall go immediately to Bem, Tafari and Nassor and show them around the lab."

Reggie leaves.

Master Howard turns back to Kookie. "Do you have the plans ready yet for the formula modification?"

"Yakov, Rudolpho and I are working on it now. It is almost ready, and I should have it to you before you leave for Judy's farm." Kookie beams, "I am very much looking forward to hearing all about *your* plans over there, sir!"

"Me too, Kookie." Master Howard says with a smile. "Me too."

The Major and Vi are getting ready for their visit to Judy. They have been discussing plans with her since the Garden Community Conference which Judy attended virtually through the communication device of Master James, the owner of Judy's farm.

Vi already sent out #5 to let Judy know of their imminent arrival.

"Honey, did you send the bird?" says the Major.

"Yes, sweetie, #5 is on his way," she replies.

"Before we leave, I should go and see our new gardeners from Johannesburg. I'm thinking that it might be a good idea to bring one of them with us this afternoon and see if we can work out an arrangement with Judy and Master James about an herb garden. As we discussed at the Garden Community Conference, a garden for growing all kinds of medicinal herbs is greatly needed as an integral part of the garden communities."

"Oh absolutely," Vi agrees. "It will also be great to have one of our herb gardeners with us when we go to Bear River Farm. I received a wonderful bit of news this morning from #1, that is, from Kenny and Lisa," she laughs. "I guess those pigeons kind of grow on you, don't they?"

The Major stops what he is doing and goes over to his honey. Hugging her and kissing her, he says, "Well Violet, you have kind of grown on me too, but I am not going to start calling you #33, or something."

Vi laughs and they smooch a little more. Then she says to him in a sultry voice, "Oh I don't know sweetie pie, maybe calling each other #33 and #34 might be a little fun when the moment is right, along with a little cooing!"

The cooing of #33 and #34, is interrupted by a knock on the door.

The Major calls out, "Whoever it is, #33 and #34 are busy at the moment!"

"What?" comes a familiar voice from the other side of the door.

"Oh! Hey there, dad! Come on in!" says the Major.

"Hi there, John, and Vi," he says walking into their suite. "Don't mean to interrupt you two, but I wanted to talk to you about your trip to Judy's farm."

"Sure thing, dad, what's up?"

"I have been thinking a few things over regarding the farm and would like to go with both of you this afternoon."

"Okay. You know we are also planning on going to see Kenny and Lisa after that. Will you be wanting to join us there as well?" the Major inquires.

"Oh my, yes! What I really want is to have a meeting with Master James *and* Master Franz, so that would be perfect!" Master Howard replies. "Oh, and of course, I would very much like to see Judy, Adam Tate, and all the others there. You know, I haven't actually seen the Chrysalenes in action yet, with their unique kind of gardening, that is."

As an afterthought Master Howard says, "Actually, this involves your mother too, so why don't we see what she is up to and invite her along for the ride."

"Oh, I would really like that," says Vi. "It will give us both a chance to share our ideas and recipes with each other for food, as well as our thoughts on what medicinal herbs to plant for Howard Pharmaceuticals."

With a smile, Vi adds, "If truth be known, I was just knocked out by her chocolate cream pie last night after dinner. I've just *got* to have her recipe!"

Master Howard laughs, "Thanks, Vi! I'll let her know you said that."

In the lab, Reggie is busy showing Bem, Tafari and Nassor around. He is introducing them to the other people there, by all of their first names. Since Master Howard's transformation, he has made a few changes in his company, and dropping the impersonal overseer/servant references to everyone was the first big change he made.

Ever since the day he first learned that the name of his Lab Overseer was Reggie, he became intrigued to discover the names of his other helpers. He also stopped referring to them as servants, and they are most definitely not called slaves anymore. But in light of these changes, and the fact that people in the service of Masters have never in his lifetime been called anything else, he just doesn't know *what* to call them yet in terms of their roles in his company. The words "worker" and "employee" have never been used in their day.

It is one of the things that he wants to talk to Master James and Master Franz about when he sees them. They are apparently in the same quandary, as are so many other members of the New Upper Crust these days.

The Major shows up and greets Reggie and the gardeners, "Hey there! How are all you good men doing today?"

"Just fine, sir! Wonderful to be here! And how are you, sir?" they all chime in.

"Okay," he says. "Say, I was wondering if any of you herbalist-gardeners would care to join us for a few days. My folks, Vi, and I, will be visiting two farms where the owners are wanting to plant medicinal herbs and become suppliers for us. Of course, they don't know much about growing medicinal herbs and will need guidance. We would all appreciate your advice based on your experience with folk medicine, and which herbs we might want to start with."

Bem, Tafari and Nassor have gone wide-eyed with excitement, which makes the Major's question rather ridiculous.

"Judging from the expression on all three of your faces it seems that I wouldn't dare leave any of you behind!"

They all laugh out loud, and the Major continues, "We will be leaving in the next couple of hours if that is enough time for all of you to get ready."

Bem, Tafari and Nassor look eagerly at Reggie, who just puts his hands up in the air and says, "Off you go then! Have a good time, you guys!"

"Great!" says the Major to the herbalists. "Just come on over to our house as soon as you are ready."

The three men scurry off with great excitement and the Major goes back to his sweetie, #34 as they must get packing.

* * *

Lady Bella has just come back into the lab. She cracks her whip on the floor to get everyone's attention. They all bolt upright instantly at the sound of that all too familiar crack.

"I have an announcement to make!" Lady Bella bellows. "I want everyone's absolute attention!"

The room is completely quiet except for the hum of the computers, and the sound of a little panel, sliding open from the side office.

"The chemical compound that we need for the reflectors will be here soon, and today I have a team of servants coming in from the mainland to help with the application of the aerosol. There are 50 Lords and Ladies who have teamed up with us for this project. They are each contributing 100 small Cloudtransporters which will begin arriving here in groups of 100 at a time, as soon as I have received word that the aerosol is on its way.

"We figured it will take about an hour for our servants to spray each group of 100 Cloudtransporters, with the next group hovering, waiting in line. We will be working round the clock, so the whole project of spraying should take no longer than about two days. Once the Cloudtransporters are ready, they will fly to the target areas which I will be assigning to the 50 Lords and Ladies, and hover over them. And when *they* are all in place," she cracks her whip sharply on the floor and screams,

"FIRE!"

A dead quiet is followed by a modest round of applause.

"Thank you!" Lady Bella says to everyone. "I figure the launch will happen in about 72 hours from the moment the aerosols arrive. What I will need from all of you between now and then is help in getting all those Cloudtransporters in and out of here smoothly. Make sure that the landing decks are all clear before one group leaves and the next one arrives. I want speed and efficiency.

"Also, there will be some of you needed to supervise the servants and see to it that they are working with speed and efficiency as well. So, let's stay focused and get ready for Armageddon! *YEEHAA!*"

Lady Bella howls, cracking her whip loud and hard on the stone floor, one more time.

Her Maniacal Highest leaves the lab, and everyone exhales.

In the side office of the lab, Lord Viktor, Lord Pavel, and Lord Igor turn to the other conspirators.

"Seventy-two hours once the chemical compound arrives," says Lady Nita, "How much time does that give *us?*"

The three Lords look at each other, nod, and then look at Nita and the others.

Lord Viktor says, "That should give us about seventy-*one* hours!"

* * *

Kookie has just made all his arrangements with Master Howard, regarding how they are going to switch formulas on Lady Bella without her being any the wiser.

Rudolpho looks at Kookie and the others and asks, "Do you think you can give Lady Bella a modified formula soon before she starts getting suspicious? And even if you do, won't they run it through analytics and see that it is not the exact same formula that they requested?"

"Aha!" says Kookie pointing his index finger in the air. "Let me tell you what I did with the Ebola bioweapon, my friend."

Kookie explains the whole thing to Rudolpho from start to finish, including how the Major was able to use the 369-Program on his Metatron device to show a different result when the bottles of bioweapons were tested.

Rudolpho is fascinated, "Whoa! You mean, you changed the bioweapon to a super-healing DNA restructuring kind of thing, which, instead of killing all the people who took them, turned them into *Chrysalenes?!*"

"Yup!" replies Kookie.

Rudolpho is stunned as he exclaims, "And *NO ONE WAS THE WISER?*... because the 369-Program that the Major zapped the bottles with said they still contained the Ebola bioweapons, when in fact they were genetically modified?!"

"Yup!" Kookie says again, tapping the tips of his fingers together, and grinning from ear to ear.

Rudolpho is absolutely flabbergasted as he shouts out, "Woof!"

Yakov is smiling and he interjects, "That's my bratan!"

Ryan is also hearing the whole story in detail for the first time. And he too is very impressed. "Wow! You guys are something else!"

They all look at him and say, "Thanks!" at the same time.

Rudolpho continues, "So Lady Bella's tech team will analyze the formula that Master Howard is going to send them and they will be convinced that it is the exact same formula that they ordered?"

"That's right," says Kookie.

"What exactly will this modified formula do, and how close are we to having it ready for Howard Pharmaceuticals?" asks Rudolpho.

Kookie and Yakov look at each other and nod. Yakov says, "It will create a kind of backdraft. So, when the laser beam is launched by her evil highest one, hitting all 5000 reflectors hovering over their targets all across One World, instead of the laser beams continuing to their targets and incinerating them, the beams will get sucked right back up to the Cloudtransporters, and **KABOOM!** No more reflectors, no more Cloudtransporters, and we are all safe from her evil Ladyship!"

Ryan thinks about this and says, "Well yes, for the time being, but can't she fire another blast?"

"Theoretically, yes," says Kookie. "Had she not been so ambitious and used 5000 Cloudtransporters. These aircraft are the properties of the Lords and Ladies, and I can tell you that she is using every last one of them for this little firework display of hers. Unless she tries to steal some of ours, there still will be nowhere near that number left in all of One World. Those are all the reserves that there are. She will then have to find the manpower to build more. And it would take her quite some time to accomplish that, if she still has any followers left by then, that is."

Rudolpho adds, "She would also have to get more chemical compound from Howard Pharmaceuticals or go to someone else. I doubt if she could find anyone else to supply her with that."

"So, you mean, we've really got a shot at this?!" Ryan asks with absolute incredulity.

"Yes," says Kookie. "But there is one more thing which Yakov has not mentioned. I will also have to use the 369-Program to work together with the chemicals on the reflectors of the Cloudtransporters. And the only way I can do that is to go back to my mega-computers at Kookie's Kastle. The box I have here by itself is just not powerful enough for this transmission."

Rudolpho's eyes suddenly pop out of his head as he gasps with excitement, "You mean I will get to see Kookie's Kastle? *WHOOOOOA!* That place is a legend! *COOWAL!*"

Everyone chuckles and nods at Rudolpho.

"Okay," says Angie, "So when do we leave?"

"That is something we will have to figure out." says Kookie. "As long as we are here, the self-cloaking and Salamander programs are keeping us protected from their surveillance systems, and we will not arouse any suspicion with Lady Bella and her Council. However, once we board a Cloudtransporter and head back to California, we become more vulnerable to their detection. It is going to be a very close call. We do not want to draw any of Lady Bella's attention and give her the idea that we are on to her. And we sure do not want them to figure out what we are doing. Or it will be all over. . . for all of us.

"No doubt we are one of their 5000 targets, as are all our friends. I would imagine that Lady Bella and the Council have a pretty good idea of who and where we all are by now."

Rudolpho looks at all of them and says, "Yes, Lady Bella does have all of that. But you guys have something that she will never have, and I believe is more powerful than anything else in all of One World."

Liling looks at him sweetly and says, "And what is that, honey?"

He smiles at them all and replies, "Love, loyalty, and trust in each other."

* * *

The 18 conspirators have reconvened their meeting on another part of the Isle of Bella. They are now gathered around a device which they have been listening to for quite some time. They decide to turn it down and just leave it on record, so they can discuss and analyze their findings.

Lord Jonah says to Lord Viktor, Lord Pavel, and Lord Igor, "Well that was probably the smartest thing you guys ever did, leaving a surveillance device on Lady Bi's Cloudtransporter."

"Yes, indeed it was," says Lord Viktor. "We figured the Cloudtransporter would return to her owners eventually."

Lady Nita asks, "But how did you manage to get it to bypass all of Lord Kenneth's cloaking devices?"

"Let's just say it is under the radar of Lord Kenneth's holographic projections. In a manner of speaking, he is projecting from above while we are receiving from below. No pun intended!"

They all have a chuckle.

"Well. However, you guys did it," Lord Jonah says, "Lord Kenneth's plan is a perfect way for us to execute our own."

"Well, not exactly," says Lord Pavel, with a sadness and fear in his voice. "There is another nightmare which Lord Viktor, Lord Igor and I are all dealing with now."

The co-conspirators look at the three Lords with confusion as Lord Jonah asks, "Well, so what is it?"

"Our highest, the sociopath, Lady Bella, is aware of our plans," says Lord Igor.

"Good Heavens!" Lady Nita exclaims, as the others all shudder with fear.

Lord Viktor looks at the floor, and stammers, choking on a lump in his throat, barely able to utter the words, "And she has kidnapped, our families, holding them hostage, as punishment, for our disloyalty."

In shock and dismay, 15 voices shout out in unison, ***"INDEED!!"***

Chapter 15 – Redemption

IT IS EARLY FALL, and the harvest has begun. Judy is thinking about her winter storage and how it will be different this year. The Chrysalenes have been such an enormous help to her, not only with the physical labor and hard work of running a farm, but also of the nurturing and emotional support they have given to her and the other farmhands.

Now that Judy is on the advisory committee of the Garden Alliance of One World, there are other responsibilities that she feels honored to take on. One of them is keeping a registry of the names, places and people of the garden communities that are being established throughout Panamerica.

Lisa and Kenny are sharing that job with her, and they are also keeping a directory of the Intercontinental Pigeons Communication Network for each garden community.

Communication networking is one of the topics that Master Howard wants to discuss with Master James. Those of the new UC who are now part of the Alliance want very much for everyone, the people and the UC, to have their privacy protected from the surveillance of the current system. And one way that the Lords have always been easily able to spy on them has been through all their communication devices.

Considering the bitter experience that Master Howard just had with Lady Bella, he intends to do all he can to allow everyone to have their freedom of privacy.

Judy thinks about how wonderful it will be for everyone to be treated with dignity and respect in a free new world of One Garden where all people, including the UC, care for one another.

As she is thinking about all of this and looking out over the field, she sees a Cloudtransporter coming in for a landing.

"Oh, good heavens! They're here!" Judy exclaims and heads out to the field to meet them.

The portal opens and out steps Master Howard, Mistress Henrietta, the Major, Vi, and their three new herbalists: Bem, Tafari and Nassor. Judy is so excited to see them all that she opens her arms to greet them with a great big hug. The people in this group who Judy knows well are the Major and Vi. The rest are all relatively new to her as she only met them briefly for the first time at the Summit.

"Welcome, everyone! Oh my, what an honor it is to have all of you here! Welcome to the farm!"

"Thank you, Judy," Bem says, who is touched by Judy's warmth and outpouring of love for all of them. He at once feels at home in her presence and bows humbly to her.

Tafari and Nassor do the same, with big smiles and respectful bows.

Master Howard and Mistress Henrietta take Judy by the hand, and Mistress Henreitta says, "Our son has spoken most kindly of you. And although we only met for the first time at the Summit, I feel as though I already know you quite well. It is quite an honor to spend some time here with you and the Chrysalenes and get to know you all better."

"Thank you, ma'am," says Judy graciously.

"The pleasure is all ours, kind lady," Master Howard adds.

Judy is very moved as Henrietta continues, "I must tell you that every time my son returns from a visit with you, he just can't stop raving about your bread! And even though he comes home with two loaves, I have barely gotten a thin slice!"

Everyone chuckles.

"I am seriously looking forward to trying your wonderful baking."

Vi chimes in, "Oh, and don't forget *your* amazing pastries, Mistress Henrietta! Your cookies, cakes and pies are just to die for!"

Henrietta thanks Vi, and she and Judy are both touched. The two women agree to bake up a storm together over the next few days.

They are walking towards the cottage when Adam Tate and some of the other Chrysalenes come out to greet them.

"Hello everybody," says Adam Tate. "May your stay here be filled with healing and love."

"Thank you," says Master Howard, and he suddenly sees something in Adam Tate's eyes. He knows that he must speak to this man right away, so he says to his son, "Uh, John, everyone, please go on ahead without me. I must speak with this man for a little while. Oh, and John, please let Master James know that we are here."

"Sure thing, dad," says the Major, and they all go off to Judy's cottage.

Master Howard turns to Adam Tate and says, "I feel like you came over to tell me something, sir. I see something in your eyes which is from that other place up there. I– I–" Master Howard stumbles through the difficult words, "I know this is going to sound crazy, but I feel like there is some kind of light in your eyes which, um, has a message for me."

Adam Tate lowers his eyes for a moment, and bows humbly before Master Howard saying, "I am here to serve you good sir, in whatever way I can."

Then Adam Tate looks into Master Howard's eyes again and says, "What do you see, Master? What is the Light saying to you?"

Suddenly, Master Howard feels an ache deep within his gut. "The Light is telling me that I am not the Master here, you are."

A sadness overcomes him as he looks off into the distance and sees a little nearby garden plot. It is earth that has been tilled and is ready and waiting for seeds.

"Can we go over there?" Master Howard asks Adam Tate, pointing to the tilled earth. Adam Tate bows, turns around and leads the way.

Master Howard walks onto the freshly tilled earth and stands there looking around. He is instantly aware of the sweet earthy aroma and feels compelled to sit down. "Wow."

He speaks softly to Adam Tate, as if not wanting to disturb the peaceful slumber of nature. "So, this is where the medicinal herbs will grow! In places just like this."

"Yes sir, it is."

Master Howard puts his hands into the dirt and starts running his fingers through it. It feels warm, soft and smooshy, and he begins to feel like a child, enjoying the pleasurable sensation of getting his hands dirty.

Adam Tate decides to sit down too and run his fingers through the good clean dirt.

Master Howard picks up a handful of dirt and smells it. Closing his eyes, he says to Adam Tate, "Ah, this smells wonderful."

Adam Tate does the same and he laughs with delight. Master Howard starts laughing too and grabs another handful, bringing it to his face again. Only this time, he rubs it on his face, with the pleasure of a little boy, and inhales.

They both laugh again when all of a sudden Master Howard's laughter turns to tears. He buries his face in his dirt-covered hands and lets go. Heavy sobs and a flow of tears are mixing with the dirt.

His new Chrysalene friend sits with him quietly, feeling the great sadness that is being released from a broken heart.

Master Howard puts his hands back down in the earth again. This time he stops crying for a moment when he realizes what he has just pulled up from the ground. An earthworm is dangling from his grasp. He begins to laugh and cry at the same time as he looks at the worm and says to Adam Tate, "Now there's a metaphor if ever I saw one!"

"How is that a metaphor, sir?" asks Adam Tate.

"Because that little guy hanging there is me. It is the story of my life. It is what I have done to others, including my wife and my son, and what I have become."

The tears fall fresh and a bit heavier this time. Master Howard starts to put the earthworm back on the ground, but Adam Tate reaches out and gently takes it from him. He says to Master Howard, "Sir, do you know what this little being of nature does?"

Rubbing his eyes with his soiled hands, Master Howard uses the front of his shirt to wipe off the muck and moisture from his face. "No," he replies to Adam Tate. "I was always a chemistry guy, not a biologist."

Adam Tate laughs, "Well then, I shall tell you. This little one eats the earth that you are sitting on. He breaks it up and cleans it, leaving his droppings behind which feed and nourish the plants. He also makes a nice soft bed for the plants so they can grow easily and happily into the healthy fruit that we harvest."

Master Howard has stopped crying and is looking at the little one which Adam Tate is still holding ever so gently in his hands. Putting his hands out underneath Adam Tate's, Master Howard takes back the critter. He picks it up and holds the little guy with his fingers, so the earthworm appears to be looking at him.

Pondering it all for a moment, Master Howard says to the worm, "I guess that means you're going to make some happy, healthy medicinal herbs for Howard Pharmaceuticals."

Smiling at the earthworm and dangling the critters face in front of his own, Master Howard say, "Thanks, buddy." Then he holds the worm in both hands and brings his hands up to his chest.

Closing his eyes and turning his face up to the heavens, Master Howard says, "Maybe even a worm like me can do some good with dirt."

Looking around at the plot of earth he is sitting on Master Howard asks Adam Tate, "Do you suppose I could use this space right here to create my own garden for something?"

"I am sure that can be arranged," says Adam Tate, happily. "And I should be most honored to help you in whatever way I can with your garden."

Master Howard puts the earthworm back on the soil and then claps his hands together. "It's a deal!" he says and puts his hand out to shake hands with Adam Tate. "Well, I suppose I had better get over to the cottage before they all come out and start looking for me. By the way, thank you my friend. Thank you for listening to my blubbering. Would you care to join us in the cottage?"

"I would be delighted to, thank you sir!" smiles Adam Tate. "Let me show you where it is."

The two men head towards Judy's cottage.

* * *

It is late at night in the Mediterranean and Lady Bella cannot settle down to sleep. She is lying in bed staring at the ceiling, anxious to know what is happening in California. She decides to message Master Howard and see how the progress is going.

When he sees who the incoming message request is from, Master Howard forwards it to Reggie back at the plant, as per their arrangement before he left. Reggie accepts the forwarded incoming message on his device and Lady Bella appears on his screen.

"You again!" she snips. "Where is Master Howard? I want to speak to him right away! Where is he?"

"Oh, I AM sorry, your Ladyship. Master Howard is gone for the day, attending to business elsewhere. He has left me in charge though if I can be of some assistance to you."

"*You?*" she sputters. "Fine! So what is happening with my chemicals? Is my formula ready yet? Overseer?!"

"Just about, My Lady. We are adding the last ingredient and expect to have the whole lot of it shipped out to you by some time tomorrow."

That news puts Lady Bella's temper to rest, for the time being. "Good! You just let me know as soon as it's on the way."

"Will do, Lady Bella," Reggie says, as she terminates the transmission.

Reggie immediately messages Master Howard who accepts it and appears on the screen. "Well then, Reggie my man, how did everything go with her Lovely, Ladyship?"

Reggie begins to speak except he is a bit awestruck and hesitant when he sees Master Howards face. "Uh, sir . . . I, uh, that is to say . . ."

"Well, Reggie, what did Lady Charmer have to say for her sweet self, then?"

Master Howard and Adam Tate have just reached Judy's cottage. He is talking to Reggie and about to open the door at the same time.

"Uh, sir, are you, um, quite all right?" Reggie inquires just as gently as he can.

"Well of course I am Reggie. Whatever gave you the idea that–" and at that moment Master Howard steps through the door. Everyone stops abruptly and stares at him.

Mistress Henrietta is walking in from the kitchen holding a tray of cookies which almost end up on the floor when she sees her husband. "Howard?" she says, in a dubious tone.

Then, all eyes turn to Adam Tate who is just smiling away, happy as a clam. He explains to all the gawking eyes in the room, "Master Howard has been making plans for a garden of his own out in the field. I have offered to help, and we are both very excited about it!"

"That's right! I'm *very* excited about it!" crows Master Howard with a big toothy grin, the only recognizable part of his features. His head, hair, hands, and shirt are all covered with grime, muck, dirt and mud.

The Major finally says to him, "I see! So, was it your *head* that you were trying to plant then, Dad?"

Everyone busts out laughing, including Reggie who has heard the whole conversation.

"Actually, with your permission, Judy, I would like very much to plant a rose garden here at your up-and-coming garden community and call it Henrietta's Rose Garden, if that is alright with you, ma'am."

"Aww!"

Everyone sighs, and Mistress Henrietta is overcome with joy.

"Of course, it's all right Master Howard. That is so sweet of you!" says Judy.

"Thank you, Howard my darling." Henrietta says, sniffling.

"Well, perhaps I should go get washed up and changed, so I will be fit to join you all for cookies. Be right back, my sugar plum!"

Master Howard is escorted by Adam Tate to the guest lodgings next door, while finishing his conversation with Reggie about Lady Bella.

"Did you get the goods from Kookie?" he asks Reggie.

"I just spoke to him a little while ago sir, and he said they are just about ready to send us the formula!"

"Excellent! Excellent! Let me know if you need me for anything else, Reggie."

"Will do. Oh, and sir?"

"Yes?"

"*DO* have fun with that garden for your lovely wife!" Reggie smiles.

"Thank you, my man! I shall!"

* * *

Today at Lord Emeka's estate, the Trader's Market is getting underway, as well as at many other locations throughout One World. More and more, the people and the UC have been turning to the new ways of the Alliance since the disappearance of PA, ES and SPA.

My Buddy transmissions have been stopped for quite some time now. And without fear dominating everyone's lives anymore, the people and the UC have been learning how easy it is to truly get along with one another, and how much better it feels to live with mutual trust. Support for the Alliance among the UC has been continuing to grow everywhere in all three Continental Territories. . . everywhere, that is except on the Isle of Bella.

Only a handful of folks know what is going on there, and what is about to happen. Kookie does not think it is a good idea to let too many people in on the whole truth of her Ladyship and the Council's plan. "For one thing," Kookie keeps telling those closest to him, "Who would believe it?"

So, while the usual plans are underway for the Trader's Market, Kookie and his companions are preparing to leave for Kookie's Kastle, at a moment's notice, hopefully staying under Lady Bella's radar. He knows that once the chemical compound leaves Howard Pharmaceuticals, it will be about 72 hours before Lady Bella hits her switch in the lab, on her island. He has got to get Metatron all connected to the super computers at his Kastle and ready to go, at the moment Bella fires her laser weapon.

The timing must be perfect for Kookie to set off the backdraft effect, destroying the 5000 reflectors before he and all the other targets are destroyed.

With Rudolpho's help in analyzing all the data of Project Laser Beam, as well as the strategic way of thinking of Lord Viktor and his people, Kookie, Yakov and Liling have figured that the best time to leave for California will be sometime after the Market is finished, and Lady Bella has received her shipment from Howard Pharmaceuticals. They know that she will be very distracted at that point, and they will have a much better chance of heading out to California undetected.

The group who will be joining Kookie and Angie at his Kastle are Yakov, Liling, Rudolpho, Ryan, Neely, Dumaka, Mimi, Eve Elli, Emeka, Phil and Doc. He has sent a coded message to the Major and Vi, asking them to be there as well. Kookie's guts are telling him that he is going to really need all the help he can get from his trusted friends, with their technological and intuitive gifts, at the showdown with Lady Bella and the Council.

He *MUST* hit the switch on his supercomputer at the exact moment *before* Lady Bella hits hers, or the 5000 reflectors will incinerate all 5000 targets.

Ryan has already prepared their companions at the Village of the Holy Ones as to what is about to happen, so that the group over there can be at the Big House and leave as soon as the time is right.

When Ryan initially asked them if they wanted to go, Mimi said, "There is no chain strong enough to hold me down and *stop* me from coming along."

The others all agreed that Mimi's sentiments reflected those of the entire group. So, they are now already on their way to the festivities of the Trader's Market. Lady Liling is especially grateful when she sees them coming, since it is not easy for her to keep up the pretense with all the folks at the Market that all is well, and it is business as usual.

There isn't too much left for the rest of them to do now, except wait it out until they hear from Howard Pharmaceuticals.

Kookie goes over to the big window in the study which overlooks the festivities of the back field and the Trader's Market. He remembers the very first one that they had there in the middle of the summer, and how it was on that same day, in their bedroom that his beloved Angie was taken from him. He is also thinking about what he recently learned, that he was originally created as one of the three children of the devil.

But the Father in Heaven took pity on them and restructured their DNA to be one of *His* own, instead.

He ruminates over all the things he had to do under the command of the Council, and how ashamed he still is of those things. In his heart, Kookie has never really been able to forgive himself for the constant surveillance of people's private lives, and occasional emotional blackmail he was ordered to do, such as that which he recently witnessed Master Howard go through at the hands of Lady Bella.

As he is watching the people in the Market below enjoying themselves and their new life of freedom, watching it grow stronger every day, he knows that it can be all over for them, sometime in the next 72 hours or so. It is breaking his heart to think their lives might end up at the mercy of a ruthless sociopath. And he knows that he will do *whatever* he must, to prevent that from ever happening.

Kookie hangs his head in sadness, not knowing if he himself has the courage and strength to do what he knows he might *have* to do once he gets back to his Kastle. It is one thing he has not told anyone, not even Angie. He knows that he might not succeed in connecting the two super computers with Metatron and the program for Lady Bella's launch. That is, he might not be able to hack into her highly secured program.

If that happens, there is one more way that he knows will work, although a desperate one at that. He can open the panels on the consoles of each computer and join them, by placing his hands directly into the open wires of the electronic circuits. The connection will be made, although it will physically lock him into both computers . . . and electrocute him.

Kookie knows that he *must* do this, should it become necessary, for all the people of One World. He prays that Angie will understand that he could not tell her about any of it and hopes that one day she will forgive him.

At that moment, his beloved comes into the study. As usual, she is wearing #3 and #4 around her neck, and as usual, they are looking totally blissful.

"Hi there, sweetie!" Angie comes over to Kookie and joins him at the window. Putting her arm around his waist, the two of them look at the Trader's Market going on below. "I'm so proud of you honey, for all you have done. You do know of course that it is largely *your* efforts and yours alone that got us all to this point so far. And I just know that everything will work out with the program and Metatron once we get back to your Kastle."

Kookie says nothing but leans into his Woman with a heavy heart. He is trying desperately to keep his secret from her that there is a very good chance he will have to make a human torch out of himself in order to make everything work.

At last, he looks at her, and with his hand brushes her hair, and #4, aside and says, "You look so pretty today, my love. You know what I think I would like to do right now?"

"No, my darling, what is it?" she says smiling up at him.

Kookie takes out his tuba mouthpiece and says, "When was the last time I played the Tuba Concerto in F Minor for you?"

Angie starts to laugh and says, "Oh, Kookie! You silly, wonderful man! I love you so much!"

Chapter 16 – Double-Cross

"REGGIE!" A VOICE CALLS from the shipping department of Howard Pharmaceuticals.

"Yes! I'm coming!" Reggie comes running down the hallway from his office in the lab to the shipping department. "Are the canisters ready, Tony?"

"All ready to go, sir!" says Tony.

"Fantastic! Great! Are they in the Cloudshipping container yet?"

"Not yet. They are ready for your inspection as you requested, sir, prior to loading them into the container."

"Yes! Thank you, Tony. Let's see those canisters and I will do a quality control check."

"Right over there," says Tony.

Reggie goes over to the two large aerosol canisters containing the chemical compound for Lady Bella. He takes out his Inventory Quality Control Device and proceeds to test them as per Kookie's instructions. Sure enough, the Inventory Quality Control Device is registering exactly what Lady Bella ordered, although the canisters are, in fact, loaded with the modified version of her formula that Kookie gave him.

Reggie is impressed, *Wow! That guy is an absolute genius!*

"Everything checks out Tony. Looking great! You can go ahead and pack these two puppies and send them off to the Mediterranean. I shall go message the customer immediately and let her know that her order is on its way."

Before he messages Lady Bella, though, he messages Master Howard first to give him the good news and to receive any last-minute instructions from him.

Master Howard accepts his message and appears on the screen. "Reggie, my man! What's the good word?"

Master Howard is all mucky again, speaking from his little future garden.

"I can see you're at it again, sir. Enjoying your garden then, are you?"

"Why Reggie, if I knew this was gonna be so much fun, I'd have done this sort of thing years ago. Why I'm just a happier than a pig in poo!"

"Yes, so it seems, sir." Reggie chuckles. "Well, I just wanted to let you know that Lady Bella's order is all packed up and ready to go. And it passed the test using the Inventory Quality Control Device with flying colors!"

"Fantastic Reggie! Wonderful to hear that! Well, let's get that thing off to Her Lady Loveliness and be done with it then, shall we?" says Master Howard.

"Will do, sir. Did you have any further instructions for me? "

Master Howard's tone changes and become more subdued. "Yes Reggie, I do. I believe you have a Woman, is that right?"

"Yes sir."

"Well, why don't you and your Woman take a little time off and come on over here for the next few days. I sure would like to have your company."

Reggie is puzzled by this suggestion. "Is everything all right, sir?" he asks.

Master Howard says to him in a casual yet subdued tone, "Maybe." There is a pause and then he continues, "I'll send the Cloudtransporter to pick you and your lady up, if you like."

"Thank you, Master Howard, sir. I shall check with Ellen, but I think it will be alright with her."

"Fine. Just let me know and I will send the Cloudtransporter to pick you both up as soon as you all are ready. You can leave Tony in charge. Oh, and just one more thing Reggie."

"Yes, Master."

"Please call me Howard."

"Sure thing," Reggie smiles. The transmission fades and so does Reggie's smile.

"Okay," he says to himself out loud. "What the bloody hell is going on here?"

* * *

It is 4 o'clock in the morning in the Mediterranean and everyone is fast asleep on the Isle of Bella. Lady Bella has her Lord's Communication Device right next to her and set to a loud volume, so she will jump right out of bed as soon as she gets the message that her shipment from Howard Pharmaceuticals is on its way.

The device begins to blast, and half asleep, Bella lunges for it. She barely manages to get one eye open and sees Reggie's face on the screen.

"Your shipment has just left our plant My Lady and should be there in about three hours." Reggie says.

"Yes. Right. Three hours. Thanks."

Transmission is terminated.

Lady Bella lays there for a few minutes allowing her body to wake up along with her brain.

"THREE HOURS! HOLY CRUD!"

In no time at all she is up, dressed, and charging down the hallway to Lord Pavel's suite. She starts pounding on his door and in less than a minute he opens it.

"Three hours Pavel! That's what we've got! Help me get everybody up and ready. I want all hands on deck, ready and waiting when that shipment arrives." Holding up her communication device she shows him the time. "I am setting the timer for 72 hours. Then we light up the skies all around One World, with a blast of fire, like it has never seen!"

And with the crazed look of a wild animal in her eyes she adds, "And all that will remain of the Alliance will be a few poor, pitiful little gardens! *HA!* Now snap to it Pavel!"

"Yes, My Lady."

Bella is about to take off and go rouse the others when she remembers something else.

"Oh, and Pavel, dear . . ."

"Yes, My Lady?

"Don't even *think* about being a naughty boy. You know what I finally did to the three of you after I caught you all being, *very, very, naughty!*"

Lord Pavel notices that she has started pulling on the whip that she has hanging around her neck. He looks down at the ground frightened and starts trembling.

In one deft move, Bella takes the whip off her neck and throws it around his, still pulling on it. "Well now, I don't think any of you would really want me to start sending little bitty pieces, of your loved ones, in little bitty boxes to you. Now, do you? Pavel, my dear? After all, they *are* rather comfortable in captivity from what my faithful AI captors are telling me."

Bella twists the whip just a little tighter around Pavel's neck as she continues, "You really don't want to spoil their comfort now do you? You know, like if I have the AI's send you a finger here, and a toe there."

She tightens the whip a little bit more. "I didn't hear you, Pavel."

He is sweating and shaking as he replies, "No, My Lady Bella, I sure don't want that."

Smiling and relaxing her grip, she says to him, "There's a good boy. Now you run along and pass that message on to Viktor and Igor, and let's get everything rolling."

As she says that, she gives a hard and sudden yank on the whip, so it comes flying off his neck and cracks loud on the floor.

Lord Pavel's knees are about to give way underneath him, when Lady Bella says, "Now, now Pavel, I didn't even break any skin. I can be *such* a softy when I want to be, you know."

Patting him on the head like a dog, Bella finishes her threat with, "There's a good Pavel." Her Ladyship smiles again and chuckles, "Now go get dressed and be off with you."

* * *

Kookie and Angie are fast asleep when the Metatron device starts beeping. The golden pyramid on the screen is rotating slowly indicating an incoming message from Howard Pharmaceuticals. Kookie accepts the message and Reggie appears on the screen.

With his eyes half open and Angie beginning to stir, Kookie yawns and says, "What's the good word, bro'?"

"Good morning, sir, sorry to disturb you at this hour over there. Just wanted to let you know that I spoke to Lady Bella only moments ago to let her know that the aerosols have just left Howard Pharmaceuticals and should be arriving at her Island in about three hours."

"Thank you, Reggie. Thanks for letting me know right away." He pauses for a moment and says, "So what are *your* plans for the next few days?"

Reggie's *red-flag-detecting-"what-the-bloody-hell," poop-ometer* goes up as he eyeballs Kookie and says, "As a matter of fact, sir, Master Howard invited me and the Woman to join him at Judy's farm. He even suggested that we leave here as soon as possible."

Kookie smiles at him in his semi-slumber state and simply says, "Good. I'm glad to hear that."

Reggie's poop-ometer is now going through the roof. "Um, My Lord . . . sir, pardon me for asking, but *WHAT THE BLOODY HELL IS GOING ON?!*"

Kookie just continues smiling at Reggie. "I'm sure Master Howard will tell you all you need to know. Thanks for everything, my good man."

And with that Kookie terminates the transmission.

He rolls over in bed and sees Angie, laying there wide awake, staring at him.

"Hi." Kookie says, softly.

"Hi." Angie says, softly, still staring.

They look into each other's eyes for a few moments and Angie finally says to her beloved, "My darling, my sweetheart, my one and only, the one for whom I went to hell and back. To quote the good man you just spoke to, *what the bloody hell is going on?*"

Kookie chuckles for a moment and then turns somber. He looks at his Woman and tenderly says to her, "Angie, I love you so much. Please, just trust me."

He takes her by the hand, as they continue to look at each other, in the predawn hours of the gloomy morning.

She touches his face and remains quiet.

* * *

Lord Pavel has rounded up everyone, and Lord Viktor has the lab up and running. Lord Igor has been assigned to supervise the servants spraying the reflectors, and Pavel is overseeing the overhead "traffic" as 100 Cloudtransporters at a time will begin to arrive shortly. The far end of the island has been cleared for Phase 4; the completion of the reflectors. A landing field has been prepared for the landing, spraying and taking off of 5000 Cloudtransporters in total.

If all goes smoothly, they should have all 5000 of them in and out of there and sent to their target areas right on schedule.

Each of the Lords and Ladies who have donated their Cloudtransporters will be arriving with them and staying on the Isle of Bella to see the so-called "fireworks" when the "show" is launched.

In the lab, Lord Viktor has most of the team working on all the last-minute preparations, right up until the moment when Lady Bella fires her deadly beam of light. A few folks in the lab however are working on something else. They have been working covertly over the past few days on trying to discover the location of Lady Bella's secret hideout, where she has the loved ones of Lord Viktor, Lord Pavel, and Lord Igor held captive. They have been making good progress so far with Lord Viktor's advanced surveillance tools.

It is not only Kookie's detection which Viktor has been able to avoid, but this time, he has also managed to stay under Bella's radar.

Lord Viktor goes over to one of his techies and says nervously, "How's everything going?"

"Fine sir, just fine." Smiling at Lord Viktor, trying to ease the Lord's fear and anxiety a bit, the techie continues, "We will find them, My Lord. We will find them in time."

"Thank you, Techie," Viktor says trying not to show the panic attack that is consuming him. "My son Ivan is only 2 years old."

"We do have a lock on their general location now," the techie continues. "They are somewhere on the coast of Benghazi. We believe they are in some kind of cove, on a beach that is not populated. That is why we are having a hard time getting a fix on an exact location. But as soon as any one of them comes out of hiding, even for a few moments if any of them can, our scanners, which are going up and down the coast day and night, will catch the movement of the DNA match instantly. Then we will have a pinpoint lock on them."

"Thank you, Techie. Thank you." Viktor says, trying to breathe, hanging onto the techie's every word, with hope.

Viktor catches Lady Nita's eye and points with caution to the back office. When they both get in there, he bolts the door and asks her, "Did you secure a large yacht for us, My Lady?"

"Yes, Lord Viktor. Do not worry about that. At 72 minus one hour, it will be there ready and waiting for all of us."

She looks into his fearful eyes and smiles, saying, "Your wife and little Ivan will be just fine.

* * *

In a few more hours, Lady Bella will receive her shipment, so early in the morning, Kookie has rounded up his group for California. He is figuring that Lady Bella is already frantic and distracted, so they can leave whenever he is ready. And the only thing left for him to do now is hack into the surveillance system of Lord Viktor so that they can follow the Council's every move.

Yakov has calculated that once Lady Bella has fired her beam of light, it will only take 0.133 seconds for all 5000 targets to incinerate. So, for Kookie to create a backdraft, that doesn't give him much wiggle room on his timing! And then there is the final challenge of hooking up Metatron and the 369-Backdraft Program to Kookie's super computers at his Kastle and to Lady Bella's computer and launch sequencing code so that they can all be in sync with each other.

Kookie is mulling all of this over, when suddenly, he, Yakov and Rudolpho see something at the same time. . . a tiny red flash on their screen (Kookie's favorite kind).

They all look at each other, somewhat baffled, as Rudolpho asks the question. "Um . . . hey guys, did someone just open a back door and let us into their surveillance system over there?"

Kookie and Yakov are thunderstruck. *"YUP!"*

None of them realize that they are hearing the desperate cry of a man saying, *Help me save my wife, my unborn child, and my son, and I will help you.*

In a moment of desperation, courage, and defiance against Lady Bella, Lord Viktor has just opened the back door of his surveillance system, to the Alliance.

At once, Kookie announces to Yakov and Rudolpho, "We're in! That's it! Let's go!"

The three of them jump up and start howling at everyone. *"We go! Now! Everyone! Packed! Angie! Birds! Liling! Dumaka! Ryan! Mimi! Eve Elli! Emeka! Phil! Doc! Now!"*

They all start heading for the Cloudtransporter and begin boarding right away, with Kookie and Angie not very far behind them.

When Kookie sees what Angie is carrying as she runs out of the house on their way to Armageddon, he is deeply touched. The one thing that his darling Angie will not leave behind, is his tuba.

* * *

The Cloudtransporter from Johannesburg is coming in for a landing at Kookie's Kastle. Kookie has already informed his staff of their imminent arrival, so his house is prepared to receive them. However, weighing more heavily on his mind is the well-being of his house staff, and friends, when Bella strikes. So, he has also asked his staff to prepare the underground shelter at the Kabin.

One of the gardeners, Molly, looks up when she sees them coming. Calling out to anyone within earshot Molly says, "Look everybody! Lord Kookie is back! He's back! He's back!" and several of the house staff go out to greet them.

The Major and Vi are also there, waiting to welcome Kookie and his troops.

The portal of the Cloudtransporter opens and out steps a bedraggled crew. The Major and Vi, along with Molly and staff, go rushing over to Kookie and company to help them, as they are dragging their things, and themselves over to the Kastle entrance.

"Oh, here!" says Molly, "Please let us help you with that," as they offer to take everyone's belongings and carry them into the Kastle.

"Thank you, Molly," says Kookie. "And thank you everybody. It sure is good to see you all again."

"It's so good to see you too!" Molly, and some of the others chime in. But the house staff, who have no idea what is going on, can tell that something is very wrong with Kookie, Angie, and the rest of them. However, Eve Elli and Lord Emeka are just fine.

As they all go inside the house, Kookie asks his staff to help the guests get situated in their bedrooms, and then come right back with all his friends and meet him in the den.

Angie is the only one left standing there with Kookie, and she is still holding his tuba. "You can put that thing down now, if you want to, honey," he says.

Angie sits down on the floor with the tuba sitting next to her. "Well, hi there!" she says. "That is the first thing you've said to me since we left Johannesburg."

Kookie just looks down at the floor and then sits down next to Angie. He reaches his hand out to hers and she takes his hand in both of hers. Angie moves in just a little bit closer to him and puts her head down on his shoulder. She finds the spot on the carpet that he is staring at and begins to stare at it with him. The others are trickling back in quietly. They see Kookie and Angie sitting together, holding each other on the floor, staring at the carpet, in silence.

The group quietly forms a circle around them, and Liling gestures with her hands that they should all sit down. The friends join hands around the ring, surrounding Kookie and Angie, giving them the peaceful, loving energy that they need; that they *all* will need very soon. The house staff are also gathered around and one by one, they too join in, holding hands and sitting in silence.

At last, Kookie looks up and smiles. "Well," he says, "I guess there's no need to move to the den. Seeing as we are all gathered, we may as well just have a chat right here."

They all look around at each other not knowing what is coming next. Then Kookie begins. "My friends, that is, *all* of you sitting here; we are facing a dangerous situation right now. As some of you already know, there is an evil force which has taken over the Council. We have come back here now because we are doing all we can to stop them, and, for that, I need the supercomputers in my workstation.

"I am confident that this is going to work, because, as my darling Angie here has told us, 'With Love all things are possible.' I cannot go into any details with you other than to say this may all be over within the next few days, one way or the other. I am, therefore, asking for everyone's complete cooperation, to trust me and just follow my guidance."

Although they are fidgeting with anxiety and uncertainty about what is going on, they respond, "Sure thing, Kookie. Yes, My Lord. We'll do whatever we can to help."

"Thank you. At any time now you will be seeing a Cloudtransporter hovering high up in the sky. There will be a shiny reflector attached to the bottom of it. I advise you not to look at it for very long when you see it, and especially do not look at it in two or three days from now."

The house staff look around rather bewildered. The others have a pretty good idea of what is coming.

"I am also asking that the house staff, as of right now, pack up enough things to take with you for a few days and go to my Kabin in the woods. For those of you who know where the Kabin is, please show the others the way. You should all be very comfortable there and have everything that you need. In 48 hours from now, I want you all to take some provisions, go down into the shelter. . . and," Kookie shrugs his shoulders and smiles, as he finishes his instructions, "just stay there for a while."

Now the staff is getting more worried, and Molly begins to weep. Kookie notices her and says, "It's okay, Molly, and everybody. You will all be just fine at the Kabin. Please do not ask me any questions at this time, just get packed and go. Oh, and by the way, I love you all. Thank you for your loyal service and your friendship."

They all look at each other, worried and a bit frightened now, as they say, "Yes My Lord," and get up and leave.

Kookie looks at everyone else sitting there in front of him and with a heavy sigh he says, "Well folks, it's time for us to get to work."

"Just one thing," Yakov says, "I'm sorry to interrupt you, bratan, but, well, are you sure you're telling us. . . you know. . . *everything?*"

Liling looks at him with the same look on her face as Yakov, and Kookie looks at them both. He gives them the same old raised eyebrow stare that their big Brother has given them their whole lives, which basically says to them, *don't ask questions, just get to work.*

Yakov and Liling look at each other, put their hands up in surrender mode, get up, and head for the workstation. Kookie and Angie do the same, and the others all follow.

Angie is still clutching the tuba tightly against her, and Kookie says to her once more, "Honey, you really can put that thing down, you know."

Angie gives him the same raised eyebrow stare that he just gave Yakov and Liling. He looks at her, smiles brighter than he has in days, lets out a chuckle, and says, "Okay, Miss Kookie! I will get to work!"

Once inside his workstation, Kookie is truly at home and begins to relax a bit more. He says to everyone, "Okay folks, listen up. There are two things we have got to get done here and not much time left to do it. What I am going to do is set you guys up into three basic groups, although that is not hard and fast. Once you see what is going on, you may go back and forth from one group to the other, wherever you feel that you are most needed at the moment. Are you all with me so far?"

"Yes, Kookie!" they all nod.

"Good. I am asking you to divide yourselves up into techies, intuitives and caregivers. The techies will be helping me out with the computers, the intuitives will be tuning in to the mental activities of Bella and her cohorts, in other words, remote viewing, and the third group is probably the most important of all; to see to it that every one of us is fed and watered. And if the caregivers see any one of us starting to show signs of exhaustion, *do* order us to lie down and take a rest!"

Everyone smiles, and they all start to organize themselves.

* * *

Things are moving at a rapid pace on the Isle of Bella. Lady Bella had originally allowed for one hour a piece to spray every group of 100 Cloudtransporter reflectors, but things are moving even faster than she had hoped. In fact, she now predicts that the laser beam will be ready for launch in another 24 hours, or so. Lord Viktor gets wind of this, and he makes sure that all the information is recording and someone is listening in on the back channel.

At one point, Viktor looks up and says very quietly, "If there is a Loving Creator up above, please let Kookie hear this. Please let him know that he has much less time than he thought to get everything all hooked up and working.

"Please, Loving Creator, if you do exist, take care of my boy, somewhere on a beach cove in Benghazi, and my wife who is due with our next child very soon. If there is anyone listening, please help my family."

Viktor hears voices coming down the hallway. He goes quiet and looks at his computer, pretending to be at work. It is Lady Bella taking the visiting Lords and Ladies for a brief tour; and he notices that she is not wearing her whip around her neck today.

"Well, my dearest Lords and Ladies," says Bella, all bright and cheerful. "This is the room where it will all happen, and in only about 24 hours from now, thanks to the efficiency of our most excellent servants. In fact, there is our very own Lord Viktor over there by that very busy, *very* large computer!" she chuckles. "He is our most faithful Lord to the cause of keeping the UC and One World just exactly as it has always been!" she chuckles again, and this time gives Lord Viktor a sideways glare, which no one else can see.

"Please, Loving Creator," Viktor whispers, as Lady Bella goes to the other end of the lab with her visitors. "Please let Kookie hear this. Please help me."

In the workstation at Kookie's Kastle, while Kookie, Yakov, Liling, Ryan and a few others are frantically putting the pieces together to get ready for their counter offense to Lady Bella's launch, Rudolpho has been listening in on the back channel. He hears the shrill boasting of that voice which tormented him every day while he was in the service of her highest.

He hears her saying, 'about 24 hours from now,' and he shouts *"EGADS!"*

Everyone stops what they are doing and looks at him. Rudolpho plays back the recording of Lady Bella in the lab and suddenly they all realize that they have much less time than they thought.

A quiet voice inside Kookie's head whispers to him to turn back the recording in the lab just a little bit further. As he does so, he hears the frightened plea of Lord Viktor. Closing his eyes, Kookie feels the terrible fear and panic of Viktor's situation and suddenly understands what is going on over there.

He looks up to the heavens and says in his heart, *Lord, we truly are One World and one people, and we all need you in this hour. Please protect Lord Viktor's family, wherever they are, and please reunite them, all safe and sound.*

***

Upon hearing the news through the back channel that there is only about 24 hours to go, Kookie now knows that he will have to be prepared for plan B. He calls over the only two men in the room whom he can trust right now with the secret that he has been holding out on everyone. Kookie calls for Yakov and the Major to come over to him.

"Let's go out on the veranda," he says to the two of them, sneaking out of the workstation while the others are all busy.

Kookie leads them through the suite where Angie stayed when he first brought her to the Kastle in what now seems to him like ages ago; where he first played his tuba for her and where they first fell in love. They go outside on, what was, her veranda at the time, and he sits down with them on the patio chairs. With his heart sinking to the ground, Kookie knows what he must say to these two men, and it will not be easy for any of them.

He says to Yakov and the Major, "We all heard the recording just now."

They both nod.

"My Brothers, I just don't know if we will be able to hook up to Lady Bella's launch system."

They both furrow their brow at him.

"So, what are you saying, bro'?" the Major says, and Yakov nods.

"I am saying that there *is* a way that this still can be done. And I am asking you, *pleading* with you both, to help me carry it out."

They just look at him very worried . . . and concerned.

"You remember how we always said that we would give our lives for the people of One World, should that ever become necessary?"

They nod, but they don't like what they are hearing.

"I believe that tomorrow, that day will come for me. Please do not ask me any questions about it right now, my Brothers, but when the time comes, *EVERYONE MUST EVACUATE THE KASTLE!* Everyone is to go to the underground shelter in the Kabin. Everyone, that is, except me."

Now Yakov and the Major are becoming agitated.

"Before I ask what it is that I need from you," Kookie says, as calmly as he can, "I must tell you something else that is very important."

Yakov and the Major are trying not to show their growing anxiety, as Kookie continues. "Do you both remember when I presented the crate of historical books at the Summit festival, and said that there were lots more, I just couldn't carry them all?"

The mood lightens for a moment as Yakov and the Major nod and smile.

"Well, when I confiscated those books years ago, I had them brought to my Kabin. They are all sitting there in an underground vault, and that is why I have been so guarded about the Kabin over the years, keeping its existence a secret from most people. There were many books which the Council confiscated, because they considered them to be a threat to their very existence. This includes a few copies of a book which is now in my underground Kabin vault that opens with a story about a garden. It is the very garden which we have been talking about recreating, and I really think people will like that book."

Yakov and the Major are thoroughly intrigued to hear all this.

"I just wanted to let you know that the vault is down there, and I am giving you both guardianship over its contents. When the time is right, you will both know when it is safe to give all those books back to the people."

The two men are worried again, as they feel a sense a foreboding in what is about to come next.

In a sadder tone, Kookie says to his best friends in the world: "Now here's the hard part, which I am asking you both to do, no matter what, and no matter how much you do not want to do this, and no matter how hard it will be. I am begging you both to find the strength and courage within yourselves to take my beloved Angie, who I am sure will be kicking and screaming, and will want to stay here with me, and carry her out of the Kastle, by force if necessary. I am asking you then to get yourselves to safety along with everyone else at my Kabin shelter. I will stay here by myself and do what I must do. Please, my Brothers, please, promise that you will both do this for me."

Yakov and the Major are stunned, and their hearts have sunk completely to the ground. With no questions asked, and a love that surpasses all understanding, they make a solemn vow to Kookie.

Chapter 17 – Fire

IN THE BOWELS OF HELL, the dark lord is watching his Lady prepare for the big light. He must speak to her, be with her, go to her. This very night he comes to her in a dream:

"Bella! Bella! My beautiful Bride-to-be! You promised yourself to me if I were to give you magnificent firepower. I shall not disappoint you, My Lady! Your blast will also be MY blast! I am Lucifer. And together, you and I will light up the world!"

Bella reminds him, "What about that big whip you promised me, Lucifer? Did you not promise me that I would go on whipping you for all of eternity, my bridegroom?"

"Oh yes, my sprightly fallen one, truly, yes! You will have unbounded pleasure with me . . . as I shall have with you, my dear! We wait but a little bit longer, My Lady, a little bit longer."

Bella wakes up with passion for her bridegroom flowing through her veins. She is overwhelmed with the anticipation of great pleasure that he has promised her, and is only slightly hesitant over his words, '*We wait but a little bit longer.*'

She reassures herself that *time is all relative, and to an immortal like Lucifer, "a little bit longer" could mean a hundred years or so.*

She shakes off the discomfort of those words and looks forward instead to the very exciting day before her. Lady Bella jumps out of bed and goes straight down to the airfield where the last leg of Project Laser Beam is underway.

The Cloudtransporters are almost all in place now, hovering over their targets. In another eight hours the laser will be ready to fire. The servants have been working round the clock to get the chemical compound sprayed onto the reflectors, and the Lords and Ladies have been transporting them remotely to their targeted areas. Lady Bella has been hobnobbing with the arriving Lords and Ladies, telling them that once this is all over and the Alliance has been crushed, things will be even better than they have ever been.

She is using the servants as an example of just how hard "the slaves" will work for them if enough pressure is applied. Lady Bella says jokingly to her guests, "I will be happy to teach every one of you how to apply pressure to people, exert your influence and use your power. You just have to show the world who is boss; yes indeed!"

They all laugh and applaud her.

But not everyone on the Isle of Bella is laughing and applauding her Ladyship.

Lord Viktor, Lord Pavel, and Lord Igor have continued to work under her radar for the last several days, while Lady Bella has been prancing around in all her glory. She has been barking orders, cracking her whip, and entertaining the Lords and Ladies who are still loyal to the Council.

Ever since she decided to put the squeeze on the three Lords by taking their loved ones hostage, Lady Bella has been able to relax and forget about their *indiscretions,* as she now refers to them. She has not even bothered with the other 15 conspirators, as she figures that terrorizing the ring leaders at the top will be enough to keep the rest of them in line. But today, she has neither the time nor the interest in bothering with those who are unfaithful to her. Today Lady Bella will gain more power than any one person ever has in known human history.

Very soon, the insurrection of the Alliance will be completely crushed, and Bella and Lucifer will begin their reign of terror together, for a long time to come.

A meeting is underway in the back room of the lab with most of the conspirators and the three Lords, where they are discussing their own plans for the day. A few are to remain in the lab at all times as lookouts, and to make sure that everything is still running smoothly with Project Laser Beam. The last thing any one of them wants to do at this point is to draw Lady Bella's attention away from her launch.

Lord Pavel speaks, "What's the latest on the location of our loved ones? Have any of you been able to pin down their whereabouts with more precision, yet?"

One of the techies replies, "Not yet, My Lord, the signal is just too weak and erratic. Keeps jumping around everywhere, probably bouncing off the walls, so to speak."

Another techie says, "My Lords, we can take the surveillance device and just head on down there with it. We will be able to comb the coast more effectively from the yacht once we are at a much closer range.

And the third techie offers reassurance to the three Lords as he says, "We will stay there and do just that until we find them."

"Thank you, thank you," Lord Viktor says.

Lord Pavel and Lord Igor sadly nod.

The others discuss their getaway plans and how they plan on getting to the yacht unseen.

"The yacht is right nearby," Lady Nita says, "And I suggest that as of this moment we start going down there quietly, one at a time."

Suddenly, one of the conspirators who is in the lab, comes knocking on the door of the back office. Lord Viktor lets her in, and she is all out of breath.

"Listen up everyone. We have just had a huge break! The visiting Lords and Ladies have been pressing Lady Bella about seeing the laser outside rather than on a screen here in the lab. We have been asked to haul a bunch of equipment out to the airfield where they will all have the best view!"

"That's it! That's our getaway! Excellent!" they all cry.

They will all be able to leave easily, about an hour before launch, without much chance of being detected.

Since Lord Viktor has left the back channel open on the surveillance device, the Kastle is now fully aware of the hostage situation in Benghazi, as well as the timing of the launch.

However, neither Lady Bella, the three Lords on her island, nor Kookie at his Kastle, are aware of yet another one with a plan, who is also waiting for the right moment to strike.

Lucifer is planning to light a fire of his own.

* * *

For the past 24 hours, no one has been able to sleep or eat much at Kookie's Kastle. The intuitives have been taking turns staying finely tuned to the mental and emotional states of the conspirators on the Isle of Bella; and things are looking more and more grim for Kookie in terms of hooking up with Bella's launch program. There have been several firewalls to cut through and the last few are just turning out to be completely fireproof, even for the genius of Kookie, Yakov and Rudolpho, combined.

At this point Kookie is relying heavily on the intuitive group, as well as using his own intuition. But he will only have one shot at it. From their data analysis given to them by Rudolpho, Kookie knows that once Bella hits the launch countdown button there will be a one-minute countdown before the laser beam is automatically fired.

Kookie's backdraft sequencing code must be fired at precisely 0.133 seconds prior to the laser beam being fired in order to create the backdraft effect when the beam hits all 5000 reflectors on the Cloudtransporters. And Kookie knows that intuition just won't be precise enough for that. Without being directly connected to Bella's launch, with Kookie's supercomputers and Metatron, they will all be vaporized—all 5000 targets across One World.

Neely has just come into the workstation from the kitchen where she has been watching the sky above the Kastle, and she has an announcement to make. "Well, folks," she says, "it looks like we were one of the last targets on their list. The Cloudtransporter designated for our demise has just arrived and is hovering about 40,000 feet above us."

Everyone looks at each other and they all take a deep breath. The intuitives are tuned into Lady Bella, and they concur with Lord Viktor's surveillance equipment that her launch is no more than one hour away.

Kookie stops what he is doing. He looks at the Major and Yakov and nods at them both. "I'm sorry Brothers, but there is just no other way anymore."

The three men have rehearsed this moment in private. And they have come up with a story to get everyone out of there and to safety, leaving Kookie behind. He just knows that everyone would be too loyal to leave if they were to know the truth. Kookie also knows that it only takes one person at this point to do what he must do. Only one, needs to be sacrificed.

"May I have everyone's attention, please!" Kookie says.

All eyes, ears and hearts are upon him as Kookie lays everything out. "Our equipment as well as our intuitives are all showing us that we will not be able to fully connect with their launch sequencing program within the time that we have left. There is one other way that I can do this, but there is a slight risk involved. I will still need your intuitive help which you can continue to transmit to me from the Kabin. I have asked Yakov and the Major to stay here with me and help, until the very last minute. Liling, I am asking you to take everyone else to the Kabin, and go down to the underground shelter, along with the house staff. As you continue to speak to my heart from the Kabin shelter, know that I am listening, and I hear you."

With a softer tone, Kookie concludes, "Thank you all . . . I love you. Please go, *now!*"

Liling nods and bows her head. She does not want anyone to see her tears that are falling, especially not her big Brother. She knows that Kookie is about to risk his life for all of them, and her heart is already breaking. But she also knows that he is doing what he *must* do, and for that she will love him forever.

*And now big Brother, I must do what **I**, must do* she thinks to herself. Liling courageously holds her head up high and stands up, as she forces a smile and says to everyone, "Okay folks! You heard the Big Kahuna! Let's get moving! Mustn't get in the man's way!" She claps her hands and continues with a chipper voice, "Not a moment to lose! Make it snappy people!"

Everyone nods and they all get up as Liling helps her big Brother evacuate Kookie's Kastle, leading them all to the Kabin's shelter, and to safety.

The only ones left in the workstation are Kookie, the Major, Yakov, and, of course, Angie. As Kookie suspected she would do, Angie has firmly planted herself like a tree, rooted to the very spot she is standing on. She too, is beginning to sense what is truly going on, and she will not follow such an order from her Big Kahuna. Angie will not leave him there to do what he must do, all alone, and without her by his side, not now, not ever.

A door in the back of the workstation closes quietly. There is someone else who is also still there and is not going to leave Kookie alone either.

* * *

Lord Viktor is supervising the set-up of all the computer and transmission equipment on the airfield. Seats have also been set up for the Lords and Ladies who will be watching, what they are all referring to as, the Laser Light Show. They will get to see the light beam "in person" as it leaves the Isle of Bella, and then watch on the big screens in front of them as it damages and destroys 5000 targets all at once in front of their very eyes, and to their great amusement. They are truly anticipating this to be a big show and greatly entertaining, but no one as much as Lady Bella. In fact, she is feeling such a kinship with this crowd that she feels comfortable enough to share her true passion with them.

The launch is about to take place very soon, and the crowd is seated waiting for their hostess to arrive.

Suddenly, Lady Bella appears and all jaws drop to the ground, as they behold a strikingly beautiful woman dressed in her favorite garb. From the bottom up, Bella is sporting thigh-high black leather boots, a black leather miniskirt that barely covers her butt and all else, and a matching skin-tight, long-sleeved, cleavage bulging, black leather top. But the crème de la crème of Lady Bella's outfit are the matching accessories she is wearing around her neck. Three long, thick whips wrap around her neck and torso, dangling down next to her ankles. And one of the "whips" appears to be moving.

Everyone is enraptured by her Ladyship's appearance and staring at the moving "whip" around her neck and waist.

"Oh!" she says, with a ladylike gasp. "I'm so sorry! Please forgive me, my dears. Allow me to introduce you to my best friend here. This is Andre!" she says while holding up the head of the snake for all to see. "I mean, no fancy outfit is complete without a boa, now is it, Ladies?"

Everyone laughs and applauds, offering their nods of approval. While they all enjoy Lady Bella's pre-show entertainment, another launch is about to happen down at the pier not far from the lab. Seventeen people on a yacht are awaiting the arrival of their captain. They have with them a few personal belongings and some food and water.

They also just discovered the exact location of the cove, which they are all headed for.

Finally, the group sees their captain, Lord Viktor, making a dash for the pier.

As he embarks on the yacht, everyone welcomes him with back-pats and hope-filled eyes. Viktor wastes no time and steers the yacht away from the pier. The little group is heading to Benghazi, where they are now racing to the cove to rescue their loved ones, and then, to face the uncertainty of an unknown future.

* * *

Kookie has been preparing Metatron and his two supercomputers with the help of Yakov and the Major. The supercomputers stand about five feet apart from each other and are six feet tall. Yakov and the Major have helped him take off the grill work at the upper portion of both computers leaving their motherboards and wiring exposed.

Angie has not budged from the spot where she has planted herself on the floor. And she does not intend to move one iota.

Kookie looks at the timer coming from the Isle of Bella. Launch is only five minutes away. He places Metatron on the floor about halfway between both computers, with a step stool directly over it. It is all set to the 369-Backdraft Program, and the Golden Pyramid is spinning. He also puts the timer down on the floor where he will be able to see it until the very last moment.

Kookie stands up onto the step stool, with his body positioned directly over Metatron. He is about to hold his arms out to either side, preparing to plunge his hands into the open motherboards. Kookie knows that he will only be able to withstand about 1 minute and 30 seconds of electrocution, while holding the connection through the exact moment of 0.133 seconds prior to launch. After that, his heart will give out.

Four minutes left, and Kookie looks at Yakov and the Major. He nods, and says to them both, just as strongly as he can, ***"GO!"***

Angie starts to scream, ***"NOOOO!"***

Yakov and the Major rush at Angie, each one grabbing an arm and a leg, swiping her off her feet and charging for the door.

Angie is thrashing and screaming, *"NO! NO! NO! KOOKIE! I WANT TO GO TO THE FATHER WITH YOU! Oh Lord! Oh, Father in Heaven! NOOOOOO!"*

The last thing Kookie hears is Angie's voice screaming and crying all the way down the hall. When all is quiet, he knows that Yakov and the Major have made it out the front door with her. He bows his head to thank the Father in Heaven for taking his beloved Angie and his two best friends in the world out of harm's way.

Kookie looks at the timer. There are two minutes left to launch. He puts his hands on the edge of each console and can already feel the energy of Metatron between his legs traveling up through his body to the top of his head.

He knows that he has a strong heart, so once the electrocution begins, there should be enough time to make the connection between the launch sequencing of Bella's computer, the 369-Backdraft Program coursing through him and his two supercomputers, and the laser beam hitting 5000 reflectors. His only hope now is to have enough time left to hear the explosion of the Cloudtransporter being destroyed above him. Then he will know that the other Cloudtransporters are also gone and everyone in One World is safe and free.

* * *

In the depths of hell, Lucifer is gloating with pleasure, *Ah! Yes! And now, for all eternity. My bride AND my son cometh unto me!*

* * *

Kookie is holding his hands in position, ready for the 1 minute and 30 second mark. He looks up to the heavens and says the only thing that comes into his heart:

"Father in Heaven; Thy will be done."

Kookie watches the timer and counts down with it; *1 minute 35 seconds, 34, 33, 32, 31, 30*—He plunges his hands hard into the open wires of his two supercomputers. A shock of searing pain goes through his entire body as Kookie closes his eyes tight.

All of a sudden, the door at the back of his workstation opens and he can barely hear the patter of little footsteps approaching. Kookie is gripped in pain and knows that he does not have much longer to live, but somehow, he can hear what sounds like Eve Elli's little voice calling to him.

"It's okay Kookie, Angel and I are here!"

The Angel of the Lord appears before him, and he feels the Monarch entering his chest. Suddenly, his hands are set free and in one swift motion, the Monarch Angel throws him to the ground with her own wings extended out to both computers.

The Angel of the Lord then speaks to Kookie saying:

"Go quickly, Abraham!
You are the father of a New World which is about to be born.
This little child shall lead you to safety,
And back to your people, to whom you belong.

And I shall die in your place.
RUN, HUMAN CREATURE! NOW!"

Eve Elli puts out her hand to Kookie and says "Come on! Follow me!"

Kookie forces himself up off the floor with all his might, just as the timer hits zero. He and Eve Elli are at the door of his workstation and a sudden explosion blows up the two computers. They can feel the heat of the blast behind them as they reach the hallway. The two of them both know that the whole Kastle could blow, and Eve Elli says to Kookie, "Hurry! This way! Follow me!"

* * *

Looking up from the bowels of hell as the timer hits zero, Lucifer lights his own fire. When the backdraft effect kicks in on the 5000 reflectors, instead of incinerating them, the laser beam rebounds *off* them going right back to the Isle of Bella. Lucifer laughs with overwhelming excitement when he sees the beautiful eyes of his bride. They look up in terror for only a split second to see the blinding white light of the inbound laser beam. Those beautiful eyes melt with the intensity of the heat as the Isle of Bella is lit up and blown to pieces. And the last thing that Lady Bella hears as she leaves this earth is the voice of her bridegroom calling:

"Come to papa!"

* * *

Yakov, the Major and Angie, do not get very far. They get a couple of hundred yards away from the Kastle and then collapse in a heap on the grass. In her heart Angie understands why Kookie did what he did, although it does not make the pain she now feels any less.

Too exhausted to move or even to cry, she just lays there with her eyes closed, not knowing how this grief inside of her will ever heal. Yakov and the Major are laying nearby, experiencing much of the same thing as Angie. They too have their eyes closed, so none of them see the momentary flash of light as the laser beam bounces off the Cloudtransporter, 40,000 feet above their heads.

But the very next thing they hear is the sound of an explosion coming from within the Kastle. The three of them sit up in an instant and watch one explosion after another in rapid succession, as Kookie's Kastle becomes engulfed in flames. From behind them they can hear the voices of everyone from the Kabin rushing towards the burning Kastle. When they reach Yakov, The Major, and Angie, the group stops to see if they are okay. Liling falls to the ground and holds the three of them tight. She, along with everyone else is weeping heavily.

Ryan, Dumaka, and Phil run to the house with Kookie's house staff to open all the outside water lines and hoses that they can find. The rest of them stay right there on the grass. They are all holding each other and crying for the loss of one whom they love dearly.

Suddenly, Mimi looks around and says, "Where's Eve Elli? Who did she leave the house with? Has anyone seen her?"

When she realizes that Eve Elli is missing, her heart nearly flies into a panic.

But it doesn't. Because at that moment, everyone hears Eve Elli's voice in the distance, "Here I am, Gramma!"

Everyone turns around to see Eve Elli, and they also see whose hand she is holding.

They all scream at once and Angie is on her feet in too seconds flat. *"KOOKIEE!"* Angie cries out and runs to her Man.

Kookie is feeling the effects of his electrical injuries so he cannot move too fast, but when Angie rushes into his open arms all he can say, over and over, are three words, "I'm *so* sorry." Kookie buries his face in Angie's hair and begins to weep.

"Shh, it's okay, my darling, I understand," Angie whispers softly into his ear.

Eve Elli calls out to everyone, "Look! It's Angel!" she says while pointing up to the sky.

Everyone looks up and, just as plain as day, they can all see the spirit of the Angel of the Lord, the Monarch Rising, above their heads. She is on her way to be with the Heavenly Father.

Angie waves to her and sadly says, "I shall miss you my soul sister."

And the Angel of the Lord speaks to the hearts of all of them saying,

For all who need me, just call out and I will be there.
My spirit will always live in the hearts of human creatures everywhere.

They watch as Angel ascends to Heaven and fades from sight.

But then, as they are looking up, Kookie notices a strange thing up in the sky that is apparently *de*scending. "Huh?" he says. "That's not supposed to happen."

Yakov and Rudolpho notice it too and they scratch their heads. The Cloudtransporter was supposed to have incinerated from the backdraft effect, but there it is, fully intact, floating gently to the ground.

Wondering what this great mystery could be, Kookie just shakes his head and says, I guess all the other targets are alright, if we are, but we may as well start messaging a few people."

"Already done, Brother," says Liling, "I just messaged several targets of the Alliance from Bella's list, and it's the same everywhere."

All is well, everyone is saying, *except for an unexplained Cloudtransporter which seems to be gently floating down to our land!"*

Kookie and Yakov just look at each other and shake their heads again. "Hm," Kookie says, pondering this inexplicable turn of events. "So, where in the wild blue yonder did 5000 laser beams go?

Chapter 18 – Birth

KOOKIE IS SITTING ON THE GROUND watching his Kastle burn and realizes that he does not feel very well. He goes pale, lies down, and starts to clutch his stomach.

Angie and Liling both become alarmed and Liling calls for a Cloudambulance.

Angie tries not to show her fear to Kookie as she holds him in her arms, "Hang in there, my darling!" she whispers tenderly to him.

Kookie just smiles lovingly at her saying, "It's okay, Angie. With you here, I have all that I need." And he closes his eyes.

Everyone else sees what is going on and they move closer to Angie and Kookie.

Looking at Angie, Neely says, "That Man of yours is one tough guy. He is going to be just fine."

Eve Elli goes over to Kookie and puts one hand on his chest and one hand on his forehead. As she speaks in a voice that is not her own, everyone hears the words that are spoken. "Abraham, father of the New World, Sarah loves you, I love you, and the whole world is waiting for you. Emeka loves you and needs you very much, too."

Eve Elli then closes her eyes and begins to sing the angel song of healing, into Kookie's heart.

All over One World, folks have sustained various injuries, mostly minor, from the effects of the backdraft. There are also some fires that were set from sparks created by the sudden heat of the reflectors. Chrysalenes everywhere are watching and doing exactly what Eve Elli is doing. They are praying for healing for all those who need it, as well as for rain.

The Cloudambulance arrives to find Kookie sitting up and feeling much better. He goes into the medical vehicle and lets the paramedics examine him anyway. They say that everything checks out and he is okay. As the Cloudambulance is leaving, it begins to rain, quickly turning into a downpour.

"Whoa! Yes! Head for the Kabin!" everyone laughs. They all start to do just that when they see Ryan, Phil, Dumaka, Molly and the rest of the house staff, coming back from Kookie's burning Kastle. They all see what Phil is carrying and Doc laughs running towards him.

Everyone else is also laughing, but none are as pleased as Kookie and Angie.

Phil managed to salvage something from the fire that is completely unharmed . . .   the tuba! As he hands it over to Kookie in the pouring rain, he says, "Well Brother, how about a little music once we get inside that nice, warm, and dry Kabin of yours?"

Angie is beside herself with joy and Kookie says with a huge smile, "You're on Brother!"

* * *

Lord Viktor, Lord Pavel, Lord Igor, and the rest of their companions are nearing the shores of Benghazi, when suddenly, behind them to the north and way off in the distance, they see a flash of light in the sky. Lord Pavel grabs the surveillance device and sees what has just happened.

He looks at everyone and says with a sad voice, "My friends, it appears that our people on the Isle of Bella are gone."

Lord Viktor looks at him, and then addresses everyone. "No Pavel, they are not. Our people are everywhere. And once we rescue our families from the cove, I, for one would like to continue to Johannesburg. There is a *very special* person there whom I would like very much to meet."

* * *

The Major and Vi have gone off to Lisa and Kenny's farm where they promised to meet up with Master Howard, Master James, Judy, Master Franz, Reggie, the gardeners, and the whole lot of them. They have so much work to do together with the garden communities, as well as the new subsidiary of Howard Pharmaceuticals called Henrietta's Herbals.

* * *

Kookie and Angie and the rest of their group are just about to land in Johannesburg, where there is a mob scene waiting to greet them. Word has gotten out about the Cloudtransporters, the reflectors, and the laser beam, and the end of Lady Bella and the Council. Stories are rapidly circulating all around One World, thanks to the Intercontinental Pigeons Communication Network and to the Chrysalenes, about the acts of heroism from the Alliance.

The Cloudtransporter lands on the back field of Lord Emeka's Estate. The portal opens, and Little Lord Emeka is the first one to emerge from the craft. He is followed by Eve Elli, Liling, Dumaka, Doc, Phil, Mimi, Ryan, Rudolpho, Yakov, Neely, Angie and Kookie. A thunderous cry of cheers goes up as the people of Johannesburg welcome their heroes home.

As everyone gathers around to thank the heroes of the Alliance, Kookie puts Emeka on his shoulders, and Emeka holds his hands up high over the crowd saying to them, "People of Johannesburg," the crowd goes quiet. "Thank you for the honor of this greeting! I am so happy to be home!"

Everyone cheers.

"Please join us at our very next Trader's Market first thing tomorrow!"

Everyone laughs and voices are heard saying "Yay! You bet!" and the like.

Then Emeka raises his hands one more time and says, "Let us sing our song as we march together in a free New World," and he leads the whole crowd in Siyahamba, as Kookie dances with Emeka on his shoulders:

"We are marching in the Light of Love."

* * *

"Ivan, where are you going?" Marie calls out to her little one.

Ivan runs down to the beach, of the secluded cove on the coast of Benghazi.

"Papa! Papa! Papa!" Little Ivan starts to cry out with excitement. He runs past the AI guards who are now shut down and laying on the beach. The waves have already carried most of them out to sea.

"No honey, Papa is not here," Marie calls out to him, as she catches up with her little one.

"Papa here! Papa here!" the two-year-old cries out with great insistence.

Marie looks out on the water and sees a yacht off in the distance. It is definitely coming their way. When the others in the cove hear the commotion, they all come out to see what is happening.

Viktor is standing on the deck of the yacht, as they come around and see a small beach cove off in the distance. Looking at the surveillance device he shouts out to everyone, "That has to be it!"

As they pull in closer to the shore, Viktor sees a little one running on the beach. Suddenly, tears well up in his eyes and he yells out for the whole world, and the heavens above, to hear, *That's my boy! My boy! My Ivan!"*

The yacht slows down when it comes closer to the shore, and Viktor can wait no longer. He tears off his shirt, rips off his shoes and socks, and dives into the water.

"Papa! Papa!" Ivan jumps up and down, and Marie now sees him too. The others from the cove are gathered around watching, as Viktor emerges on the beach, runs to his little boy, and scoops Ivan up into his arms. Marie rushes to his side and they all throw their arms around each other. And little Ivan discovers that sometimes there are just not enough hugs and kisses in the world to say, "I love you."

On the yacht, the techies have been busy with the surveillance device. They have been watching as, one by one, the Cloudtransporters of Project Laser Beam, have all come floating back to the ground. And now they have spotted one on the screen that is not very far from their present location. They waste no time in telling their companions about it, and they proceed to board the loved ones of Viktor, Pavel, and Igor onto the yacht.

As soon as they reach the downed Cloudtransporter, Viktor and his techies have it up and running in no time, and everyone climbs on board. They are friendless and do not know where to go.

But as Viktor has already said to them and now reiterates, "Well my friends, there is someone I would very much like to say thank you to. Shall we go there?"

They all nod in consent.

* * *

With little Lord Emeka on his shoulders, Kookie dances and sings through the crowd, with all the people of Johannesburg.

Eve Elli suddenly cries out, "Look Everybody! It's Mama Eve Zula and Papa Adam Makena!"

The Chrysalenes from the Village of the Holy Ones are coming down the road, making a joyful noise and joining in on the excitement and celebration. Everyone starts to dance around in a great big circle, rejoicing in the glory of Freedom and Love.

As the singing and dancing continues, Liling looks up and sees that another Cloudtransporter has appeared in the sky. She points it out to Dumaka and Yakov who both notice something strange about its appearance. As it gets closer, Kookie and the others notice it too, and the revelry quiets down.

The Cloudtransporter is about to land on the back field of Lord Emeka's Estate when Kookie, Yakov and Rudolpho recognize the strange-looking thing on the bottom of the craft. It is a partially burned-out reflector.

Everyone looks on with uncertainty and some trepidation as the craft lands. The portal opens and out steps a group of anxious-looking men, women, and children. One of them comes over to Kookie who recognizes him immediately.

The man says nothing as he bows his head to Kookie and drops to his knees.

Kookie takes the man's hands and lifts him up, saying, "It's all right, Lord Viktor. You are all welcome here."

Viktor breaks down crying and Kookie puts his arms around him. He smiles at Viktor and says, "Why don't you bring your family and all of your companions over to the Big House, and we shall all break bread together.

"Thank you, My Lord Kenneth," says Viktor, overcome with gratitude. "Thank you for everything."

* * *

That night as Kookie is laying is bed, he mulls over in his mind many things that have happened in his life. He thinks about the promises that he, Yakov and Liling made to each other as children, as well as the promises that he made to the Major and the people of One World. They have basically been the same promise: to help all people *and* the UC alike, to live an authentic life, where each person is free to choose his or her own destiny. And now that day has come where people can start to live the life of their highest calling and discover who they truly are.

As he is about to drift off to sleep, Kookie is thinking to himself that *we, the people do not belong to the Council anymore, but to ourselves, to the spirit of love that lies within each of our hearts, and if we so choose, to each other.*

"EACH OTHER!" Kookie suddenly exclaims, bolting upright in bed. *"AHA!"* he howls pointing his index finger in the air, almost waking Angie up.

Talking out loud to himself, Kookie says, "I don't care what time it is, here, in California, or in Oregon. Every Bro' I know is about to get a wake-up call from me!"

* * *

It doesn't take long for Kookie to make all the arrangements for the big event. Mama Eve Zula and the Chrysalenes from the Village of the Holy Ones are invited, as well as all of Kookie's friends from Bear River Farm, Judy's Farm, Howard Pharmaceuticals, Lord Emeka's Estate and all the UC and people of the Alliance.

The guests have all assembled in the back field of Lord Emeka's Estate as Kookie asks Mama Eve Zula to come forward.

Kookie begins, "Dearest friends gathered here today, thank you all for being here on such short notice. There was a promise that I made to my Woman a while back which I am standing here today before you to fulfill. I know that many of my Brothers and Sisters gathered here feel the same way. Without further ado, let us all fulfill that promise together.

"Will those of you who have come here to partake of this auspicious occasion, please step forward."

The following people come forward: Lisa and Kenny, the Major and Vi, Phil and Doc, Mimi and Ryan, Jackson and Rita, Yakov and Neely, and Liling and Dumaka. Last, but not least, Kookie and Angie take their place among the others.

Mama Eve Zula steps forward and speaks to those standing before her. "It is my greatest pleasure to be offering my services to all of you gathered here today. Will the couples please face one another?"

They all do, and Mama continues, "As you gaze into each other's eyes, always remember that you are looking at the Light of the Heavenly Father gazing back at you. He sees you in all your imperfections as well as all your glory, just as you see your beloved standing now before you. And He loves you for all of eternity. May you all hold each other in that same loving gaze of the Creator, with all the love that you have in your heart; today, tomorrow, forever, and ever.

"And now, will all of the men repeat after me:

"I, (your name), take you (her name), to be my wife, to have and to hold, from this day forward, for better, for worse, for richer, for poorer, in sickness and in health, to love and to cherish, till death us do part."

Mama Eve Zula then says, "And now for the women:

"I, (your name), take you (his name), to be my husband, to have and to hold, from this day forward, for better, for worse, for richer, for poorer, in sickness and in health, to love and to cherish, till death us do part."

Mama Eve Zula concludes with: "In the name of the Heavenly Father, I now pronounce you all husband and wife. You may now kiss each other . . . very much!"

Up in the heavens above, a voice is heard saying, *A New World has been born, and may no human creature, man, or woman, put it asunder.*

Amen!

* * *

Eighteen years have passed since that day. Garden communities are flourishing and thriving all over the world, along with the people. New kind of loves have been blossoming; the high and pure love of friendship; the courageous love of self-sacrifice; and the noble love of the greater good.

A higher form of humans has also been blooming, as the young Chrysalenes all over are marrying and having children.

Lord Emeka is now 23 years old. He has already helped to established free trade, higher education for all, and a medical system that combines ancient wisdom and modern technology. His wife and soulmate, Eve Elli, is 21. She is a leader in healing and in worship of the Father in Heaven. Lord Emeka and Eve Elli have just given birth to their first child, a little girl named Lady Bi. And like her mother, there are times when Lady Bi glows in the dark.

Since the fall of the Council, Kookie and Angie have become a powerful force of unification and healing. They travel all over the New World as ambassadors of Love and Light, bringing all kinds of people together. With their love and support, walls between old adversaries are coming down, and people are learning every day, through all their ups and downs, how to honor, respect, and live together and how to grow in spirit with one another.

Suzie of the Seashells and Rudolpho, who are now 19 and 30 years old, respectively, have also teamed up as ambassadors of Love and Light to share their stories of courage and strength, bringing hope and faith to all people everywhere. Suzie wears her necklace proudly, honoring all those little ones who lost their lives in the dark days, now behind them.

"Henrietta's Herbals" is growing and thriving all over the world with medicinal products that are endowed with the healing properties and love of the Chrysalenes.

The Major and Vi have given Master Howard and Mistress Henrietta three grandchildren. Thanks to Howard Pharmaceuticals and the new herbal products, the fertility rate of the people all over the New World of One Garden, is greatly improving.

Master Howard and Mistress Henrietta are now enjoying their golden years. He still calls her his Peach Cupcake, bounding up the stairs like a charging rhino. And the little garden which he started 18 years ago at Judy's farm is now blossoming with roses, all for the love of his Sugar Cookie.

Coffeehouses and Free Trade Centers are flourishing throughout One Garden. People everywhere are learning to accept others as they are, on the road to healing the divide that was created by fear. They are truly learning the lesson that Angie and Kookie are now sharing with everyone all around the world:

"With love all things are possible."

And way up above in the House of the Heavenly Father, a voice is heard saying:

Well done, human creatures,
With you the Master is well pleased.

* * *

Somewhere in the polar region, a blanket of ice from the great ice storm has been slowly melting. The light breaks through to a small portal of an underground palace where three faces peer out and see the sun. It is the first time that PA, ES and SPA have seen natural sunlight in 18 years.

As the three men of the former Council look up to the heavens above, a voice speaks to their hearts, saying:

"For I will be merciful to their unrighteousness,
and their sins and their iniquities
will I remember no more."

(Hebrews 8:12 KJV)

Amen

A MESSAGE FROM ANGEL

Bless the human creature whose cup is half empty:
The fearful, the scorned, the lost and the lonely.
Bless the one who is suffering in pain.
This is your time to rise,
To spread your wings in all your glory
And share your sacred gift.
Do not fear the dark hour; run to embrace it,
For it is the cry of a new day, about to be born.
Have courage human creature as you bring forth Love,
Shining from your soul like a path in the storm.
With nothing to lose there is all to be gained,
As you travel the road to Heaven.
For a cup that is full runneth over,
But the human creature
Whose cup has been spent,
Is the Holy Grail set to be filled.

Much love to you all,
From the bottom of my heart,
Forever and ever . . .

Acknowledgements

A HUGE Thank You goes out to my Dream Team:

Leanne Sype, thank you for your fantastic editing, constant encouragement, brilliant insights, and wonderful friendship.

Wendy Garfinkle, thank you for your beautiful formatting, incredible patience with me, and all the other things you have helped me with, above and beyond.

Taylor Dawn, thank you for your magnificent, magical graphic design, and the way it makes everyone go, "OOO and AHH" and "WOW" when they see the book cover.

Glenda Nowakowski, thank you for your very much appreciated, long-term friendship, enthusiasm, and excitement over my book, and taking the time to offer me wonderful insights on the tiniest detail.

Pooja Lama of the UPS store in Sherwood, Oregon, thank you for your help in printing out the preliminary manuscript. I have really appreciated your joyous enthusiasm over the whole concept of the story, as I shared it with you in the early stages of development.

Once again: thank you, thank you, to the truly awesome baristas at the Starbucks in Sherwood, Oregon. You have made me feel like a part of the family in your very special Coffeehouse, setting a whole new standard of excellence for the hospitality and retail industry.

About the Author

Sylvana C. Candela, L.Ac. MATCM, licensed acupuncturist, Master of Acupuncture and Traditional Chinese Medicine, resides in Sherwood, Oregon. She has supervised in community acupuncture clinics in Los Angeles, California, including Samra University and Yo San University of Traditional Chinese Medicine.

She received her bachelor's degree in special education from Queens College of the City University of New York, and taught children with autism at the Sybil Elgar School in London, England.

Sylvana has five children and six grandchildren.

She is the author of *Gently Heal Thyself: Healing the Soul with Energy Medicine*, and the first two books in the *Monarch Rising Series: Awaken* and *Gather*.